Patricide

Madonna Dries Christensen

PATRICIDE

iUniverse books may be ordered through booksellers or by contacting:

iUniverse LLC
1663 Liberty Drive
Bloomington, IN 47403
www.iuniverse.com
1-800-Authors (1-800-288-4677)

ISBN: 978-1-4917-4329-4 (sc)
ISBN: 978-1-4917-4330-0 (e)

Printed in the United States of America.

iUniverse rev. date: 08/08/2014

Patricide is a work of fiction. Any real names, characters, places, and events are used fictitiously.

All royalties from this book go to Down Syndrome Association of Northern Virginia.

Cover design: Jeff Owenby (www.autumnwindstudios.com)

Author's Note

Author John Barth stated, "We live in an ocean of story, and wherever you decide to drop your bucket, when you haul it up it'll be overflowing."

When I dipped into the digital files of my hometown newspapers, I ladled up two stories that grew to book length: *The Orator And The Sage*, a biographical sketch of John and Lyn Glover, Osceola County Iowa pioneers, and this novel.

Patricide is based on a homicide that occurred in this actual locale in 1920. Some of the characters are real people, but their actions, thoughts, and dialogue is fiction. Some characters are entirely fictional. Some news articles are verbatim (no longer under copyright protection); some are altered, still others are fabricated. The local papers carried no byline on their stories. The *Des Moines Register* story had the byline Rae McRae. Research told me that she was a Features Editor at that time. Her gender led me to create the character Augusta Duvall.

People have asked, about other books I've written that are based on true stories: What part is true and what isn't true? I strive to blend both ingredients until the story is seamless. Truman Capote called *In Cold Blood* a nonfiction novel. Some publishers today are calling this genre *faction*. For Osceola County readers in particular, your memories of the setting and people will not always match my created story.

— THANK YOU —

Jeff Owenby for the stunning cover design (www.autumnwindstudios.com) *

Nephew Mike Harlow for information about firearms *

Granddaughter Grace Buzby for lending me her lovely name for one of my characters, and for helping me name Willis Overholser's cat, breed, and background story *

JB Hamilton Queen, G.L. Christensen, and Marshall Cook for aiding and abetting *

I plead guilty to any and all errors, but I reserve the right to blame someone else.

Madonna Dries Christensen
Sarasota, Florida
e-mail iowagirl1@aol.com
www.madonnadrieschristensen.com

. . . but we were born of risen apes, not fallen angels, and the apes were armed killers besides. And so what shall we wonder at? Our murders and massacres and missiles, and our irreconcilable regiments? Or our treaties whatever they may be worth; our symphonies however seldom they may be played; our peaceful acres, however frequently they may be converted into battlefields; our dreams however rarely they may be accomplished. The miracle of man is not how far he has sunk but how magnificently he has risen. We are known among the stars by our poems, not our corpses.

-- Robert Ardrey
African Genesis

CARL JESS

In the distance, a church bell rang, and then another with a different sound. On Sunday mornings the various bells pealed from early morning until the later services. Carl Jess, his father, and *Oma* belonged to the Lutheran church. None of them would attend the service this morning.

Carl's father snored in the double bed. Carl didn't want anyone to know he slept beside his father most nights. He didn't like sleeping alone. *Oma* once said it was because he'd lost his mother at age five. He barely remembered his mother so he couldn't think what that had to do with it. But these days nothing *Oma* said made sense. She was ancient, a word he remembered from vocabulary lessons at school. It meant really old.

The hand-tinted bridal photo of his mother on the bureau next to the bed revealed a young woman with blue eyes and reddish hair, braided atop her head and with a veil falling from the braid. She looked sad.

What Carl actually remembered about his mother, he wished he could forget. He felt certain it happened the day she died, and it involved a baby, and his father. His grandparents were there, too. He'd once told his grandfather about this dim memory. *Opa* said it must have been a dream and Carl should forget it. But the images returned without trying. The blurred scene arose now and he pushed it away. Like *Opa* said; forget it.

Carl tumbled out of bed without aid of an alarm clock. As far back as he could remember of his fifteen years he'd risen before the sun streamed through the windows. That was—if the sun could break through the grime. He raised the shades on both windows to let in what light was available. People talked about electricity but they said it would be a long while before farm folks had it. Carl's father said they didn't need electric lights; you went to bed when it got dark and got up when it was light. Or, in Carl's case, before light, to do chores. The morning and evening chores were his job.

Shivering in his long underwear he dressed in a denim overall, a flannel shirt, and wool sweater and socks. Seated on a ladder-back chair he laced his high-top work shoes as best he could with the ragged strings. He couldn't say the last time his clothing had been washed or he'd had a full bath, and he now caught a whiff of unpleasant odor.

The cows were grumbling in the barn and the old horse would soon begin his snorting and stomping for attention. *Oma* used to say: First things first. That meant chores before playtime. As if he'd ever had playtime. He had an extra chore this morning. He would carry out the plan he'd made last night. He'd thought about it before, for maybe a year. The time had come.

From the closet, he removed the 32 calibre rifle he'd placed there last night after taking it from the pantry where his father stored the loaded gun. His father had taught him to use the gun for killing feral varmints or hunting for game birds and animals.

His father stopped snoring and lay as still as the snow-covered fields surrounding the northwest Iowa farm.

As Carl approached the bed, his father's eyes blinked open and he glared at Carl, as he usually did. The eyes were pale blue, almost colorless. Scary and cold, like the glass marble Carl found in the snow yesterday.

When his father mumbled something, Carl went rigid as a tree trunk. Then his father closed his eyes again.

Carl waited. The eyes stayed closed.

Claus Jess had seen his son for the last time.

In one fluid movement, Carl planted his feet on the floor, spread apart for balance and to steady himself, leaned slightly forward, placed the gun at his father's head, and pulled the trigger.

Carl's scrawny frame reared back as the blast vibrated through his body and echoed through the house. He immediately recognized that the sound had been different from shooting outdoors; a sharp snap, like the time lightning hit a tree and brought it down near the house. The power of this shot rattled the storm windows and loosened the frost that had been etched on the glass in a lacy pattern. For a moment it looked as if a light snowfall had settled on the windowsills; the flakes mixed with furry dust and peeling paint. Outside the window, a chunky fringe of icicles along the eaves thudded to the ground.

Without looking at what he'd done, the noise ringing in his ears, Carl worked his jaw to ease the pressure. His ears felt like they were filled with water, like when he swam in the river.

He walked to the bureau and opened his mother's Bible. Using a pencil, and checking the calendar on the wall, Carl entered his father's date of death: March 7, 1920, in the allotted space. Guessing at the time, he added: about ten minutes before seven in the morning. His father used terms such as six-forty-one, but Carl had never been able to figure time that way. Later, he would use pen and ink from school and go over what he'd written. His ink bottle had the word permanent on the label. That meant it couldn't be erased.

Carl searched through the pile of dirty clothing on the floor and lifted his father's denim overall, which smelled of dried manure and pipe tobacco. Digging into the pocket, he pawed out a handful of coins, chose a nickel, and dropped the soiled garment and the other coins back into the pile.

CARL JESS

In the hallway, with the gun hanging at his side, Carl no longer felt like a frightened boy. He had stood up to a man. Like the Bible story, David and Goliath.

Carl paused at the door to the parlor, where *Oma* slept on the daybed since deciding she no longer wanted to climb stairs. Anyway, the upstairs was closed off to keep the lower floor warmer. Carl hadn't worried that the gunshot would awaken *Oma*. She used to say she slept like a baby, didn't hear a thing. These days she absolutely didn't hear a thing; she'd gone deaf as a turnip a couple of years ago. She no longer said much either, except to screech orders at him in German.

Carl ejected the casing from the rifle, put it in his pocket, reloaded the gun, and placed it in the pantry. His father had told him to always reload in case the gun was needed quickly. Carl built a fire in the kitchen cook stove and when it was roaring he laid two already boiled potatoes in their skin on the burner plate. By the time he did chores, the potatoes would be warm enough to eat. Then he lit a fire in the other stove, used for heating the room. He downed in one gulp a half cup of bitter black coffee from the pot that had sat on the heater overnight.

Dressed in his rummage sale coat, cap, overshoes, and gloves Carl waded through the snow to the barn to feed and milk the cows and feed the horse. Those were the main chores in the wintertime; plus cleaning the barn. Which he was supposed to do yesterday but he fooled around in the snow and caught hell from the old man, plus a whipping.

Why clean a barn? It made no sense. It's where animals shit and pissed and puked and belched and farted and sweated and breeded and gave birth, and doves and pigeons roosted in the rafters and their crap plopped to the floor along with bat and vermin pellets. Carl never said these bad words aloud; his father didn't stand for cussing or swearing. He said Christians did not use such language. When Carl got mad he said the words in his

4

mind. Boys at school used even worse words, some of them names for body parts for boys and girls.

Opa once explained that it was important to clean the barn and other buildings because people could tell if a German owned a farm because it was tidy and clean enough to eat off the floor, like *Oma's* kitchen. *Opa* should see the kitchen now. *Oma* had slowed down. The house was falling apart and stunk as bad as the barn. *Oma* refused to use the outhouse in winter, so of course it was his job to empty the enamel pot she kept by her bed in the parlor.

With chores finished, Carl headed back to the house. The sky, streaked with blue, purple, and yellow, reminded him of a bruise when it's starting to heal. The old mutt, Baxter, trailed after him. Carl ruffled Baxter's matted fur and then pointed to the barn. Baxter loped off to his nest in the hay. There were cats there, too. Who knew how many? Sometimes cats showed up and had kittens and Carl's father took them to the creek and drowned them. Other people did that, too, so it wasn't just his father being mean.

Carl left one milk can on the enclosed porch and stepped into the kitchen. The creamery man would pick up the cans by the barn when he made his rounds. Carl looked back at the porch to see if he'd covered the can. He had. One time he forgot to put the lid on the pail and a mouse drowned in the milk. His father scooped out the mouse with a dipper and made Carl drink the milk down to the mouse. His father laughed and said next time he'd make Carl eat the mouse for dessert.

The potatoes on the stovetop were warm, so Carl brought in a chunk of butter from the porch, their icebox in the winter. After biting off the end of one potato, he slid it across the butter and ate the potato like he would an apple. He dipped into the butter with each bite. He loved butter and it was one food they always had. His job to churn it, since *Oma* got old.

While eating the second potato, Carl heard what sounded like a groan. He went to the parlor to see if *Oma* might need something. Or was maybe talking in her sleep. Or awake and mumbling as she did most of the day. He heard not a sound, not even her usual wheezing. The room stunk; either from the pot or *Oma* had peed the bed. Probably both.

Carl detected another muted whine. The wind in the chimney? Sometimes the wind whimpered, or whistled a sound like his father made when he couldn't find Carl and wanted him to appear. He'd put his fingers in his mouth to make the shrill sound. "Carl, come here," he'd call.

No; this sound came from the bedroom.

Could his father be alive after being shot in the head? That would destroy the brain, wouldn't it? Maybe not. Carl thought now that his hand might have slipped when he pulled the trigger. Maybe he should have shot the heart. People always said a dead person's heart stopped beating. They never said the brain stopped working. Maybe his father had enough brain left to know Carl had shot him. Maybe he'd had time to think about it. That would serve him right.

Carl, come here.

Carl took the rifle from the pantry and stepped into the bedroom. The smell of gun smoke lingered. He hadn't noticed it before. The body in the bed lay still. Maybe it wasn't a groan he'd heard; maybe it was body noise. A girl at school whose grandfather was an undertaker said that after someone dies the body makes noises from the organs inside settling down or some such thing. Like when your stomach grumbles from hunger. Her grandfather said that one time a dead body sat up partway. She wasn't supposed to hear this; her grandfather had been telling the story to friends.

Carl noted that there wasn't much blood on the bed or even anything messy from inside his father's head. He expected it to look like a watermelon that had burst apart. He sometimes used watermelons for target practice.

Resuming his stance from earlier, he aimed the rifle, held steady, and pulled the trigger. This time it made a helluva bloody mess.

Trembling, his ears roaring again, a glob of puke clogged Carl's throat until he coughed and spit it out. He grabbed the dirty clothes from the floor and wiped at the blood and pieces of brain on the bed and wall. The goop looked meaty, like the sausage *Oma* used to make on butchering day. It smelled as bad, too.

Using quilts from the cedar chest, Carl covered some of the blood on the bed to hide it. Then he grabbed the pile of bloody clothes and carried them to the kitchen.

Removing the rifle casing, he put it in his pocket with the first one, reloaded the gun and returned it to the pantry.

Still dressed for outdoors, he left the house, carrying the bloody clothes wrapped around the rifle casings. He had planned last night how he would explain his father's death. He rehearsed it now.

Taking the shortcut to Frank Hromatko's farm, he tramped through the fresh snow that muffled sound in the countryside. As the sun rose higher, its rays cast on the snow, the glare hurt Carl's eyes. At school, a nurse had tested everyone's eyes. She said Carl needed glasses for distance; he couldn't see the blackboard well enough. When he brought home the note, his father read it and scribbled across the bottom that he'd take care of it, and sent the note back to school with Carl. Nothing had come of it.

Partway to the neighboring farm, Carl stopped at a woodpile in a grove. After removing some of the stacked wood, he tossed in the bundle of evidence: the bloody clothes and shells. The wind caught the stirred up snow and slapped it in his face—icy, biting. He restacked the wood and scattered snow on top so the pile wouldn't look disturbed.

Ahead, something sprinted across the field, a slash of rusty color against the white landscape. It might have been a fox but Carl couldn't be sure because of the distance. Glasses would help. Whatever it was he'd seen, the color brought to mind blood splattered on the pillow at home.

Shaking away the image, Carl stooped and scrubbed his hands clean in the snow and then continued to his destination.

SHERIFF JOSEPH GILL

Osceola County Sheriff Joseph Gill had investigated one previous murder. It had not, however, involved a child at the scene—a wretched boy who huddled in a corner repeating that his father had been kicked by a horse yesterday and didn't wake up this morning.

Sheriff Gill and Constable Chris Wassmann had arrived from Sibley, the county seat, after being notified by Frank Hromatko that a man had died at the Jess farmhouse in Ocheyedan. Hromatko reported that Carl Jess had come to him for help this morning. Hromatko and his teenaged son were here now, along with three doctors, one of them the coroner.

Coroner Winkler and the doctors wore white surgical masks and rubber gloves. Gill wore gloves but no mask; that would mark him as an amateur. Wassmann's complexion turned green when he viewed the body in the bed but his natural color had returned.

While the medical men examined the body, Gill questioned the boy and took notes.

"Your name is Carl Jess?"

"Yes."

"How old are you?"

"Fifteen since last December."

Gill would have guessed twelve, maybe thirteen. "Your father's name?"

"Claus Jess, Junior. His pa was Claus Jess, too, but he died."

"And you say your father was kicked by a horse late yesterday. Did you call for help when he got hurt?"

"We ain't got a telephone and he don't want doctors."

"I see. So he went to bed and was okay during the night? You checked on him?"

"I slept with him and he snored like usual."

"And this morning, was he awake at all?"

8

"I guess he was sleeping. The cows was bawling so I did chores and then I went to the neighbor."

"If he was sleeping why did you go to the neighbor?"

"Um, he didn't wake up when I got done from chores."

"Joe," Dr. Winkler interrupted and Gill nodded to go-ahead.

"Son, a kick in the head last night, outdoors, did not produce brain matter on the bedroom wall. And it's fresh, not several hours old."

Carl cowered; his eyes darted from Gill to Winkler, who said, "He wasn't kicked by a horse. He was shot in the head, twice."

Gill gave Carl a moment. "Did you hear what the doctor said?"

The boy nodded, or maybe his whole body had trembled.

"Do you want to tell us what really happened?"

Carl erupted in heavy sobs. "I s'pose I done it, then."

"You suppose you did what?"

"The gun's in the pantry. I hid the shells and bloody clothes."

Gill glanced toward what would be the pantry. "Carl; I'll need to take you to Sibley so we can talk about this more."

"I ain't been there before."

"You stay here right now, with Constable Wassmann. I'm going to look around the house."

Wassmann placed his hand on Carl's head and led him to a chair and stood guard over him. While the doctors attended the body, Gill paced through the house to see what might be amiss. Leave no stone unturned being a smart adage to follow.

Passing a window he noted that the creamery truck had lumbered into the yard. The two milk haulers were dawdling, their breath billowing in small clouds as they talked, wondering, no doubt, what had brought the sheriff's car and others here. They would spread the news on their route and soon the telephone wires would flicker with activity. Tillie Holman, who operated the switchboard out of her home, swore she never repeated anything she heard through the headset. True or not, she didn't need to; every man, woman and child with a spark of curiosity picked up the receiver whether or not the long and short rings indicated the call was theirs. Rural folks were offered the option of a private line, but it was more expensive, and besides, why pass up the opportunity to hear other people's conversations? Might as well get their money's worth.

The grandmother had been wandering, but had retreated to the parlor, where she sat in a rocker by a window with a shade hanging loose on one end. Bewildered by the commotion and still in her nightclothes, she seemed frightened when she saw the sheriff. At six-one and twenty pounds heavier than he should be, he filled the doorframe.

"*Was ist geschehen?*" the woman mumbled.

Gill thought that meant: What has happened? Knowing she couldn't hear, he held up one finger to indicate: wait a minute. He tore a page of paper from his notebook and wrote: Claus is hurt in an accident.

She took the note and leaned toward the lantern to read it. She said nothing more, so Gill moved on. Could she even read English? The smells from the room followed him: urine, body odor, mentholatum, and the lighted kerosene lantern on a table. The smell of kerosene bothered him more than spilled blood did.

He slid open the pocket door to the upstairs, obviously closed to keep what little heat there was downstairs from drifting up. Many people closed off unneeded rooms in winter. This might explain why the boy had slept with his father last night. That's what he'd said, that he'd slept with him. At age fifteen? That seemed peculiar. Beyond peculiar. Might this be a case of sexual abuse and the boy put an end to it?

He slept with his father—involuntarily or voluntarily?

Then he rose and shot him in the head. Twice.

And composed an alibi. Premeditated murder.

Fifteen-years-old. He seemed younger than that.

Gill glanced at the boy in the kitchen. He didn't know enough to wipe his nose. Gill pulled out his handkerchief and took it to Carl. He used it and made to give it back but Gill indicated he should keep it. Carl still wore his coat, buttons missing, and a cap with earflaps hanging to his chin. The house was cold enough for a coat and cap. He needed a bath and his breath smelled like, what? Vomit. Behind Carl and behind the stove the wallpaper glistened with spattered grease. Strike a match too close to the wall and this room would go up in flames.

"Anyone upstairs?" Gill asked.

Carl shook his head but Gill climbed the stairs anyway. He'd heard of cases where a child or adult was kept in a bedroom or attic; someone grossly disfigured, feeble-minded, epileptic, even someone like the grandmother downstairs. Not many people lived to her age; one of the doctors said she was eighty-seven or -eight.

The three bedrooms were vacant and, although the attic had no light, Gill could see enough to know that no human lived there. Plenty of mice, though. Vermin had a distinctive smell, of decay. A rag had been stuffed into a broken window; the tail of the cloth waving like a flag in the wind.

In the hall, Gill ducked under a flypaper strip hanging from the ceiling. Brittle and covered with dead flies, the strip had to have been here since last summer.

From the window, Gill looked out over the farmland. When he came to Iowa years ago, the county looked desolate, forbidding, and he decided to open a livery instead of farming. He hadn't regretted that decision. Farming was risky; work all year and the crop could be set afire by a lightning flash, trampled by hail, carried away by a tornado, flooded with too much rain, withered by drought, or devoured by grasshoppers. The hoppers were gone now but there wasn't a farmer around who had forgotten their ferociousness.

Yesterday's snow had partially covered the corn stubble in the fields. Footsteps were visible through a grove. A scruffy looking dog out by the barn barked sporadically as people entered or left the farmhouse. In the distance, a windmill spun, like a child's top at full speed. Gill couldn't hear the sound from here, but he knew its metal against metal creak.

Descending the stairs, his foot nearly went through the boards on one step. Wassmann met him in the hallway, keeping one eye on the kitchen. "We've wound things up here. The coroner took the body. Shall I handcuff the boy?"

Gill considered that. "He might be covering for someone."

"What? Seriously? The old woman?"

"I doubt it, but it's too soon to be sure."

"He led me to the woodpile so I could retrieve the evidence. The pile looked undisturbed but he knew where to pick off the logs. He knew enough to cover them with snow after he'd messed it up. It had to be him."

"All the same; he's a child. Forget the cuffs. Have you checked the barn, the machine shed, the other buildings, the cellar?"

"Everything, even the outhouse. The doctors watched the boy while I looked around."

"Okay. Now, the grandmother. We can't leave her here."

"The neighbor said he'd take her home with him. She seems to know who he is."

"Tell him she asked what happened and I wrote her a note saying it was an accident. Hromatko said earlier that she has another son. He's met him and knows how to get in touch with him."

Gill looked toward the living room. "Tell him to be sure that lantern in the parlor is turned off, and any others. There's a fire waiting to happen."

"Ya ask me, this place should be burned to the ground."

"Not our job. You can drop me and Carl at the depot in town."

"The depot? Why?"

"I want to talk to him, get a feeling about what all went on here."

"You could do that in the car."

"I could, but humor me. Maybe I feel like a train ride."

"You're the boss. The sooner we leave here, the better. This place stinks to high Heaven."

THE REVEREND JOHN GLOVER

Fourteen miles from the Jess farm, the Reverend John Glover hung his vestment in the closet, having finished Sunday service at Sibley's Congregational Church. Although he'd felt the call to ministry in college in Wisconsin, he'd also been drawn to the law, and farming, local and state politics, and other occupations. His ordination had come at age sixty-two, but it gave him more satisfaction than any of the titles and robes he'd worn. Under his one-year pastorate at the Ocheyedan parish, the congregation had grown by thirty percent. Since that time he'd served as a substitute minister, locally and at other Iowa churches, in Minnesota, and once in Missouri. It amused him to think of himself as a modern day circuit rider—one who rides the rail instead of a trail. He also enjoyed preaching at tent revivals, one of which was recently disrupted when an attendee sat on a bee's nest. He didn't know who had been more frightened, the woman or the bees, all of whom created quite a stir before settling down. To lighten the situation he'd tried to quickly recall a mention of bees in the Bible but could think only of honey, so he quoted Emily Dickinson instead of scripture. "To make a prairie it takes a clover and one bee. One clover and a bee. And reverie. The reverie alone will do, if bees are few."

John slipped into his suit jacket and headed for the church proper, where his son waited for him. But Lyn wasn't alone; Sheriff Joe Gill had entered. Lyn had been at the service but Joe had not. He had stopped attending church after his son died in the war more than two years ago. Fred's funeral was the last time Joe had come to a service. John had tried friendly persuasion but had met a brick wall of silence from Joe. They were best friends but Joe had politely told John to butt out.

"Judge, I need you at the courthouse," Joe said now. "We have a situation."

No longer a judge, John held the office of Justice of the Peace, but folks still called him Judge or by other past titles.

"What's happened?"

"Out near Ocheyedan. Looks like a boy killed his father."

"Looks like?"

"I'll tell you on the way." Joe turned to Lyn. "I assume you were waiting for your father."

Lyn nodded, and John said, "Don't wait dinner," knowing that Lyn would open a couple of cans and call it dinner. They'd done plenty of that after Lyn's mother died when he was nine. As adults, they'd lived together at various times, but now Lyn had a place near the depot and for the past several years John took room and board at the Windsor Hotel. The widower and the bachelor had many of their meals in the dining room, always on Sunday noon.

Lyn departed and John quickened his pace to catch up with Joe. "Fill me in," he said when they were side by side.

"The boy said his father got kicked in the head by a horse last night and went to bed early and he found him dead this morning."

"And?"

"The coroner said the holes in his head came from a rifle. Two shots. The kid broke down and admitted he shot his father."

"Dear Lord. Is there another suspect?"

"Not likely. No one else around except a senile grandmother who can't hear a word or understand much of anything."

"How old is the boy?"

"Fifteen. Name's Carl Jess."

A rattle-trap automobile drowned out the last name and John asked Joe to repeat it. "Carl Jess. The father is . . . was Claus Jess."

John jerked to a stop. "Claus Jess? I know him."

Joe turned a corner, and John followed. "His father homesteaded about the time I did. I've done business with Claus. He's the town assessor; owns a lot of valuable land, farms and in town."

Arriving at the courthouse the men paused out front. "I'll bring the kid over from the jail," Joe said.

"The jail? You know the law—"

"No need to cite law to me. He's not locked up; he's with Chris."

"And call the coroner, and the doctor. Where's the body?"

"Funeral home. The coroner brought him and I brought the boy on the train." Joe paused. "He'd never been on a train. Acted like it was a joy ride."

"He's probably in shock. Does he have a lawyer?"

"I sent someone to see if Lou Dwinnell will represent him."

"Is there a court reporter available?"

"It's Sunday. But Myrtle from the assessor's office knows how to use the Stenotype. She's across the street, if she's not at her mother's this weekend. I'll call her."

"I'll wait for you to get everything lined up. See you inside."

The two men parted company; each to his own duty.

JUSTICE OF THE PEACE JOHN GLOVER

As Justice of the Peace, John had no particular office; he might be called anywhere to hear a case. One time when a brawl began on the street corner downtown, Joe Gill hauled the men into the backroom of Joe's Place and John heard the case from behind the bar.

This being the courthouse, he stepped into the familiarity of the judges' chamber. He probably had a robe around here somewhere, in moth balls, but this was a fifteen-year-old boy. Maybe a clerical collar would put more fear of God into him than a black robe.

While waiting for Joe, John did a quick memory check on some of his past cases, in more than one role: Justice of the Peace, County Attorney, County Judge, Mayor, defense lawyer. Now seventy-four-years-old, he'd had pretty much everything come before him, from disputes over chickens and pigs to school children fighting on the playground to drunks and bullies causing trouble, and even a couple of shootings and attempted murders. He'd had teenaged boys appear before him for speeding, drinking, and the usual shenanigans of youth after they'd had too much illegal exhilaration juice. As a Civil War veteran, John had seen death many times, and he and Lyn had witnessed a murder five years ago. John had held the initial inquest on that one. But he'd never before had a boy of fifteen who might have committed patricide, on Sunday, the Lord's Day.

When Joe Gill opened the door and told John the group had assembled, he strode into the courtroom. His eyes fell directly on a child-like form. John had imagined a corn-fed, brawny, muscular, almost grown man. He said a quick prayer at the tragedy of it all. Lady Justice, from her seat in the mural on the wall, had never viewed a scene like this.

Carl Jess and his lawyer, Lou Dwinnell, had risen when John entered, as had Sheriff Joe Gill, Constable Chris Wassmann, Coroner Winkler, a couple of doctors John recognized, and Thomas Betts, a reporter for the local paper. It didn't take long for this kind of news to hit the streets and for reporters to show up. John had done it plenty of times, in what seemed a lifetime ago.

At least this was John's paper of choice, *The Gazette*, and not that rag from Ashton, *The Osceola County Tribune*. No, that wasn't fair; the *Tribune* wasn't a rag, but its publisher had long been a rival, in politics and when John had been in the newspaper publishing business. *The Gazette* was edited and published by W. W. Overholser, a like-minded crony of John's.

From the high-back leather chair behind the desk, Justice Glover said, "Be seated." While he made notes in his register on the nature of the proceedings, Myrtle Foster bustled into the room. She looked as if she might have just gotten out of bed; her hair could use a bit of tidying. Then, using the old chestnut among judges, John asked himself: Who am I to judge? It never failed to draw a laugh among jurists.

"Good afternoon, Your Honor. I came as quickly as I could."

"We appreciate it, Miss Foster."

Sheriff Gill pulled a chair close to the witness stand and she settled herself and her stenography machine.

"For the record," Justice Glover said, "I'd like each of you to state your name and why you're here. Miss Foster, you go first, and then begin recording the proceedings."

"Miss Myrtle Foster, and, for my record, Your Honor, why are we here this morning?"

"A Coroner's Inquest into the death of Claus Jess, Junior, farmer, Ocheyedan, age? Does someone know the deceased's age?"

Lou Dwinnell whispered to the boy beside him and waited for a reply. Lou stood to speak. "Your Honor, my client says that next month Claus Jess, Junior would have been, my client thinks, fifty-two-years of age."

Justice Glover tapped his gavel. "Let's begin."

THOMAS BETTS

On Monday morning, awake with the roosters and armed with a new spiral notebook and a half dozen sharpened pencils, Thomas Betts arrived in Ocheyedan just after the businesses opened their doors. En route he had stopped at the Claus Jess farm; the scene of yesterday's shooting. The place looked vacated and derelict, although he did hear a cow lowing. Thomas took a few photographs with his Kodak Autographic. The dim light would make the photo grainy, highlighting the eeriness of the scene.

The Gazette publisher, W.W. Overholser, had sent Thomas to do "man on the street" interviews regarding the murder. Thomas had been around small towns long enough to know that any news out of the ordinary spread like measles among school children. A murder in a small town—now that was news.

General stores were usually the center of activity, so Thomas headed for Grole's Department Store. What better place to pick up conversation than around the pot-bellied stove, if stores still had such a thing. With a little warmth he could shed his gloves and write well enough so that he could transcribe his notes later. He'd won no penmanship awards in grade school, but he'd done well in high school English, edited the school newspaper, and had a year in journalism school under his belt. This job gave him a chance to get his feet wet. Actual experience would be an advantage when he returned to the classroom.

Thus far the stories he'd covered had been boring: Grange meetings, church and school events, a Golden Wedding, a box social. The most fun story had been a truckload of hogs tipped over on a country road. The swine had run amok and scared the wits out of a schoolmarm peddling her bicycle to school. "Pigs will eat a person," she screamed at Thomas.

As Thomas stepped into the store a bell jangled overhead. Yes, there was a pot-bellied stove but no old gents holding a meeting around it. Nor was there any sign of a clerk. Thomas sat down, pulled off his gloves, and held his hands over the stove. When his fingers warmed he took out his notebook and pencil and made notes. The 1920 Federal Census was in progress now, and the 1910 population for Ocheyedan was 595. That was only the town; the farm people were counted by township. Whatever the current count, it was down by one, Claus Jess, Jr.

"Good morning," a woman said. "I didn't hear you come in."

Startled from his thoughts, Thomas bolted to his feet as if he'd been caught at something untoward. "Good morning."

"Help you with something?"

"I hope so but not in the usual way."

The woman's raised eyebrows indicated puzzlement. A pencil dangled precariously from a bird's nest of gray hair atop her head. The tag pinned to her dress read: Elsie Grole, Prop.

"I mean, I'm not shopping. I'm Thomas Betts, from *The Gazette*."

"Bet you're here about the Jess family."

"You're very intuitive."

"A shooting and a reporter go hand-in-hand." She began tidying a table piled high with piece goods.

"Do you know the family?"

"I own a store."

That apparently answered the question. Thomas picked up a bolt of pale green satin and wrapped the tail end around the cardboard holder. He offered it to her and she stacked it where it belonged.

"When I heard about it, my heart nearly stopped." Elsie Grole laid her hand over her heart as if it had just begun beating after being stopped yesterday.

Finally; a reaction from the woman.

"Tell me about the family."

"Father, son, elderly grandmother. I haven't seen her for years but the father trades here. Pays cash, never uses credit."

Thomas noted the present tense. "The boy?"

"He comes in with a list from his father. Sometimes he buys penny candy."

"What's your feeling about him? Would you have expected him to shoot his father?"

She crossed her arms across her bosom. "I'd never expect any child to shoot a parent. Or vice versa. But, I'm a Christian. Judge not lest ye be judged."

"You're entitled to an opinion."

"Not when I run the only store in town. I'm a widow and I can't alienate customers by spouting off one way or another about anything."

Thomas thought: Where else would they shop without driving fifteen miles? But he said, "I never thought of it that way."

"I don't talk religion or politics and I certainly won't talk about a shooting we don't know much about yet. I've heard only gossip."

"I'm here to gather facts. Okay, you say you won't judge, but if you were on a jury you'd have to judge."

"That's different. Until that happens, and it will now that women finally have the vote and can serve on juries, I'll reserve judgment."

"I respect that. Do you mind if I hang around and talk to your customers? They're entitled to an opinion, aren't they?"

"They are. I expect to hear plenty of opinions today."

"And you'll keep your own counsel?"

"I will."

Thomas sat down by the stove while Elsie puttered around the store. Soon the bell tinkled above the door and two women entered with cloth shopping bags looped over their arms. "My business comes first," Elsie told Thomas as she walked past him. "You can talk after that. If they're interested."

After a few minutes Thomas hadn't picked up a word about the shooting. Maybe there were people who hadn't heard, or weren't interested. It appeared that the women were lollygaggers and that Elsie did her best to encourage their purchasing and discourage his waiting.

Thomas stepped outside. Across the street, a man had stopped to look in the window of Arnold's Shoe Store. By the time Thomas got there the man had disappeared into the tavern next door. Given prohibition, liquor was off the table so maybe the establishment served coffee and doughnuts.

Inside the shoe store, Thomas introduced himself to Ben Arnold. "Sure, I know the Jess family," Arnold said after Thomas stated his business. "The kid came in recently and bought a pair of Sunday shoes. Said he earns money selling milk."

In court yesterday Carl claimed he never had more than a nickel to spend, if even that. But two store owners had now told Thomas that Carl made purchases—candy and shoes.

Arnold shook his head. "What a tragedy. Claus was always decent to me. Town assessor, you know, so I had business with him now and then. But you never know what goes on in someone's household."

"Do you think he abused Carl?"

"Oh, I couldn't say."

Thomas speculated that, like Elsie Grole, this businessman would hold his tongue for now.

Arnold readjusted his suspenders. "He'll have his day in court."

"That's our system. Thanks for your comments."

"Are you going to use my name in the paper?"

"I might. Is that all right?"

"Sure."

Any mention of the man's name probably brought recognition to the business, even when the story had to do with murder.

Back outside, Thomas shot photos of the business district, only a block long and with stores on both sides of the street. A sign on Kirby Furniture announced they were closed for a funeral. Kirby must be the undertaker; the two businesses were usually of a piece. Thomas had once read that in colonial times the village furniture makers undertook the job of making coffins; thus the term undertakers.

A woman approached and Thomas paused in place. "Morning," he said, lifting his hat. She responded with a cautious smile.

"I'm a newspaper reporter. Mind if I ask you about the shooting yesterday?"

"The what?" She tugged her bonnet away from her ear.

"The murder, out in the country."

"You must be joking."

"Ma'am, I would never joke about—"

"Murder?"

"Claus Jess was shot. By his son, fifteen-years-old." Thomas realized he should have said "allegedly by his son." Innocent until proven guilty. And he shouldn't call it murder; it might have been an accident.

The woman sucked in a breath. "You don't say. The Claus family."

"So you know them?"

"Oh, my goodness; I knew the mother. That dear woman. I heard the father is a brute. And you say the boy killed him? That child? Merciful Lord. I feel faint."

Thomas took her arm and steadied her. "My car is just ahead. Would you like to sit down there?"

She gulped fresh air. "My friend lives yonder. I wonder if she knows. I was sick in bed yesterday. I didn't see or talk to anyone all day."

"Would you like me to walk to your friend's house with you?"

"No, thank you. You're very nice but I'll make it." She hugged her pocketbook under her arm and scurried off. He hadn't even learned her name.

As the morning progressed, more people appeared on the streets, seemingly for no other reason than to tell what they knew and find out what others knew. Without actually talking to anyone, Thomas jotted down comments.

"I heard the boy took coins out of the collection plate at church."

"They say the murdered man is rich and the boy wants the money."

In front of the tavern, a man yelled to a listener, "Hell, my old man licked me. Beat the crap outta me. I'll tell you this, though. It didn't happen twice. I left; only sixteen, I was. I up and left and never looked back."

Further along a man offered, "They say the boy is simple-minded."

"I saw him acting up in town one day and he seemed like a wiseacre to me," his companion said.

"What will people think of us?" a woman wondered to another.

"Us? It's nothing to do with us. One person did this."

Just before noon Thomas saw a familiar face. As he walked toward the man he couldn't remember his name. "Sir," Thomas called and the man halted at the doorway to Good Eats Café. Thomas extended his hand and introduced himself. "I saw you in court but I'm sorry I don't recall your name."

"Frank Hromatko."

"Thanks. I'll remember it now." Hungarian, maybe Bohemian, Thomas thought. "May we talk?" he asked. "I'll buy dinner."

Hromatko opened the door and had found a booth by the time Thomas caught up with him. Thomas shrugged off his coat and hat and tossed them into the booth and sat down. "Thanks for the time, Mister—"

"Call me Frank. And you're Thomas?"

"Correct." Thomas grabbed a menu from behind the condiments.

"The hot beef sandwich is their specialty," Frank said, and when the waitress appeared he ordered the special for both of them.

"How you doin', Frank?" the woman asked. "Bad news from out your way."

"Terrible, Lois. Unbelievable."

While Frank and Lois expressed concerns, Thomas raised his hand for attention. "Glass of milk, please," he said. He didn't drink coffee and didn't want his guest ordering for him.

"Coffee for me," Frank told Lois, and she bustled off. Frank slipped out of his jacket and cap and laid them aside. "It's been a helluva couple days." He ran his hand over a day's growth of chin stubble, a mix of gray and black.

"I can only imagine," Thomas said to keep Frank primed. Thomas had heard about Iowa reticence but surely this man would want to talk; he'd been there at the house. He knew the story. He'd played a role.

"I had to tell the grandmother," Frank said. "I told her that Claus died. She didn't ask for details and she doesn't remember from one minute to the next. I told her Carl is staying with friends. Her other son arrived this morning. He'll take her home with him after the funeral. If he wants to tell her different, that's up to him. My son, Willie, is doing chores at the farm."

Thomas wanted to use his notebook and pencil but it didn't seem polite. Instead, he made mental notes. He had a good memory and he had notes from yesterday's inquest. This chat would be the human interest angle.

Lois returned with two steaming plates of roast beef between slices of bread, a mound of whipped potatoes, and brown gravy topping the whole thing. Thomas took a sip of milk and then a forkful of potato.

"So have you talked to anyone else?" Frank asked.

"I spoke to several people on the street."

"What's the consensus?"

"None that I see. Mixed feelings. One woman wondered what others would think of the community. The other snapped at her that the community didn't do this; one person did."

Frank swallowed a bite. "I expect tempers are short and folks are saying things they wouldn't ordinarily say."

Thomas nodded. Of course, this was not an everyday topic.

"Are you from Sibley?" Frank asked.

"I am right now. I grew up in St. Paul."

"A city boy. All right; let me tell you about small towns." Frank laid down his fork and knife. "You have your ethnic and religious groups. Protestants who don't like Catholics and vice versa. You'll hear that Baptists are too strict; Presbyterians too lenient; that Episcopalians and Lutherans are only dehorned Catholics. There's anti-German prejudice since the war, and even the Scandinavian groups tell jokes about each other. The Irish are the butt of saloon humor. There's a wheat farmer from the Ukraine who speaks no English. He and his wife keep to themselves."

Thomas wondered if Frank might be from that part of the world, but he carried no discernable foreign accent.

"That said," Frank continued, "when trouble strikes, folks come together. A tornado, a flood, or a farmer has an accident and crews show up to pick his corn and the women bring food. Someone dies, and within minutes condolence calls are made. Food like you wouldn't believe."

Thomas believed it; the latter was true in cities, too. "And when someone is murdered? How do folks react?"

"Well, this isn't like a city. This is a first for us. Thank God. It hasn't sunk in yet. There's a state of disbelief. At least I assume so. That's the way I feel."

A man on his way out stopped at the booth. "Hey, Frank."

"Zeb," Frank said.

"Hear there was trouble out by you yesterday."

"Sure was. I'll stop by later if you're gonna be home."

"I'm heading there now."

Thomas had consumed more of his hot beef sandwich while the two men had their brief conversation. "How well did you know Claus Jess?" he asked now.

"We were neighbors, but not close friends. Neighbors help each other when needed. Other than that, Claus wasn't one for socializing."

"An introvert?"

"I suppose. Controlling. I sensed a lot of anger. His own father was a hard man, but he apparently liked his only grandchild. From what I've heard, from a reliable source, Claus's father left his estate to the boy, not to his wife and not to Claus."

"That follows what Carl talked about in court yesterday. He wanted half of the money from the sale of the farm. But he wasn't exactly coherent in his confession."

"That's the first I heard that Claus had sold the farm. Willie said Carl bragged about being rich but I didn't put much stock in it. What's rich to a kid? I once thought a hundred dollars was a fortune."

Thomas smiled. "Isn't it?"

Frank laughed. "Anyway, I imagine Claus resented his father's estate skipping a generation and going to Carl. Of course, Carl isn't old enough to claim the money so Claus has, or had, the reins. That's what I was saying about him being controlling."

"And Carl would resent that," Thomas said. "So we have a household filled with resentment and repressed anger, both father and son. Carl was fighting not only his father but struggling with himself. Wouldn't you think he'd a least try to run away? Where did the idea come from to kill his father? Do you think he even considered what would happen if he killed his father and got away with it? He had a lame alibi, but what if it worked? His father is dead and he owns the farm and let's suppose there is a fortune. He's fifteen. Is he going to farm the land? Or if he got caught in his deceit, did he even consider the consequences—"

Frank held up a hand, a stop sign of sorts. "Slow down. You've asked a half dozen questions as well as crediting deep thinking to a kid who isn't real smart."

"I heard that from someone else. But he planned a murder and carried through."

Frank nodded. "There is that. I suppose experts will be called in to decide on his intelligence, or lack of it."

"If he is simple, that would make it even harder for him to make sense of the conflict in his mind. To come to a rational decision. Let me ask you this. When he came to your house that morning; how did he behave?"

"Agitated, but that seemed natural given that he said his father got kicked by a horse and was bleeding, maybe dead. I know for a fact that a horse kick can kill a man. When we got there, it didn't look like a kick to me and then I smelled gun powder. I told Carl his father was dead and I needed to call the sheriff."

"And that was okay with him?"

"I didn't ask him. Willie had followed us over and was outside. I sent him home to call the sheriff."

Thomas's mind reeled with questions. "Was there a drinking problem?"

"Claus? He didn't touch the stuff. His father did, too much."

Thomas pushed aside his plate. "That was a fine meal."

Frank smiled. "My sister is the cook."

"No kidding. Tell her it was real good."

"I'm thinking about a wedge of pie. Sour cream raisin."

Sour cream didn't entice Thomas. "You go ahead. Not for me."

"No dessert," Frank told Lois as she refilled his cup.

"No pie? You feelin' okay?" she asked with a smile. She tore a sheet off her order pad and waved the bill. Thomas took it.

"If you have a few more minutes," Thomas said to Frank. "A couple of questions. One, did you see this coming? The shooting?"

Frank rubbed his eyes. "How could anyone foresee that? Not even with hindsight can I think of any red flags." He seemed to maybe reconsider, but said no more.

"Carl says he was being abused. Did you know that?"

"I never witnessed it."

"That's not the same thing. Did you know it?"

"No; not for a fact." Frank's voice rang angry, as if he were being accused of neglect; as if he might have somehow prevented this from happening. "Willie mentioned it. But kids tell stories. I saw bruises on Carl but for all I knew he got into a fight at school and told Willie his dad did it. Willie said Carl got into scrapes at school."

"If you knew for certain Claus was abusing Carl; would you have reported it?"

Frank sighed. "If I'd actually come across Claus beating him, I'd have stepped in. I don't know that I'd have reported it. I've always believed in live and let live."

"Okay, let me think out loud. Then I'll let you go." Thomas pulled out his notebook and pencil, wrote something and showed it to Frank. "I'm sure you're familiar with these journalism details: Who, what, where, when, and why."

"I've heard that, sure."

"Okay, who?" Thomas asked.

"Claus and Carl Jess."

"What?"

"Shooting. Murder."

"Where?"

"In the bedroom, at the farmhouse."

"When?"

"Yesterday. March seven, about seven in the morning."

"Why?"

"Well, that's not clear yet."

"Right; and neither is when."

"I don't understand."

"We know *when* in the sense of the date. But I'm thinking in terms of *when* Carl went from thinking about murder to doing it. *When* did things become so unbearable that he felt he had no other recourse? *When* did Carl slip over the edge? That moment, that second, and there was no turning back."

Thomas paused. "And, *why*? Not the motive, but *why* that morning out of all the times the act must have crossed his mind?"

Frank took a moment to respond. "If you ever answer those questions, let me know." He picked up his coat and cap. "And now I need to go to the feed store and get home."

As Thomas gathered his belongings he thought: A jury will need to answer those tough questions.

"Thanks for dinner," Frank told Thomas.

"My pleasure. Well, not the occasion, but it helped talking to you. Oh, by the way, who's in charge of the funeral?"

"That would be Reverend Fiene, Saint Paul's Lutheran, a block west of here."

"I'll find it. Thanks again."

The Reverend's wife answered the door and told Thomas, "Pastor is in his study. I don't disturb his meditation hour. He's particularly distraught today." She curled together the fingers of both hands beneath her bosom, the way female choir members do when singing. "I can tell you that the service will be held Wednesday at the Jess home."

"Why not from the church?"

"The man's half-brother came to look after his mother. He called and said the family wants privacy."

"That's understandable. Thanks for your time."

Walking to the car, cold raindrops pelted Thomas's face. That could mean sleet. He'd best get on the road. He could make calls from the office. He wanted to know more about the money situation. Maybe talk to someone at the bank.

He'd taken the town's pulse and temperature. Passions ran hot and cold regarding the Jess family. He knew only *who* and *where*.

Why does one person kill another? Beyond having a motive, *why*?

When does the decisive moment come?

What propels one to that moment?

Intellectually, Thomas knew there were no satisfactory answers to those questions. Not now, and probably not ever.

THE SHERIFF'S WIFE: GRACE GILL

That same Monday morning, while making breakfast, Grace Gill kept her eyes on the back of the head of the dark-haired boy at her table. Joe had brought Carl Jess home late yesterday after the inquest and her heart had immediately gone out to this child whose ragged clothing bore clots of his father's blood. Grace called a neighbor whose son was about Carl's size. By the time Flora arrived with clean clothing and flannel pajamas, Grace had banished Carl to the bathtub, and she'd washed his hair, as well. That accomplished, he'd eaten supper with them, speaking only when spoken to, politely covering yawns, and then shyly asked if he could go to bed.

Later, as Grace and Joe settled onto their pillows, she said, "All that waif needs is mothering."

"This is no ordinary boy," Joe warned. "Keep your mothering to a minimum."

Joe had told Grace that Carl confessed to killing his father and Justice Glover had bound him over to a Grand Jury and remanded him to Joe's custody. The boy had been upset that he couldn't go home and do chores. Frank Hromatko, the neighbor Carl had gone to and who had been at the inquest, assured Carl that he and his son, Willie, who was Carl's friend, would do chores. They had taken his grandmother home with them.

This morning, Carl hadn't come downstairs until Joe checked on him and invited him to the kitchen. He probably didn't know what he was supposed to do. Now Joe had gone to his office at the jail and Carl was in Grace's hands for a few hours. Monday was usually wash day, but she never fretted about altering routines. If they had clean clothes and bedding, the laundry could wait a day or two.

"Do you drink coffee?" she asked Carl in a welcoming tone.

"Sometimes," he replied, not loud, but audible.

"Or would you rather have milk?"

"I drink plenty of milk. I like coffee."

Grace set a cup of coffee at Carl's place and waved her hand to the lazy Susan in the center that held nearly every condiment stocked at the mercantile. "Help yourself to cream and sugar."

Back at the stove, she filled a plate with fried potatoes, two eggs, and four bacon strips. "The eggs got a tad hard," she said. "I hope they're okay."

"*Oma* used to ask how I liked my eggs cooked and then she'd laugh and say that didn't mean I was going to get them that way."

Grace smiled. "That's right. Joe likes them over easy but if the yolk breaks he doesn't mind."

"*Oma* doesn't cook much anymore. She's real old. One time she was cooking and started a fire."

"The sheriff's no hand at cooking so he's grateful for what anyone puts on the table. I ate earlier with him."

Carl snapped a piece of crisp bacon in half with his fingers and ate both halves together. "This is good. I ain't had bacon for a while."

Joe had told Grace that at the farm there'd been little food in the cupboards and pantry. You'd think they'd have meat, at least; hams or bacon. The poor kid was probably starving. "Oh, for goodness sake," she said, rising. "I didn't make toast."

"This is plenty."

"Are you sure? It won't take long."

"I'm sure."

She told herself to stop hovering. "Did you sleep all right?" Now she wondered if she should have asked. How would a boy sleep after a day like yesterday?

"I slept some. The room looks like a boy's room. Do you have a boy?"

Fighting to control her emotions, Grace said, "He died in the war, in France. His name was Fred. He was nineteen."

Grace realized Carl probably didn't know what to say. Even adults didn't know how to respond to a comment about a deceased person, so she filled the space. "We have a daughter, too. Mildred. She lives on a farm near Spencer. Married with two girls. One is about your age, the other younger."

Fred had been a surprise baby, ten years after Mildred, but Grace didn't burden Carl with details. He'd cleaned his plate so she picked it up and took it to the sink. "Would you like more coffee?"

"No, thank you." Carl brought his cup to Grace and then stood looking out the window over the sink.

While she considered what to say or do next, Carl said, "I had two sisters what died. I don't remember them. One died when she was two and the other was a few days old. I saw their names in the Bible."

"Oh, I'm sorry." Grace felt certain that her mentioning Fred's death had brought this comment, but she liked that Carl was conversing. Last night he'd hardly spoken. She sat at the table and he joined her.

He twirled the lazy Susan with his finger, as if it were a toy he'd never seen. "The one who was two was Margaret Cecilia. It didn't say why she died. The other was Annalise Barbara. She got pneumonia."

"Pneumonia can take someone quickly, especially a baby."

"By my name in the book there was a scrap of paper from a newspaper that said I was born and weighed nine pounds. I don't know why that was in the paper."

"Probably because most babies don't weigh that much. Even eight pounds is a big baby."

"Her name was Marta Anna Grabow. Before she got married."

It took Grace a second to understand that he meant his mother. "It's nice you have all that family information."

"Why?"

"Well, we should all know where we came from."

"I'm from Ocheyedan."

Grace ducked her head and smiled.

"I think I remember my mother."

"How old were you when she died?"

"About five."

"Oh, my; that's young. I don't remember much from that age. But then I'm much older than you are. I've lost names and places."

"Lost them?"

"I mean, sometimes I can't remember a name or place from long ago."

"*Oma* doesn't remember who I am lots of times."

"I understand she's quite old."

"She can't hear anymore."

"That must be difficult."

Carl stopped the lazy Susan. "I have one memory about my mother. *Opa* said it's a dream."

"It's hard to tell sometimes. Dreams we usually forget but memories stay in our mind and then come back from time to time. At least that's what I think."

Unsure where this was headed, or whether or not to encourage it, Grace waited for Carl to continue or change the subject.

"*Mutter* came from the outhouse. She was holding her dress and apron between her legs. It looked like blood on the cloth. She stumbled to the ground and said *kleinkind*. That meant baby. We talked German. I didn't talk American until I learned at country school. And during the war we had to speak American, no German allowed. Teacher said the governor made a law that we couldn't talk German anywhere. Not in school or church or even at home."

"I know," Grace said to let Carl catch his breath. His story had poured from him like syrup on pancakes; as if he'd been waiting all his life to tell it.

"*Oma* still talks German. She understands American and can read it but she won't talk it. She can't hear so we don't talk much now."

Grace nodded, again letting Carl lead the way.

"I didn't know what *Mutter* said about a baby but *Vater* told her to go back to work. He yelled about shelling corn. Then . . . I think, *Oma* and *Opa* came and later there was a man, maybe a doctor. He and *Vater* talked loud. They were mad. Then it might have been another day and *Mutter* was in bed and there were people in the house. That night *Oma* put me to bed and told me that *Mutter* went to Heaven and I should pray for her every night but forget about her."

Carl had stared out the window while telling this, as if the details lay in the distance, back at the farm. Now he glanced at Grace, his blue eyes wide in his round face. "Do you think that's a dream?"

"I doubt it, Carl."

"How could I forget about her but pray for her every night? If I forgot about her, I wouldn't remember to pray for her."

"That makes sense."

"Anyway, that's all I remember about my mother."

Grace had read about doctors who claimed they could help people remember things buried in their brain. But in Carl's case, she could not see what purpose that would serve. Or in anyone's case. If it was buried, leave it alone.

Carl jittered in his chair, seemingly uncomfortable, so Grace offered, "If you like to read, there are books in your room, stories my son liked. I know there's a copy of *The Call Of The Wild*. That was one of Fred's favorites."

"I've heard of it. I've read *Tom Sawyer*."

"That might be there, too. Do you go to school now?"

"Not regular. I'm a farmer."

Grace knew that farm children had time off from school to help at home, but she doubted that any, at fifteen, called himself a farmer. Least of all a boy this small.

"What will happen today?" he asked.

"I don't know, but don't worry about it." Another hearing would be held, but she'd let the lawyer or Joe tell him about that.

"If you want to go upstairs and read, that's fine."

He slid from the chair and pushed it under the table.

Good manners. The sheriff didn't always put his chair out of the way.

Grace put one arm around Carl and hugged him. He stiffened, as if this were the first time anyone had hugged him. It occurred to Grace that Joe might not approve of this gesture, but he didn't understand that mothering happened of its own volition; one could hardly keep it in check. But if it made Carl uncomfortable, she'd hold back.

"You go upstairs and rest," she said. "I'll call you for dinner."

GRACE GILL

Grace stacked the dishes by the sink. With just her and Joe here, she usually left the dishes until it was worthwhile heating water for a bigger batch. She cooked for prisoners at the jail, but that happened rarely. Most of the guests there had imbibed too much and spent the night to cool off and were released in the morning. Carl's plate, cup, and utensils added little to the accumulation. She primed the pump and ran water into the sink, then added the plates with congealed egg on them. They'd wash easier later.

Wiping the table clean and setting it in order for the next meal, Grace went over what Carl had told her. Perhaps his first memory, it reveals his father abusing his mother, and details about her death. All these years his father had silenced him with threats and now his grandmother had become childish and of no help to him. If he'd had someone to talk to this terrible thing might not have happened. Didn't anyone see his need, a teacher, their pastor, a neighbor, a relative?

What would she have done if she'd seen indication that he needed help? People didn't appreciate someone telling them how to raise their children. Her childless sister, rest her soul, had sometimes criticized Grace's parenting. She let it slide because it was only a matter of opinion. Faith had been extremely conservative, while Grace gave Mildred and Fred a long leash as long as there was no harm in their conduct. Of course, they were never in dire straits like Carl.

Now she wondered if she should tell Joe about Carl's memory. Was it relevant to his defense? The question went unanswered when she glanced out the window and saw Alma Lundberg chugging up the walk to the house. That's the way she looked, chugging like an engine, her breath preceding her as she huffed and puffed in the cold air. Grace had a good idea what Alma the gossip wanted, but it was too late to pretend she wasn't home; Alma had seen Grace at the window and waved. Might as well get it over with it.

"You're home." Alma feigned surprise when Grace opened the door.

"Hi, Alma." Grace backed herself into the kitchen, out of the way.

Alma made short order of taking off her coat and headscarf and mittens and then grunted as she bent to remove her overshoes, a man's four-buckle style.

"Don't bother," Grace said. "I need to mop the floor anyway."

"If you're sure." Alma sat down; the huffing waning now. "They're a pain to get on and off. I'll be glad when the snow is gone. And the cold. It brings on my lumbago."

"Coffee's still warm if you want some."

"Oh, sure; I can always drink coffee."

Grace poured a cup for Alma but passed on refilling hers. She'd had her limit for today. She scooped a few gingerbread cookies onto a plate and put it on the table. Ginger soothed the stomach and hers felt topsy-turvy since hearing Carl's story.

"So," Alma said, craning her head toward the hallway. "Where is he?"

Grace nibbled a cookie and played dumb. "At the office, like always."

Alma looked at Grace. "Not Joe. I heard Justice Glover gave the sheriff custody of the boy."

"That's right. By law, they can't hold a child in the jail."

"I didn't know that."

"No reason you would."

"So, how does he seem; the boy?"

"Quiet. Polite."

"Is he locked up?"

"He's in the upstairs back bedroom. Fred's room."

"Door locked? Windows locked?"

Grace shook her head, remembering what Joe always said about court; a witness should answer only what he's asked and not offer any information.

"If I'm not mistaken, Fred's room has an outside stairway."

"Alma, Carl isn't locked in but he's not going anywhere. I have no qualms about his being here. He promised the sheriff he wouldn't leave. A person's promise has always been good enough for me. In this case, too."

That was more than Grace intended to say and she now opened her mouth to change the subject, but Alma jumped ahead of her.

"He killed his father."

"We don't know that."

"I heard he confessed in court yesterday."

"People confess to things they didn't do."

"Why would anyone do that?"

"Joe says it happens. Sometimes to protect someone else."

"Who could that be? The crazy old woman?"

"I understand she's deaf; not crazy."

Alma made a point of staring into her cup, as if reading tea leaves, but Grace had emptied the pot and wasn't going to make another. It would only encourage Alma.

"Do you know the family?" Alma asked.

Again, Grace played dumb. "What family?"

"The family we were talking about. Jess."

"I'd never heard of them until this happened."

Alma leaned forward on the table. "Well, my cousin, she lives in Ocheyedan. She's friends with Lizzie Hromatko. They farm next to the Jess place. Lizzie told my cousin that Claus was mean as a rattlesnake. He beat the kid and his wife. She lost two babies, born dead. She miscarried the day she died."

Grace wasn't about to tell Alma that Carl's sisters had not been born dead. Their names and ages were in the Bible. But from the story he told it seemed likely there'd been a miscarriage the day his mother died.

"Lizzie told my cousin she remembers when Marta died. The boy's mother. A couple days before, she'd been spotting and Claus wouldn't take her to see the doctor and wouldn't let her lay down neither. The day she died she began hemorrhaging and it was too late."

"We can't know any of this for sure, Alma. And, you know, I've told you before, Joe doesn't want me to talk about anything that goes on at the jail or courthouse, any of that business."

"You're not telling me anything. I'm saying what I heard. Folks are talking on the street. No one seems to be mourning for Claus Jess."

"He didn't live here. I doubt that anyone knew him personally."

"They say the branches of that boy's family tree are riddled with disease. They're Germans, you know."

Grace almost laughed. "I declare, Alma. That's nonsense."

"Really? Have you forgotten that war we just fought?"

Grace's heart fluttered and then her anger flared. "Alma Lundberg, I'm not likely to ever forget that war. Nor that you asked that question of me."

Alma's face reddened. "Forgive me. Sometimes I don't think before I speak." She reached for Grace's hand but Grace leaned away.

Grace almost felt sorry for Alma's chagrin, but now she just wanted her to leave. Glancing at the clock, she said, "I need to go to Richardson's for some liver. Monday is Joe's liver and onions meal."

"Sounds good to me." Before standing Alma added, "I'm sorry for what I said about the war."

Grace knew she should acknowledge the apology but did not.

Alma pulled on her coat and scarf and gathered her mittens and handbag. She glanced toward the stairs to the upper floor and Grace knew what she was thinking: Are you leaving him here by himself? The answer was yes.

"Thanks for the coffee," Alma said on the porch. "I guess we'll hear the full story when the paper comes out. I heard there was a reporter from the paper at the inquest. My cousin said he came to Ocheyedan."

"My father always said you can't believe everything you read in the paper. But let's hope we get the correct story."

While dressing to go outdoors Grace wondered if she should leave Carl in the house alone. Well, she'd stop next door at the jail and tell Joe she was going to the market. If he felt better about having someone with Carl, then he could go home for the half hour it would take to run her errand.

On the way to the jail it occurred to her that Carl might not like liver and onions. Kids were finicky. She'd buy enough hamburger to make a couple of patties. She still thought of it as hamburger, although during the war anti-German sentiment had folks calling it ground beef or ground steak.

Grace bore no grudge against Germans in general, even though the war with them had taken her son. The Germans here had nothing to do with that.

True; she'd had a hole in her heart since the morning the telegram arrived on their doorstep. She didn't understand how a hole, which is supposedly empty, could have weight, but the pressure persisted every waking moment, and in sleep, too. Like carrying a child in the womb, or like breasts filled with milk, the ache felt at once burdensome and comforting.

JOHN GLOVER

On Thursday morning, Alma Lundberg wasn't the only one eager to see the weekly paper. Rather than wait for a house copy to be delivered to the hotel, John walked to the newspaper office to get a copy hot off the press. He chatted with Willis Overholser about the murder, and then begged his leave. Along the street, as merchants opened their doors for the day, John heard snatches of conversation: Abuse . . . money involved . . . the bastard . . . what's this world coming to?

Yes, the world had changed; the town had changed, the people had changed. Things should change. They must not stagnate. Twenty years ago, when John was mayor for the second time, he'd instituted The Mayor's Walk. Once a month, on a Saturday evening when the stores stayed opened late to accommodate farmers who couldn't come to town during the day, he donned the silk top hat given him by the town council and strolled through the business district greeting shoppers and entering each store to inquire of the owner how business was going. Back then many of the merchants and townsfolk still spoke a native tongue: German, Dutch, Scandinavian, Italian, Polish, French, and Irish and Scottish brogues so thick one had to listen carefully to gather the gist of a comment. John wished he had a tenth of the fire and spirit he'd had back then. Still, it pleased him to see how the town he'd helped found had grown and prospered. He still enjoyed watching the activity on the street.

Rounding the corner, John spied Alex Tossini and Joe Massa ahead, in front of their side-by-side businesses across from the hotel. Friends since childhood in an Italian village, they'd emigrated about five years ago. Alex sold confections, ice cream, and fruit. Until prohibition set in, Joe's Place, run by Joe and his brother, Louie, offered alcoholic beverages. Louie had recently returned to the old country, and Joe had snubbed John for a while because he'd sided with prohibition, but he'd become friendly again as business picked up. Joe's Place now offered pool, billiards, snooker, card tables, short order meals, and nonalcoholic drinks. A kind of men's club without actually saying women were not allowed. A weekly poker group met there. Watching the two businessmen as he approached, it amused John to see their arms flailing as they talked. He once playfully offered to tie their hands behind their back to see if they could still speak.

"*Giovanni*," Alex called, making John's name sing as only an Italian can. Joe raised his arm in greeting, too.

"*Buongiorno*," John replied, trying for the same melodious inflection, and failing.

Coatless on this crisp morning, each man wore a white apron tied at the waist and had rolled his shirtsleeves above the elbow, anchored with a red garter, ready for the day's business. Noting the newspaper under John's arm, Joe must have anticipated the front page story. Crossing himself he uttered, "*Che Dio ti benedica ragazzo,*" which John interpreted as God bless the boy. Alex nodded in agreement.

"He needs our prayers," John said. Eager to move on and read the paper, he added, "Enjoy your day," and jaywalked across the street.

In the hotel dining room, awaiting coffee and oatmeal, John donned his reading glasses and opened the paper. In the blackest, largest font he'd ever seen in this particular paper, the headline and subtitles under the byline Thomas Betts read:

PATRICIDE: CARL JESS KILLS FATHER
Fifteen-Year-Old Lad Of Ocheyedan Shoots Father In Bed Sunday
Slept With Father Night Of Homicide
Coroner's Inquest Held Sunday
Funeral Yesterday

The story ran several columns, so rather than trying to read the lengthy story and eat at the same time, John scanned the other front page stories. Bids were taken on street paving; the Shorthorn Breeders Association held a meeting; personal news from the small towns surrounding Sibley and, tragically, the death of a one month old baby. John knew the parents, from the Congregational parish, and would need to make a condolence call today.

Finished with breakfast, John went to the reading nook off the lobby, turned on a lamp, adjusted his glasses, and sat down to read the reporter's account of what had happened last Sunday.

Bound Over To Grand Jury

When someone dies in a small community where everyone knows everyone, folks gather to support the deceased's family. When death is the result of murder, the town is draped in a veil of shock, distress, and bewilderment. Residents at once discuss the crime and stand back until the chaff of gossip is separated from the grains of truth. While the winds of March have brought frigid temperatures, it is a vicious murder that has chilled residents to the bone. Some of what Carl Jess claimed in his confession is disputed by the townsfolk and merchants. But on everyone's mind is the question: Why? Why did this happen? If there is an answer, we don't yet have it.

According to evidence submitted at the coroner's inquest, Carl Jess, a fifteen-year-old lad, shot his father, Claus Jess, Jr. early Sunday morning with a 32 calibre rifle. The revolting crime was committed while the elder Jess was asleep in bed, Carl having slept with his father the last night of his life. Carl said his father mistreated him and did not give him money.

Carl arose before 7:00 o'clock Sunday morning intending to shoot his father. Noticing that his father's eyes were not closed he went to the kitchen and built a fire in the cook stove. He then returned to his father's room with a 32 calibre rifle, shooting him in the side of the head. After committing the rash deed, he went to the barn to do chores. Returning to the house, and noting that his father was groaning, he reloaded the rifle, shooting his father the second time. The whole transaction was said to be most deliberate and had been premeditated for some time past. The boy's grandmother, 87-years-old, lived with the father and son, but being hard of hearing knew nothing of what happened.

After shooting his father the second time, Carl went and told Frank Hromatko, a neighbor, that his father had been kicked by a horse and was bleeding badly. In court, the young man seemed indifferent to the awfulness of the crime committed. Only once or twice did he show any evidence of remorse. At the coroner's inquest held Sunday afternoon he made a frank and full confession of the crime. He appeared in court with his attorney L. A. Dwinnell, who waived examination for his client, and he was bound over to the grand jury by Justice Glover and is now in the custody of Sheriff Gill. He was greatly dissatisfied that he was not permitted to return home in order to take care of chores.

Before the coroner's jury, Carl said he was dissatisfied with the amount of money he was receiving and thought he should have half of his father's property, valued at from $100,000 to $150,000.

Coroner Winkler deputized Dr. Padgham to hold the inquest. O.J. Frey, Heke Henderson, and Lee Poole were sworn in as jurymen. County Attorney Butler assisted the coroner in the investigation. The jury returned the following verdict:

Said jurors upon the oath do say that the said Claus Jess came to his death in his own home in Ocheyedan, Iowa, on March 7, 1920, at or about the hour of 7 o'clock a.m., as a result of two rifle bullets entering his brain and said bullets fired from a 32 calibre rifle held in the hands of Carl Jess, his son.

(Signed) O. J. Frey, H. H. Henderson, Lee Poole.

Testimony Of Carl Jess

Carl Jess being first duly sworn testified as follows: That he is 15 years of age, a son of Claus Jess; that his mother has been dead since he was a baby 2 or 3 years old, that he has been going to school.

"Last time I saw my father alive was at six a.m. this Sunday morning when I got up. I slept with him all night. I got up at six o'clock this morning, built a fire, went out to milk, and then got my rifle and shot my father. The rifle was loaded when I got it and after I shot my father the first time, I went back and got another bullet and shot him again. When I shot him I think he was awake but his eyes were closed. After I shot him the first time I then went back and shot him a second time. I didn't know where I hit him the first shot. I did not see any blood fly. I didn't go the second time for about ten or fifteen minutes after the first time. This gun is the one I used. It is a thirty-two calibre single shot rifle. He did not bleed until after the second shot. I wiped up some blood off the floor. After I shot him the second time I did not stop to look at him. I then put the gun in the pantry because I was afraid to go in the room again. I took the shells and threw them in the snow.

"My father got kicked last night and I helped him to undress and to bed. This happened about eight p.m. I went to bed about eight-thirty and slept with him all night. I planned this whole thing out before I went to sleep. I planned to shoot him in the morning and then tell that the horse kicked and killed him.

"I don't know why I shot him a second time, but I wanted to make sure I killed him. I thought of killing my father for a year. I slept with my father because there was no other place to sleep. There was another bed, but I didn't want to sleep alone. I killed him because I wanted to. I killed him because he whipped me, abused me, made me work, and wouldn't give me any money for two or three years. He whipped me pretty near every day; he whipped me for the last time yesterday. He would whip me with a stick, blacksnake, buggy whip.

"I loaded the gun the second time. I shot him the second time because I wanted to. When I shot him the second time he was in the same position as first time. The gun shoots true. I tried to hit him in the head. I did not aim it. I glanced along the barrel a little. I got front sight on his head. I aimed a little but I did not put it right up to my shoulder. I got the sights up a little.

"After I shot him the second time I went to Hromatko's. Then I came back and wiped up some blood off the floor and his face. I then went to the barn.

"I planned in bed last night to shoot my father this morning. I did not load the rifle for the first shot. My father loaded it about a month ago, but I knew it was loaded when I went to bed.

"I knew my father sold his farm but did not know what he got for it or what he did with it. He had made me hate him. If I had to do it over again I wouldn't have killed him. I wish I had him back now.

"I spend quite a little money uptown. My grandmother would give me money every week, more than twenty-five cents a week. After I shot my father I went over and took five cents out of my father's pocketbook which he kept in the pantry cupboard. This was at noon sometime. I wanted some of this property myself and I wanted about half of it, but never asked my father for it.

"I usually get up and build fires. My grandmother was not up this morning when I got up. I got my own breakfast and ate alone as my grandmother does not eat breakfast.

"My father was awake when I went to bed last night. After I went to bed I planned and thought I would get up in the morning before he would, start the fire and come back and if my father was awake that I would wait. I planned to get the rifle and shoot him. I planned to shoot him twice.

"When I woke up this morning I remembered and decided to do as I planned last night. When I got the gun I started to leave and then stopped and looked at him and his eyes were closed. Then I shot him. When I shot him the first time I was scared. I did not see any blood and did not see him move. I then went out and did chores and left the gun in the pantry. While out in the barn before I got chores done I came in to see about the fires and got the gun to put back in the room. I looked at him. He was groaning so I wasn't sure he was dead. I went and got another bullet and shot him again.

"When I shot him the first time I knew I hit him because he kind of jerked and moaned. I felt if he were dead that I wouldn't be bossed around so much. My grandmother is very hard of hearing. I looked at the gun last night and saw it was loaded."

John paused, trying to follow this repetitious statement that segued from that of an incoherent child to that of a cold-hearted killer. The story ran all over the place; Carl was in the house and then he was in the barn and back again and he built a fire before killing his father or he did it after. Did he wipe up blood before or after he went to the neighbor's farm? He didn't have any spending money, and then he spent quite a bit. The confusion was understandable; this had obviously traumatized the boy.

John paced the floor to stretch his legs. His back troubled him lately and he found it difficult to get comfortable in bed or a chair. Might as well visit the men's room while he was up. To make certain that no one borrowed his paper, he tucked it under the chair cushion. Five minutes later, refreshed, he resumed reading.

Among the witnesses examined were Constable Chris Wassmann, A.D. Fritz, F.J. Boyd, Dr. L.G. Lass, Dr. W.E. Ely, Frank Hromatko, and Willie Hromatko, all of whom were called to the home soon after the homicide.

Frank Hromatko, who lives within a half block of the Jess home, told of Carl coming for him Sunday morning and saying that his father was kicked by a horse and bleeding badly. How he found the man in bed dead. Carl said his father had been kicked Saturday night and he (Carl) didn't send for a doctor because his father seemed all right.

In telling Willie Hromatko what had happened Carl broke down and cried. Mr. Fritz told of walking home with the deceased Saturday evening. About nine o'clock Sunday morning he saw Carl Jess sitting by the stove and asked him where his pa was. He pointed to the bedroom. He told of finding the man dead in bed. He said to Carl, "How was Pa killed?" Carl said, "He came into the barn, slipped and fell, and I guess he grabbed the horses by the back leg, and the horse kicked him. I was on the wagon throwing down straw when I heard a noise and went into the barn and found him laying there; I took hold of him, lifted him up and helped him into the bedroom about eight o'clock Saturday night."

The funeral was held yesterday from the home of the deceased and was largely attended. Rev. Fiene conducted the services. Interment was made in the Ocheyedan cemetery.

Claus Jess, Jr. was born in Germany April 24, 1867, and died March 7, 1920. With his parents he came to Osceola County in 1873, homesteading a farm south of Ocheyedan. His wife passed away about ten years ago. He leaves a son, a mother, aged 87, and a half-brother, Claus Bohr.

John checked to see if there might be more information continued on another page, but that was it. Considering what he'd read, from several views, John formed more than one opinion. From the standpoint of an editor and publisher, he considered Thomas Betts an unskilled writer. His opening, with a line or two of purple prose, tossed readers a hook, but the story was unorganized and confusing. Both Fritz and Hromatko said they'd found Jess dead in bed. When had Fritz come to the house? It sounded as if it were Saturday evening, and again Sunday morning? Again, playing editor, John deplored sentences such as: Mr. Fritz told of walking home with the deceased Saturday evening. He walked home with the deceased?

From the standpoint of an attorney, both for the defense and for the State, John noted gaps and inconsistences in times and dates. The boy said he was two or three when his mother died, but in another place her death was placed at ten years ago. That would make Carl five when she died. Some of this didn't make much difference, but depending on how the case evolved, lawyers might have a hey-day with it.

As an ordained minister, John felt pity and forgiveness for Carl Jess, but the Lord's commandments were clear: Honor thy father and thy mother. Thou shalt not kill.

John wanted to discuss this story with someone and, as luck would have it, Lyn stepped into the lobby and glanced around. John waved from the corner and Lyn shuffled over to join him.

JOHN GLOVER

"I haven't seen you since church on Sunday," John said. "Where have you been?"

"I had a job in Melvin and stayed at the man's house. I told you I'd be away." Lyn peeled off his coat and let it drop to the carpet. John picked it up and draped it over a chair.

"Come to think of it, you did tell me. I've been preoccupied. I hope it wasn't outdoor work."

"No; all the walls in his house needed replastering."

"You're the man for that." John held up the newspaper. "Have you read it?"

"Over at the café. Everyone has an opinion."

"Human nature."

"People either liked Claus Jess or hated him. His name is familiar. Do you know him from the early days?"

"That'd be his father. We homesteaded at the same time. But I knew this one, too."

"After reading the story it came to me that I worked for the guy years back. He added a bedroom to the first floor and I did the lathing and plastering."

"That's where it happened, the murder, in the downstairs bedroom. How long ago did you work there?"

"Umm; ten years seems about right."

"Was the mother around then? Claus's wife?"

"There was a young woman. Friendly, but . . . I don't know, timid. Nervous."

"She might have had good reason."

"I recall she looked younger than Claus. A lot younger."

"She was barely out of childhood when she married him. How about the boy?"

"He hung around while I worked. About four, five years old. Wanted to help. Got himself covered with plaster dust and looked like a little ghost. I recollect his father yelled at him and took him out and dunked him in the horse watering trough. Held him under longer than I thought he should but what do I know about raising kids? He did a lot of yelling, Claus did. The kid and the mother seemed to stay out of his reach."

"That follows with Carl's story."

"That his father beat him?"

John nodded. "What do you remember from age five?"

"Hmm, that's a tough one. Some things I probably remember only from stories you've told."

"How about your mother? What do you recall?"

"I have actual memories of her. She read to me sometimes. Mostly, it seems they're about her being sick. And other people helping in the house. Aunt Addie and Grandpa Upton."

"Do you remember her death?"

"I do. Why all the questions?"

"Just wondering what the boy might recall about his mother. He was younger when she died than you were."

"His thought process seemed odd. The confession was rambling and confusing, a lot of contradictions."

"I thought so, but that's to be expected. He was a frightened boy there in the courtroom."

"Did anyone examine him for abuse?"

"There were doctors at the inquest who had been at the house. I don't know what they'd done at the crime scene. I noticed a bruise along Carl's wrist."

"Now, Papa, the prosecution would object and say that kids get bruised all the time." Lyn pushed up the sleeve of his whipcord shirt and exhibited a black spot. "I get bruised and don't even know when or why it happened."

"Objection well-taken. Did you ever see Claus hit his wife?"

Lyn laughed. "I was working, not standing around watching people. And do you think he'd do it front of others?"

"Did you see any bruises on the wife?"

"Papa, it was a decade ago."

"But you have good recall. You're observant."

"Need I remind you that Claus Jess is not on trial? His son killed him."

"So he says."

"You mean there's another suspect?"

"Not likely."

"One fella on the street was saying maybe the grandmother did it and the boy is covering for her."

John shook his head. "She's close to ninety."

"Anyone else around? A hired man?"

"Joe says no hired man. Claus had sold the farm and cut down on livestock. A couple or three cows and a horse."

"A tramp wandering around bothering people?"

"Not likely in this weather and tramps aren't usually violent. And why would the kid cover for a stranger?"

Lyn shrugged. "Just asking questions."

"Right. Me, too. Say, maybe you'll be called as a witness."

"Witness to what?"

"You worked for Claus."

"Papa, again, it was ten years ago. I saw nothing relevant. Besides, I've had my turn as a murder witness."

"Ah, that was a night to remember."

"So, is he crazy, the Jess kid?"

"I'm not a doctor but—"

"That's the only profession you haven't tried. That and undertaker."

"That's one I never considered, but I started to say, I'm not a doctor but if I were his defense attorney I'd start with state of mind."

"Would you like to be the defense lawyer?"

"He's in good hands."

"Would you like to be the sitting judge?"

"Hutchinson will handle it well."

"You're evading questions."

"I will say I wouldn't care to be on the jury."

"Where's the boy now?"

"He was with the Gills. By law juveniles can't be imprisoned while awaiting trial, but at the hearing on Monday, Judge Hutchinson ordered he be held in jail."

"It should be an interesting trial. But it's back to work for me. Father O'Reilly wants me to check his chimney for loose bricks. It might need to be repointed."

John patted his middle-aged son on the shoulder. "Watch yourself on the roof. We've had sleet."

Lyn raised his hand in an obedient salute, grabbed his coat and shuffled out the door.

He'd begun using that gait after his mother died. John used to tell the child to pick up his feet when he walked, but mentioning it only seemed to enhance it; a form of defiance, it seemed, particularly in the teen years.

A young child losing a parent had to be highly traumatic. A child killing his parent opened a Pandora's Box of ills.

JOHN GLOVER

Later that day, John laid hands on a copy of the other local paper: *The Osceola County Tribune*, published in Ashton. It carried a different headline, a different lead-in to the story, and used the term parricide for the boy. John hadn't seen that word used for years, meaning the person who committed patricide.

Murdered By His Son
Claus Jess Shot While He Slept
The Youthful Parricide Tells The Coroner's Jury A Graphic Story
Of His Unusual Crime

Claus Jess, a wealthy retired farmer of Ocheyedan, was shot and killed in his bed early Sunday morning. His son, Carl Jess, aged 15 years, confessed to the commission of the crime before a coroner's jury Sunday afternoon.

The murdered man, his mother and son, were members of the Jess family. The woman is aged and very deaf. Sunday morning Carl Jess went to the house of the nearest neighbor, Frank Hromatko, and told him that his father had been kicked by a horse, was bleeding, and asked him to call a doctor.

Youthful resentment at parental restraint and a desire for money are indicated in Carl Jess's confession as motives for the crime. His father had a life interest in the estate of his deceased father that would descend to the youth.

The testimony of the parricide before the coroner's jury tells graphically and grimly the story of the crime. The youthful assassin was brought before Justice Glover in Sibley. By his attorney he waived examination. The court held him without bail and committed him to the custody of the sheriff. Under the juvenile laws imprisonment in a jail of a person under 16 years of age is forbidden and no provision is made for the safekeeping of juveniles who commit high crimes. Sheriff Gill consulted Judge Hutchinson, who ordered the prisoner taken to jail, where he is now.

This version of the story again suggested a motive. Carl knew he had money coming to him from his paternal grandfather. He understood that his father had control of the money, but if he were out of the way, Carl would be in charge. Unfortunately, his alibi didn't hold up. A kick to the head by a horse doesn't resemble a rifle shot. Two shots, as it turned out.

John's thoughts wandered to Grace Gill. He'd known her for many years, well enough to know that even before she lost her son to the battlefield she'd had a soft spot for boys. As a motherless boy, Lyn had spent time at the Gill house when John had to be away. Grace would be plenty upset about Carl being taken out of her home and locked in a cell. She'd probably already been there with blankets and pillows and food and books and even hung pictures on the wall. Maybe even wallpaper, with a boyish pattern. Boats or airplanes. Well, that might be exaggerating but Grace did pamper boys, especially those in need.

It being time for his daily constitutional John decided he'd walk over and pay a call on Grace. First he'd stop by Tossini's Fruit and Confectionary and buy a box of the chocolate covered cherries Grace favored. Those would end up with Carl Jess, too, but that was fine.

John wanted to see Joe Gill, too. There'd been another patricide years back; another teenaged boy shot his father. John couldn't recall the details and wanted to read the file.

JOSEPH GILL

Before running for the office of Osceola County Sheriff, Joe Gill had owned a prosperous livery and stable. Then he became involved in local politics, encouraged by John Glover, and learned that some years back there'd been a problem with a sheriff who was involved with graft. Hoping to restore luster to the department's tarnished reputation, Joe promised to devote himself full time to law and order. He'd had no complaints about his service. In his seven years thus far, he'd handled bootlegging, burglary, horse thieves, fraud, domestic violence, gunfire, a disastrous train wreck, the aftermath of a horrific tornado that struck Melvin, the usual accidents and drunks, and now the second murder in his jurisdiction.

The first one, five years ago, involved two migrant railroad workers who lived in a railroad boxcar southwest of town. After a night of drinking they got into a hassle and one killed the other with a knife. It turned out Lyn Glover witnessed the killing from the window of the rooming house near the depot where he and his father lived. Lyn alerted the town marshal and the killer was apprehended in Le Mars after fleeing on the train.

Last night Joe had dug out records from as far back as the county's founding and found a murder in 1904. Rather, the man had been accused of murder but he committed suicide in jail. In 1909, a seventeen-year-old boy shot and killed his father, and in 1910, a young man killed a woman because she wouldn't let him court her. He then turned the gun on himself. It was the patricide in 1909 that interested Joe now.

He finished reading the file just as John Glover came into the office and seated himself with a heavy sigh. He seemed a tad out of breath from his walk. Although Joe was a decade younger than John, they both had more past than future. Joe didn't know if John had any serious ailments, other than old age, but Joe's nagging hernia gave him fits.

"What brings you out on this cold day?" he asked his visitor.

"My daily walk. It keeps me spry. So to speak." John shrugged off his coat and laid it aside, a package atop the coat. "How's your day?"

Joe leaned back in his chair and stretched his arms behind his head. That put a strain on his hernia so he lowered them. "I went to Ocheyedan and met with Harry Leo at the bank. We opened Claus Jess's safety deposit box. He was a wealthy man."

"I notice that in the papers they tend to call any farmer wealthy. I should have held on to my land but I needed the money for other things. Often, farmers have valuable land but not much cash."

"True, but Jess had both." Consulting the list on his desk, Joe said, "Besides checking accounts in more than one bank, he had a thousand or so in checking at Leo's bank. We found a trove in his private box. Some ten thousand in personal property and real estate holdings. More than a thousand in gold coins. Leo said those are scarce these days. He had bonds, stocks, and mortgages worth upward of thirty-thousand, about ten thousand in Liberty Bonds and another twenty-five hundred in war savings certificates. There are notes and mortgages in excess of twenty-thousand. He not only owned realty in his own right but possessed a life interest in two-hundred acres of land in the county that should descend to the son, who shot him dead."

Joe glanced up and found his friend with his mouth hanging open. "That's the first time I've seen you at a loss for words, John."

"Holy Toledo. I knew he was well-fixed but not to that extent. He was a good businessman, I know that. Better than I ever was."

"So, you're the lawyer, refresh my memory on what happens to those assets if Carl is put away?"

"If he's convicted of murder, he gains nothing, ever. Since his grandmother is still living the estate will transfer to her. Now, if Carl is acquitted and set free, he claims the estate. If he's acquitted but, let's say, he's committed to the state hospital, the estate is held on his behalf. When he dies, and has no heirs, it goes to the state. Escheat, that's called."

"Got it." Joe placed his hand over his abdomen, a habit he'd developed since the hernia appeared. "I heard an interesting story about Claus, besides all the accumulated wealth. After Harry and I finished at the bank we had dinner at the local eatery. The county engineer joined us. Wilson, his name is."

John nodded, indicating he knew Wilson. Joe would bet that he could mention any name around the county and John would know him or her.

"Wilson said that last fall, Claus Jess came to him and said he was interested in buying swampland that was not going to be drained by the state. He wanted to operate a farm for fur-bearing animals, where he could raise muskrats, mink, skunks and other cute little quadrupeds for their skins."

Joe grinned. "That's what he said—cute little quadrupeds. Wilson told Claus of several places that would work for that purpose. Pratt Lake in Dickinson County wouldn't be bad. It has both high and low land. Skunks and other dry land animals could feed on the higher land and beavers and muskrats and other such animals would thrive in the low land. Wilson mentioned a couple of other places that might be good: Rush Lake near Ocheyedan and maybe Iowa Lake." Joe paused for a breath.

"Wilson told Jess he was inclined to think this fur proposition was a money-maker. He joked that he had observed women wearing fur stoles summer and winter, and that maybe someday the fashion would go back to the vogue of the cave woman and they'd wear a simple girdle of fur about where a one-syllable bathing suit hits the eye. Then the swamp farmer like Jess would be strictly in the swim."

John laughed. "If the magazines I've seen left around the hotel are any indication, with women's swim fashions, it's anything goes. So, what happened with the swampland?"

"As far as Wilson knew Jess never followed through."

"So, have you seen the papers? The Jess story?"

"Not yet. Grace will pick up copies." Joe looked at his watch and grabbed his coat. "I nearly forgot; I need to go see Zeke Frome."

"What's up with him?"

"Ah, Ed Guertin asked me to talk to him. Ed took his prize stallion to Zeke's farm to breed a mare and says Zeke didn't pay him. Zeke says Ed owes him money so they should call it square."

"Good luck. They're both stubborn as a two-year-old."

"This could end up in your court."

"Could be. Oh, before you go, I came to read a file. A patricide from maybe ten years ago. The kid was a teenager. Where can I find it?"

Joe handed John the folder. "I just read it."

"Mind if I sit here? It's warm and cozy."

"Be my guest. I shouldn't be long on this call."

"I admire your confidence, my friend."

JOHN GLOVER

Joe's file included the sheriff's reports and two stories from *The Sibley Gazette*, the first from January 7, 1909.

George Groen, a well-to-do farmer west of Ashton, was shot by his son, Ernest, Wednesday evening. Mr. Groen returned from Ashton about 4 o'clock Wednesday afternoon. His sons John and Ernest were testing each other's strength by pulling each other with a stick. Their father suggested he could pull both of them and wagered a dollar to that effect. He lost, and when the boys asked for the dollar he became enraged and suggested they might trust him until tomorrow. He then suggested he could pull Ernest with one hand, and failed. He again wagered he could pull Ernest, and won. He demanded his money and the boys said they were even now. He became angry, took Ernest and sat him on the stove and a general melee ensued in which the elder Groen was struck over the head with a chair as he left the house. He returned with an iron bar and swore vengeance on Ernest who had fled up stairs. He was told Ernest had gone to the neighbors, but up the stairs he went, where he saw Ernest with a shotgun. He was warned to keep back or he would be shot. On he came and Ernest blazed away the entire charge of the gun, entering Groen's left side in the region of the lung. Just after he had been shot, he asked for a revolver, saying he wished to shoot Ernest.

Drs. Langenhorst and Buckmaster of Ashton, and Cram of Sheldon, were called. Nearly 200 buckshot had entered the unfortunate man's body and the wound proved fatal. Groen died Saturday morning, the funeral being held on Tuesday.

Ernest Groen went to Sibley Saturday and voluntarily gave himself into the custody of the sheriff, to await action of the grand jury. He is a young innocent-looking boy of 17-years-of age. It seems he and his father have disagreed for years, but his father refused to consent to his leaving home.

The father has been addicted to drink and of late had often been under the influence of liquor.

For over a year a divorce case has been pending, in which his wife has been the plaintiff. The deceased owned a fine quarter section of land aside from other property.

Dr. Hough and County Attorney Garberson went to Ashton, Saturday, where a coroner's inquest was held, C. Aykens, J. W. Clark and Hans Seivert were empanelled as jury. They returned the following verdict: We the jury find the deceased, Geo. Groen came to his death by reason of a gunshot wound inflicted at the hands of his son Ernest Groen.

The deceased was born in Germany 45 years ago. For the last 15 years he has resided in Osceola County on his farm two miles west of Ashton. Aside from the widow he leaves seven children: John, Ernest, George, Hattie, Maggie, Dena, and Ollie; and three brothers and a sister, John, Dick, Sidney, and Maggie Groen, all of Kossuth County, Iowa. His father John Groen also resides in Kossuth County.

John laid aside that story, took off his glasses and rubbed his eyes to refocus. He remembered the outcome of the trial but not all the details. He helped himself to a glass of water from Joe's pitcher and then sat down and picked up the second piece, dated March 25, 1909.

Jury Finds Young Man Not Guilty of Murder

Ernest Groen is a free man again. At 5 o'clock Thursday evening, the jury of twelve men returned a verdict of not guilty. Ernest Groen, who is but 17-years-old, shot his father last December. On the stand Wednesday afternoon the young man, in a dramatic manner, described the homicide. He said he fired the gun which caused the death of his father. He claimed he did it in self-defense and had not intended inflicting a mortal wound. He also admitted having struck his father with a chair previous to the shooting affray, also in self-defense.

Mrs. Groen, mother of the unfortunate boy, and John Groen, his brother, and Drs. Langenhorst and Buckmaster were the material witnesses for the State. The mother and her son told of the events leading up to the shooting. How the deceased had quarreled with the boys and had been drinking heavily. How the father struck Ernest and that Ernest had struck his father with a chair. The enraged father went outdoors, secured an iron handle to a riding plow, came into the house looking for Ernest, who had gone upstairs. The father started up the stairs when Ernest fired the shot from the top of the stairway. The physicians told of the nature of the wound and the condition in which the deceased was found.

The evidence was concluded Wednesday evening. On Thursday morning, Attorney Garberson made the opening and closing arguments for the State while Attorney Hunter made the argument for the defendant. The arguments were eloquent throughout and held the closest of attention. The judge gave his instructions to the jury who retired about 11 o'clock. They returned a verdict about 5 o'clock.

According to the instructions of Judge Gaynor, the jury was instructed to return a verdict for the state, should the evidence show even an assault. They could find the defendant guilty of any lesser crime than the one charged, should the evidence so determine.

John left the file on Joe's desk and moseyed over to the courthouse, where he passed the time of day with the clerk of courts. Later, he saw Joe return and wanted to talk to him about the Groen case, so he went back to the office. "How'd it go with Zeke and Ed?"

Joe laughed. "Ed conceded that he owes Zeke money but not as much as the breeding fee so it wasn't a fair barter. I left them charitably talking things over but I smelled liquor on both of them so we probably haven't heard the end of this. At least those two are mellow when they drink, unlike that Groen fella, who got nasty and ended up dead."

"I'd forgotten most of the story," John said. "I was astonished at the similarities to the Jess case. Both teenagers, both rebellious, both wanted to leave home because of his father. Carl didn't know where to go or how to get there and Ernest's father wouldn't let him leave."

"He was seventeen. He could have gone without permission."

"True. Maybe he stayed to help his younger brother and mother."

"Both boys were from German families who owned valuable land. Both had long-standing disagreements with an abusive father. If what Carl says proves to be true."

"You don't believe him?" John asked.

"I do, but that's up to a jury. I hear there are witnesses to back up his story. Groen got off under self-defense. The same might be said for Carl. His father wasn't an immediate threat that morning. He was asleep. But he'd long been a threat. Supposedly."

"I doubt that Lou will claim self-defense for Carl."

Joe shook his head. "I don't understand it."

"Understand what?"

"Why people kill."

"Well, that's incomprehensible, of course. We're repelled when we hear about it. Even when it's someone we don't know—a stranger in a newspaper story. And, of course, it's more disturbing when a child is a victim, or in this case, the perpetrator."

"Why not walk away, leave the situation?"

"Rational people do. It's not always possible. Take Ernest Groen. He first used a chair to fend off his father. His father left the house and came back with an iron bar. Ernest fled upstairs. The mother told the father that Ernest had left the house but he didn't believe her and went upstairs wielding the bar. Ernest said he warned his father that he'd shoot but the man kept coming. Now, put yourself there, in that moment. You have only seconds to react. Would you have thought—he's too drunk to hit me with that iron? I'll butt him with the gun and knock him down the stairs and then get out of here. Or would you fire that gun in your hands?"

"John, I understand that self-defense is different. And manslaughter is often accidental. But to calculate to kill someone and carry through, like Carl did. And he's just a kid who's supposedly not very bright. I haven't formed an opinion on that yet."

"Nor I. But this killing has polarized the community. Some pity the poor boy; some say he's dangerous, crazy like a fox. Joe Massa said a prayer for him out in front of his business."

"The clerk at Brunson Hardware said he had to drive to Sioux City for a supply of door locks. The last time that happened was when that Mexican murdered his friend. I guess that's why the judge wanted Carl in jail instead of at my house. To appease those who think he's a danger to the town."

John stood, stretched his legs, and then paced back and forth, as if he were in the courtroom trying a case, thinking on his feet. "There are people who are insane, mad, who kill on impulse, perhaps a voice telling them to do it. They might kill a stranger, at random, or more than one person. Many reasons we can't explain or understand. Murder is older than time. Look at Cain and Abel, the sons of Adam and Eve."

"That's your area, Reverend. Refresh my memory."

"Cain was the first born, a farmer. Abel was a shepherd. One day Cain offered part of his harvest to the Lord. Seeing that, Abel killed a lamb and offered that as his gift. The Lord highly regarded Abel's gift but not Cain's. Cain was jealous and killed his brother. The first case of fratricide."

"That doesn't sound like a fair Lord. Why did He spurn Cain's gift?"

"Perhaps killing a lamb was considered a greater sacrifice than a basket of grain."

"The lamb was a living thing. God condoned killing innocent animals? Why not accept both gifts in the spirit in which they were given?"

"I can't argue with that." John sat down. "But then Cain lied to the Lord about the murder. When questioned as to Abel's whereabouts, Cain withheld the truth. He asked God if he must be his brother's keeper."

"Was Cain punished for his crime? The family had already been tossed out of Eden."

"He was no longer able to work the land as a farmer."

"That's it?"

"He was cursed, too. But the question, as I see it, is not God's judgment and punishment but Cain's reaction to the disappointing result of his offering. The Lord tested his tolerance and he failed the lesson. He killed his brother. It was a bad decision, but we all make them. Again and again. We fail to see the lessons someone tried to teach."

"We're imperfect," Joe said. "Our crimes and misdemeanors become lessons to others. Carl Jess killed his father and we ask how could he do that? We each claim we would never do that. And most of us don't."

"But if we'd stood in Carl's shoes that morning? After years of being bullied by the man?"

The two men sat quietly for a moment, and then John spoke, "As for patricide, mythology is rife with it. In literature, *The Brothers Karamazov* is centered on patricide. Then there's *Oedipus Rex*—"

"You've gone from theology to scholarly on me, John."

"In the latter, the son kills his father so he can marry his mother."

"Whoa. Now you're getting a tad queer."

John laughed. "Do you want to hear Freud's Oedipal Complex theory?"

"Spare me."

"Well, we must—"

The ringing phone spared Joe but while he picked up he let John finish his thought.

"Juries must deal with these eternal moral questions in a practical, but imperfect, way. It's the system this country chose."

Joe attended to the phone. "Sheriff Gill speaking," and John trailed off to the men's room. When he returned, Joe said, "That was the editor of the *Des Moines Register*. He's sending a reporter here today to cover the Jess case."

"Our little county has hit the big time."

"I've been fielding wires and calls from reporters and lawmen from all over the state. One deputy asked if the killer was in custody or did he need to warn his residents about a murderer on the loose."

"I'm not surprised about the interest. Newspapers thrive on such stories."

"I'll handle the reporter when he gets here. Right now I need to go home and smooth Alice Grace's ruffled feathers. She's upset about Carl being in jail instead of with us."

"I figured she would be. You call her Alice Grace?"

"When I need to sweet talk her I do."

John picked up the box he'd brought along. "I was going to stop by and take her these chocolates."

"She'll be happy to see you. Come on along and break the ice for me."

"I'm meeting Lyn for supper. I'll tell you what, you deliver the candy. And it's not from me; it's from you."

"If you insist, but I owe you one."

"I'll enter it in the friendship ledger I keep. Give my regards to the lovely Alice Grace."

AUGUSTA DUVALL

From the front window of her room on the second floor of the Windsor Hotel, Augusta Duvall looked down onto the avenue that ran north and south off Sibley's business section. Across the avenue, Joe's Place seemed to have something to offer men. A stream of customers flowed in and out, but with prohibition now the law of the land, Augusta thought it might be camaraderie they sought, rather than booze. Some men, and women, now harbored a flask, although carrying liquor was illegal, along with making it, selling it, and buying it. In other words, one could drink the hard stuff, as long as you didn't make it, buy it, or carry it. It made little sense, but Augusta didn't care, booze wasn't her choice of beverage. Even in college, she'd avoided it for the most part.

She could use a bite to eat, though. Supper, they called it in small towns like this. They ate dinner at noon. She'd grown up in Chicago in a home where meals were served by a maid, and the evening meal was dinner, promptly at seven. Having eaten only a sandwich on the train, whatever the meal served downstairs, she needed nourishment.

Adjusting the skirt of her navy blue gabardine suit, she opened two buttons on the slit at the side. The shorter hemlines since the war made for more comfort and movement. She fitted a gray felt cloche over her bobbed auburn hair, picked up her oversized handbag and went downstairs.

A half hour later she had finished a tasty chicken pie, a biscuit that melted in her mouth, a cup of coffee, and a mound of rhubarb cobbler. While eating she heard part of a conversation between two men at a table in the center of the room. A reporter needed a talent for eavesdropping. She thought she'd heard the name Carl Jess, the reason for her trip here, and now she picked up on the word patricide. Bingo—her lucky day.

Augusta sat a few minutes, pretending to write in her notebook. When the men finished their meal and were drinking coffee, she gathered her belongings and, striding with pretend purpose, she passed the men's table.

Then she halted, as if she'd just thought of something, and turned back. "Gentlemen, please excuse my interruption . . . ."

The older, distinguished-looking gentleman rose, and the other man bobbed up, too, spilling his napkin to the floor.

"May I be of assistance?" the older man asked.

"I do hope so, but please, be seated."

They remained standing, both taking her measure, so she continued. "Of course, you might be strangers here, too. Traveling salesmen, perhaps?"

"No, no, we're local folks," the younger man said.

"You see, in the morning, I need to speak with the sheriff. I believe his name is Gill." Actually, she'd already called and made an appointment; she simply wanted to find out what these men knew. Before leaving town, she hoped to talk to every Tom, Dick, and Harry, and their wives; anyone who knew the Jess family.

"Joseph Gill is sheriff. I'm John Glover and this is my son, Lyn."

"Augusta Duvall. Pleased to meet you both."

"Will you join us?" Lyn dragged a chair from the next table and held onto the back while she sat down. Both men resumed their seats and Augusta felt two pair of eyes studying her.

"I do feel I'm interrupting."

"Not at all," John insisted. "We've heard the sounds of our own voices long enough. We're happy for a diversion."

"Good. I'm not quite ready to retire either. I arrived mid-day and hoped to see Sheriff Gill but I was weary from the train ride so I took a nap and didn't awaken until an hour ago."

"If you don't mind my wondering," Lyn said, "it seems unusual for a young lady to be looking for the sheriff. I hope it's nothing serious."

"I don't mind your asking. I'm a reporter for the *Des Moines Register*. I'll want to talk to the sheriff about visiting with Carl Jess, the young man who, allegedly, killed his father."

Augusta sensed that John picked up on the word allegedly. Possibly an attorney. He looked the part.

John eased into the conversation. "You'll find Joe at the jail, next to the courthouse, bright and early. I might add, he'll be surprised to find a female reporter on his doorstep."

No, he won't, Augusta thought. He'd expressed surprise when she called but now he knew. "We're a rare breed," she said. "I'm the only woman on staff. Even in my hometown of Chicago there are no women reporters on the big newspapers."

"I'm impressed," Lyn said. "Women are moving in many directions."

"Indeed," John added.

Augusta raised her hand to wave away the compliments, but then she thought: Why should I? It's a feather in my cap.

John said, "My guess is that you'll need to ask Carl's lawyer for permission to see his client."

"Who is the lawyer?"

"Lou Dwinnell. He's a good man. He won't object. Listen, I have business at the courthouse tomorrow. I could escort you there."

"That is most chivalrous. I accept. Tell me, are you an attorney?"

"I am."

"Among other things," Lyn said, without elaborating.

Augusta crossed her legs, the split skirt allowing a peek at what her boss called gams. Focusing on Lyn, she asked, "Did you follow your father's footsteps into law?"

"I've been following him around all my life, but in the courtroom I'm only an observer. I'm a laborer. Masonry, lathing, plastering, that sort of thing."

"He's too modest," John added. "Lyn is as skilled at his trade as any lawyer is at his."

"Your father admires you," Augusta told Lyn.

"We belong to a mutual admiration society. It meets here at the hotel whenever we feel inclined to hold a meeting."

Augusta smiled and quickly gave Lyn the once-over. He had a tinge of quirkiness about him, but he wore it easily. She liked his manners and obvious affection for his father.

Suddenly she recalled something and she wagged her finger at John. "I knew your name was familiar. I know your byline. You write for *The Sioux City Journal*."

"I do," John said.

"Among other things," Lyn repeated, this time with a grin.

Augusta waited for more from Lyn.

"Preacher man, too. Ordained, Congregational Church."

"My goodness," Augusta said. "Or should I say, *Your* Goodness?"

"Please, no," John said, "but Reverend is the work I enjoy most."

"If I recall your resume from the paper, you've been a judge, a state legislator, a justice of the peace—"

"Guilty on all charges."

"Some call you The Great Orator." Was she pushing her attention too far? But she had read his newspaper articles and the details of his biography.

Lyn added, "The traveling men here call him a walking encyclopedia. One man said that John Glover can go home with Susan and come back for Annie."

Augusta tipped her head, puzzled. "I don't know that expression."

"It means he can take both sides of an issue, in debate, or as a lawyer. He's worked both sides of the law, for the defense and for the State."

"I'm duly impressed. *Thee* John Glover. I've thought about doing a profile piece on you for *The Register*." The idea had never entered her mind until this moment, but it might be worth pursuing.

"Ah, I would bore you quickly. In my dotage I tend to repeat and embellish. Enough about me. What—"

"No one bores a journalist. There's always a story. But, listen; I've taken enough of your time." Augusta rose and picked up her handbag.

Both men leaped to their feet. "Our pleasure," John said. "What time would you like to leave tomorrow? The courthouse opens at nine. Oh, by the way, I live here, so I'll meet you in the lobby."

"You live here? Then please let me buy you breakfast before we go."

"I'd be delighted to share breakfast, but it's on me."

"I never argue with a judge, or a man of God. I'll meet you at, shall we say, eight o'clock?"

"Perfect. But I'm in no hurry to retire just yet. We could all move to the lobby where it's more comfortable."

"I'd like that. Perhaps I can twist your arm into telling me about some of your cases."

"His arm is permanently twisted in that direction," Lyn said.

"If you like stories about disputes over chickens and hogs. Or, I heard an amusing story today about a fella wanting to buy swampland."

Augusta laughed and then introduced a possible topic for discussion. "I'd welcome your opinion about the Jess case."

"Yes; certainly. My newspapers are around here somewhere, with the whole story."

"Really? I'd love to see them."

"Miss Duvall," Lyn broke in, "if you'll excuse me, I'll take a rain check. I put in a hard day. I hope I'll see you before you leave town."

"I look forward to it. And please, call me Augusta." She allowed her eyes to follow him out the door. Something about him intrigued her.

"Do you play chess?" John asked.

The out-of-the-blue question threw Augusta for a second. "I do," she said, and added a fib, "but not well."

"Then you're my favorite kind of opponent. But my guess is you're being modest. There's a board set up in the reading nook. Shall we?"

Augusta took his offered arm. "But I do want to hear your stories, and your opinion on Carl Jess. And perhaps you'd loan me those newspapers for bedtime reading."

JOSEPH GILL

Joe straightened the mess of papers on his desk, emptied the ashtray, and brushed cookie crumbs off his blotter. It wasn't often a woman made an appointment and for that reason he tended to slack off on housekeeping. He depended on Grace to notice when the debris became too thick.

Joe had been taken by surprise when the reporter who called was a female. She sounded young. She said she'd be here about nine-fifteen and sure enough, here she came now, with John Glover a few steps behind. Caught at once by her youth and good looks, Joe noted that she had a couple inches in height on John. The judge, never what you'd call lanky, had shrunk a bit with age. He was winded; his nose red from the cold, while Miss Duvall's cheeks appeared a healthy pink, and not from rouge.

"Miss Duvall, you're very prompt," Joe said. "Morning, John."

"You two have met?" John asked.

"I called ahead," Augusta replied to John. Joe had no idea what this exchange meant.

Joe helped Augusta remove a long, heavy black wrap like those worn by soldiers during the war. Great Coats, they were called, and this one looked as if it might be an actual coat from the war, not a mass produced look-a-like. Perhaps she had a brother who served. Although masculine in style, on Miss Duvall the coat looked feminine.

The same went for her suit, which had a trouser bottom instead of skirt. He'd seen pictures of this style in one of Grace's magazines, but hadn't seen anyone wearing it. He couldn't imagine Grace in the suit, but the style looked fetching on this young woman with long, slender legs. He guessed her age at early twenties. She wore a fedora, which she didn't remove. He half expected to see a card reading PRESS stuck into the hatband.

"So, Miss Duvall, you'd like to visit with Carl Jess."

"That's my mission. And please, call me Augusta."

"Thank you; I will. It's a lovely name."

She offered an indulgent smile and tapped her red nails on the chair arm, which Joe took as indicating impatience.

"It's fine with me if you talk to Carl. I spoke with Lou Dwinnell, Carl's lawyer, and he'd like to be there, too."

"I've nothing to hide. I've worked my way around lawyers. They stop me if I've gone too far. But this won't be an inquisition. I'd simply like to visit with the boy. Hear his story."

"He has a court appointed guardian *ad litem*, too. Frank Hromatko."

"Do I need his permission, too?"

"Lou probably called him; just to keep him informed. Carl is excited about the visit. He said that before now, he'd never had anyone come especially to see him. His father didn't let kids come to the farm except for one neighbor boy. He's had visitors here but only in this office. For you, we'll take him to my house where you'll be more comfortable."

Noting that John had tried to get a word in edgewise, Joe paused.

"Who's been visiting?"

"Some days it looks like pretty much all of Ocheyedan has moved in. They've closed ranks around him. Ladies from the local churches come with food and sympathy. Father O'Reilley stopped by. Relatives of Carl's, a half-brother of the father's. Oh, and a man with the same name as Carl's. Carl Jess and his wife. Said he's a cousin and came to look at some land he owns around here. He's from Minnesota."

Joe returned his conversation to his female guest. "Miss Duvall, Augusta, the lawyer won't be available until after dinner, around one."

"Fine. That gives me time to call on Willis Overholser. He and my boss are friends and—"

John interrupted. "I'll be happy to take you there and introduce you."

"You have an appointment this morning," Augusta said, causing Joe to wonder why these two knew so much about each other's schedules.

Joe said, "Mike Hicks was looking for you, John. Said you were going with him to Rock Rapids."

"I'm speaking at Rotary and then he wants me to look at some land he's thinking about buying." John turned to Augusta. "I should be back to take you to the newspaper office."

"Well, since I need to wait to see Carl this afternoon, I might go there this morning. I can find my way around. I live in a city, you know."

While they continued their discussion, Joe stifled a sneeze with one hand and placed the other across his abdomen. Jolting eruptions like a sneeze or cough aggravated the hernia. Grace had made him a couple of flannel-lined elastic bands to girdle his midsection. She teased about him wearing a corset, which didn't set well with him. He could understand why women had tossed away their corsets. Girdles would probably go next. He'd like to be rid of his support belt, too. But then; it held in the pot belly most men his age acquired.

Augusta's trim figure didn't look held in by undergarments.

"Sheriff Gill, maybe I could just say hello to Carl this morning."

"Well, Grace, my wife, wants to groom the boy before you see him."

"Is she in charge of prisoners?"

"Of course not, but Carl is a special case. She keeps him well-fed and bought him a couple sets of clothing, down to skivvies and socks. She brings his meals and sits with him while he eats."

"She sounds like the perfect mother."

"I go home and take my food out of the warming oven and eat by myself. Which reminds me; Grace will want you to have dinner with us. Carl will be there and you'll have a chance to meet him before the interview."

"Perfect. I won't turn down that offer."

"If you have time on your hands this morning, I'll give you a tour of the courthouse. We have a lovely mural in the courtroom. And a great view of the countryside from inside the dome."

Joe chided himself internally for vying with John for the young woman's attention. Like a couple of old fools. John had been around since the Biblical flood and some days Joe felt like he'd come on Noah's boat, too. Joe had never looked in the mirror and been so distracted by his good looks that he cut himself shaving; still, he figured he leaned more toward handsome than homely. John had always charmed women, without trying. More than one had set her cap for him, starting way back after his wife died. His support of suffrage didn't hurt his popularity. Joe supported the vote, too, but it had taken a while for Grace to convince him without, as she said, beating him over the head with a broom.

"I'd like that," Augusta said through Joe's thoughts. What was it she'd like? Oh, the view.

John told Augusta. "It's nothing like the view from the capitol in Des Moines, but we like our little town. And yes, the mural of Lady Justice—"

"Ah, here's the deputy now," Joe said as Grace appeared in the doorway.

He rose behind his desk. "Grace, meet Augusta Duvall; come to see Carl."

Each woman said she was pleased to meet the other, with Grace's eyes taking in Augusta's suit and hat and bobbed hair. "Joe told me you were coming," Grace said, "from the newspaper. *The Sioux City Journal?*"

"*The Des Moines Register*."

"Oh, yes. I like Des Moines. Joe took me with him to a convention there and we ladies had a grand tour of the city."

"I'm originally from Chicago, but I like Des Moines."

"I spent some time there myself," John interjected. "One term in the legislature."

Yes, John, Joe thought. We know that.

Grace continued as if John hadn't spoken. "We take the Sunday *Register*. Joe likes to keep abreast of the state news. Not to mention the comic strips."

Grace reached over to Joe, signaling she wanted the key to Carl's cell. "I'll take Carl home now," she explained to Augusta, "and see you later."

"I look forward to it."

"There's something I'd like to discuss—"

"Grace." Joe raised a cautionary finger to his lips. He knew what Grace meant. She'd told him Carl's story about when his mother died, and he advised her to tell only Lou. He could decide if it had relevance.

Grace left, and then Mike Hicks poked his bald head around the doorway, looking for John. Gathering his coat and scarf and hat, John told Augusta, "I'll see you this afternoon at the hotel. I'd like to take you to the Opera House tonight. There's a musical comedy playing, *Oh, Girlie Girlie*—"

Joe interrupted. "Grace mentioned she'd like to see it. Maybe we could meet there and sit together."

John ignored the comment and addressed Augusta. "I hope I'm not delayed by business."

"Right; I'll look for you later."

"She's in good hands here, John." Joe knew that if John hadn't business elsewhere he'd have wrangled his way into this interview. Sometimes friend John seemed to think this town would go to sleep and never wake up if he weren't running things.

"Joe," John said, "let Augusta read the Groen file." He turned to Augusta, "It's a patricide with many similarities to Carl's."

Joe laid his hand on the file and noted how eagerly Augusta reached for the folder. Reporters were the hungriest people he knew and he didn't trust most of them.

This one he liked.

CARL JESS

Carl stood in the doorway between the Gill's kitchen and dining room. Mrs. Gill had gone to answer the front door and was now talking in the parlor with Miss Duvall, the lady who wanted to visit with him. Miss Duvall told Mrs. Gill that the sheriff would be along soon; someone had come into the office to see him.

On Carl's first night in Sibley, after Sheriff Gill brought him from the farm and they'd finished in court, he had eaten in the kitchen with the Gills. This would be his first time eating in a dining room, anywhere. The farmhouse had a dining room but his father closed the sliding doors to keep the other rooms warmer. Not that the house was ever warm in winter. In summer they never ate in the dining room, either.

This room had lace curtains, plants by the windows, a flowered carpet, and a white tablecloth under the dishes with a blue and white pattern that looked like a place in Japan Carl had seen in *National Geographic* magazine at school. There were also pictures of naked people in a jungle, not Japan.

Mrs. Gill said the dishes were for company and Carl thought that meant Miss Duvall until Mrs. Gill said, "You're company, too, Carl."

He'd never been company before. He'd never eaten anywhere other than at home. Oh, wait, he'd been to church picnics. He'd had pie there.

Carl helped set the table. Mrs. Gill wasn't bossy about it. She didn't tell him he had to; she asked if he'd mind carrying in the dishes and silverware. The silverware was for company, too. She wiped each knife and fork and spoon with a cloth before handing it to him. She showed him where to place each piece, some on the left side of the plate, some on the right.

Oma had a chest of silverware that came with her from Germany. It stayed packed in a trunk with other things that looked unused. What tools they used in the kitchen, if they used any at all, were scratched and dirty.

The room had pictures on the wall; one Carl especially liked showed a wolf standing in the dark on a snowy hill looking down on a village, like

Ocheyedan, with a moon and stars overhead. The scene made him think of *Silent Night*, or as *Oma* used to sing it, *Stille Nacht, Heil'ge Nacht*.

The picture reminded Carl that in Geography class the teacher said the Ocheyedan Mound was one of the highest points in Iowa. It covered forty acres and had been formed by a glacier thousands of years ago. The Sioux Indians used it for meetings and pioneers used it as a landmark for giving directions. They might say: "It's four miles due north of the mound. You can't miss it." Carl had trouble remembering most stuff from school but he liked Geography so that helped. He liked reading about Indians who actually lived here. One time he found an arrowhead. His father asked to see it and then tossed it into the cornfield. Carl wanted to go look for it but he'd been warned to stay out of cornfields because kids had wandered into them and gotten lost and weren't found until harvest—dead. One boy claimed he'd found a skeleton in their field. Carl didn't believe it because everyone called the boy a liar, liar, pants on fire.

Carl liked pioneer stories. Sheriff Gill told him one about grasshoppers that ate all the crops and almost everything else in sight. Sheriff Gill wasn't real friendly but Carl supposed a sheriff had to be tough, like Wyatt Earp in Wild West stories. The jail wasn't so bad. It had once been part of the Gill's house so it looked more like a regular room than a cell. Mrs. Gill brought over some things to make him comfortable and Sheriff Gill left the lights on at night. Carl didn't mind sleeping alone now. It was quiet, no snoring or tossing and turning from his father. He didn't feel nervous anymore.

Now Mrs. Gill and her guest came into the room. One glance and Carl thought: Jeepers, she's the prettiest girl I've ever seen. Prettier even than the lady in the wedding picture who had been his mother. But why did Miss Duvall wear men's clothes?

"Carl," Mrs. Gill said, "This is Miss Augusta Duvall."

The pretty woman reached for Carl's hand, like men do, and he responded with a shake. "I'm happy to meet you," she said.

Carl didn't know what to say but Sheriff Gill came in then and saved him from trying to make conversation.

Five minutes later, with his head lowered while Mrs. Gill said a prayer called Grace, Carl peeked at Miss Duvall. She caught him and smiled. Something that felt like butterflies tingled in his belly. Her fingernails were painted red. He'd never seen such a thing and wondered what it meant. Right now he couldn't remember her first name but it didn't matter. She was like a teacher; children called teachers Miss Froke, or whatever.

With the prayer finished and food being passed, Carl still didn't dare look at Miss Duvall, although it was hard not to; she sat directly across from him. It wouldn't be mannerly to keep his head lowered, so he sat upright. Sunlight coming in the window just over Miss Duvall's head made her hair shine like the copper horse weathervane he could see out of the high window in the jail.

As the adults talked, Carl figured he wasn't expected to join the conversation. Miss Froke said children should be seen but not heard, unless called on. He ran his finger under his shirt collar and scratched. Mrs. Gill had given him a haircut this morning before she sent him to the bathtub. He must not have gotten all the clipped hair washed off his neck, although he'd dunked his head and washed with soap. He liked baths. Maybe it was the newness of the shirt that made him itch. The material felt stiff.

Deep in thought, Carl hadn't noticed the conversation had stopped until Mrs. Gill said, "Carl, you've been very quiet. And you've barely touched your food."

"Sorry; I was just listening." He forked a dollop of mashed potatoes and let it rest on his tongue before swallowing. He'd never had mashed potatoes like Mrs. Gill's. He sometimes smashed his own with a fork, but they were dry and lumpy. These were creamy and smooth and buttery.

"The meat is real good," he said. Mrs. Gill called it Swiss steak.

"Carl," Miss Duvall said.

When he looked at her the butterflies tickled again.

"What grade are you at school?"

"I don't go regular, but I graduated from Sixth Grade at country school. We got a paper diploma. That was a couple of years ago." He didn't know what else to say so he took a bite of green beans, hoping someone else would talk.

"Carl is a good reader," Mrs. Gill said. "People have brought books of all kinds."

"I'm sure that helps pass the time," Miss Duvall said, and Carl nodded. He continued eating to catch up with the others. They had finished and he knew Mrs. Gill had made chocolate pudding for dessert. He'd watched it bubble on the stove and she'd asked him to tell her if it got too high. She didn't want it to boil over. "They say a watched pot never boils, but it surely does," she told him.

After dessert and coffee, Mrs. Gill checked the watch clipped to her dress and announced that it was almost one o'clock. She began gathering dishes, and Miss Duvall helped.

Mrs. Gill said, "I usually don't let guests help but Lou is as punctual as Father Time and will be here shortly."

Carl wondered if Father Time might be another priest. One had already been to see him. A lady came and made him kneel down with her and pray the rosary. She left the rosary for him and also something called a scapular to wear around his neck. Another woman called him bad names and Sheriff Gill asked her to leave but she wouldn't and he lifted her off her feet and carried her out of the jail. Carl and the sheriff laughed about that.

When the doorbell rang, Sheriff Gill said he'd get it and soon returned with the lawyer. Carl knew and liked him.

Lou Dwinnell gave Carl a quick shoulder rub, from which he flinched. He hadn't gotten used to anyone touching him in a kind way.

"We men will get comfortable in the parlor," the sheriff said, "and the ladies will be along shortly. Grace will bring in a pot of coffee and a batch of cookies. She's kept the cookie jar filled, what with this boy around. Boys can't have too many cookies, can they?"

"I reckon not," Carl said, and Miss Duvall winked at him.

Butterflies; big as barn swallows this time.

JOHN GLOVER

March had blustered in like the proverbial lion, this particular beast in the body of a boy who roared with anger and bit off his father's head. Then, a few days ago, with spring on the cusp, a gust of fresh air blew into town in the person of Augusta Duvall. John knew a woman named Augusta who preferred being called Gussie. That suited the matronly widow, but the diminutive did not suit this Augusta. No shrinking violet; the word gust belonged in her name, with emphasis.

Augusta had departed too quickly to suit John. He'd been delayed with business the day he left her at Joe's office, and when he returned to the hotel, the desk clerk said that Lyn had stopped by as Miss Duvall was leaving and had escorted her to the depot.

John's thoughts returned to the day he took her to the courthouse. She turned more than one head, and not only the males—she left even the secretaries aflutter in her wake. Before the day was out, there probably wasn't anyone in town who didn't know her name and why she was here. As for Joe and Lyn; they'd both taken a proprietary interest in the young reporter.

Come to that, if he were honest, so had John Glover.

He'd scoffed at Lyn when he suggested with a sprinkle of humor that Augusta might have sparked Papa's fancy—it being spring—that time of year when such things are said to happen.

Well, really, what man could resist her? Besides being pleasing to look at, she was intellectually stimulating; inquisitive, and quick of mind. They'd stayed up late that one evening at the hotel; first over a chess game, which John won but he suspected she had not played as well as she could, and then discussing all manner of things. It pleased him to learn that she was a Civil War buff, and they had conversed intelligently about battles. When she commented that this had been her grandfather's war that put their ages in perspective and John came to his senses. Or had he? Here he stood now, thinking about her, peeved that she hadn't hung around town longer. A girl who could be his granddaughter.

She was too young even for Lyn. If he were interested. He'd courted young ladies in his youth, but nothing had come of it. It wasn't too late, in John's opinion, Lyn being only . . . what was he? Forty-three, it must be. But matchmaking, even in John's mind, was foolish. Augusta Duvall had gone back to Des Moines and Lyn lived here, contented, as far as John knew.

Augusta had left a note, written on Windsor Hotel stationary, thanking John for his hospitality and hoping they'd meet again. She added that she'd been eager to return to Des Moines and write her story. She had enjoyed meeting Mr. Overholser. Joe Gill had driven her to the newspaper office. Best of all, she'd had a successful meeting with Carl Jess, that sweet boy. She hoped John would be able to read her story in the *Des Moines Register* and she would welcome his thoughts on it. He could reach her at the paper's business address.

Not a word about the proposed evening at the Opera House. But then, she hadn't said she'd go. The conversation had barely gotten off the ground, and then Joe Gill horned in and invited himself along.

She signed the note: Warm regards, Augusta M. Duvall.

What did M. stand for? He liked the idea that it might be Mary because that had been his wife's name; his beloved Mary Frances. How she'd suffered from scrofula and the consumption that took her life at not quite thirty. Looking at the calendar he did the numbers in his head. Thirty-four years ago this May.

Well, Augusta had come, and turned his head, and gone. That was the end of that story.

John had gone to the library to read her piece in the *Des Moines Register*. It made the front page, above the fold, the prime spot, and had been picked up by the wire service around the state. John was reminded of the old yarn about the reporter who handed a lengthy story to the editor and said, "If I'd had more time, I could have made it shorter." Yes, succinct was best, but when a story lay across the whole front page, it conveyed the message that this is important. Readers took notice.

This week, both local papers had printed Augusta's story verbatim. *The Gazette* used the photos from the original *Register* story, a wedding picture of Claus Jess and his wife, one of Joe Gill, one of Grace Gill, and, in the center, Carl Jess, whose boyish countenance belied the inhumanity of what he had done.

The Tribune didn't use the photos, but they introduced the story with a brief editorial opinion that provided food for thought, not only about Augusta's content, but on her writing style.

THE OSCEOLA COUNTY TRIBUNE

Is The Slayer A Hero?
Was His Victim A Brute?

The *Des Moines Register*'s sensational account of the Ocheyedan tragedy would make it appear so. Last Sunday's *Des Moines Register* published a spread on the late Ocheyedan murder, along with pictures of Carl Jess and his parents and Sheriff Joe Gill and wife. The story was written by staff writer Augusta Duvall and is sensational to a degree. How much is true and how much is fancy and malicious gossip cannot be said. It is to be remembered, however, that Claus Jess cannot speak for himself. *The Tribune* republishes the story for those who may not have seen it originally.

Is Carl Jess a criminal? Is he a moron?

Or is he a heartbroken, soul-crushed little boy, driven by German cruelty to become a murderer?

When the news that a 15-year-old boy at Ocheyedan, Ia., had killed his father flashed over the state perhaps you said, "How horrible. He must be insane."

If you could see this bright-faced, likeable youngster, all "slicked up" for company, bashfully awkward at the sudden kindness the world is showing him, and consuming more jelly and cookies per hour than your own little boy might if he suffered as Carl has. Carl is a curious combination of childhood and age, of guilt and innocence, of gentleness and steel.

He is a murderer.

He has the heart of a child.

He has worked as hard as a man of 50 years.

He is as innocent of life as a baby.

He feels no grief, yet he cries because he unwittingly did wrong.

Love of Money, Root of Evil

Carl has over $100,000 in his own name, but he has never had more than a nickel to spend at a time.

Though $1,000 in gold was found in the house when the coroner investigated, Carl was ragged, dirty, and half frozen.

Last Thursday, Carl and I sat on the davenport in the sheriff's parlor at Sibley, the county seat, where Carl is held in jail, and talked about many things—murder, and death, and airplanes, and Tom Sawyer, and cruelty, and rifles, and apple pie, and Santa Claus, and jails, and sheriffs, and moving picture shows.

Carl, you know, has never been more than fifteen miles from home.

He had never ridden on a train until Sheriff Gill took him from Ocheyedan to Sibley.

Sibley has two or three thousand souls. Carl said when he saw it, "Gee, this is a big town, ain't it?"

Was he afraid?

"Just once," he told me, "the train kind of tipped going 'round a curve."

He has seen only two moving picture shows.

He has never seen a streetcar.

He has never had a Christmas present.

He has lived on bread, potatoes, and meat.

He has had pie to eat on Christmas and the Fourth of July, when neighbors brought it in.

He has worked harder in fifteen years than many men in a lifetime.

He has never played.

He has never had more than a nickel to spend for himself.

Did a Man's Work

Since his tiny fingers could pick up corn cobs and drag baskets of firewood to the kitchen door, little Carl was made to work.

As the boy grew older, Claus Jess put upon his small son's shoulders a man's work, and denied him every right of a child.

He taught him to kill varmints with a rifle.

He taught him too well.

When existence under his father's brutal hand became more than a human could endure, Carl took the rifle and shot his father as he lay in bed.

It was the only way he knew to get out of bondage.

Before you can understand how this could be, before you can see how a child might in cold blood raise a rifle to his shoulder, aim at his father's head, and pull the trigger, you must hear the story of Claus Jess, the father.

"Claus Jess killed himself, his son pulled the trigger, that's all," is Ocheyedan's way of disposing of the subject.

Not a tear was shed when the man's body, riddled by bullets from his son's hand, was laid away beside his wife.

Ocheyedan and the whole county know that frail little Mrs. Jess would be alive today but for her husband's atrocious brutality.

At 17-years-of age, she married Claus Jess, then 35 years old. Little Carl was the first baby. There were two more, but they were born dead.

Shelled Corn As She Died

When Carl was 3-years-old, his mother suffered from a hemorrhage and lay for days, dying. Claus Jess refused to call a doctor.

Neighbors brought a doctor, who asked Jess to remain at home until his wife's death, which would be a matter of hours.

He refused, saying he had a job shelling corn for which he would receive six dollars.

Little Mrs. Claus died, unattended, her weary-worn body in a pool of her own blood, at 4 o'clock the next morning.

Claus Jess would not spend ten dollars to have her body embalmed. She was buried at 3 o'clock of the afternoon of the day she died.

It was the same when the old grandfather, Claus Jess's father, died.

Little Carl grew up in daily, deathly fear of this man who had let Carl's mother's life ebb slowly away with each beat of her heart.

Every day of every year of Carl's life, with rare exceptions, Claus Jess beat his son.

Blacksnake, leather thong, tree limb—whatever fell to his hand he brought down on his boy's shoulders.

The boy got up at 4 and 5 o'clock in the morning, milked cows, did chores, fed the hogs, got his own breakfast of bread and potatoes, dabbed out the dishes, made a feint of sweeping out the dungeon-like hole in which he lived, dressed and fed his querulous, childish, invalid grandmother, 84 years old, who babbled in German by the hour, "Carl, don't! Carl, don't do that. Carl, you mustn't."

Not Temper, Just Nature

Then the boy went out and did man's work in the fields, and if his childish efforts displeased his father in any respect, as they always did, it was, "Carl, come here," and then a beating.

Claus was not a man of temper. He never cursed. He did not grow angry, rage about, whip the child and then repent. His was the cold, inhuman, unfeeling brutality that smiles while it lashes, that is coldly, cruelly, deliberate, and knows no remorse. It was his nature.

Is it any wonder that Carl, the son of such a father and trained in such a torturing school, decided to get out of his suffering by killing his father?

"I thought about it for a long time, a year, I guess," he says.

But he put it off.

Then one Saturday he went out and slid on the ice with little Johnny Graves.

Johnny tells the story: "Carl's father came out and looked on a minute, then he called, 'Carl, come here.' He took out his jackknife, cut a limb off a tree and beat him with it. Carl screamed. I ran like everything."

That night when Carl went to bed he planned to get up and shoot his father in the morning.

He woke Sunday morning, lying beside his sleeping parent in the bare, black, ill-smelling room.

"I remembered what I'd been thinking about the night before," he explains simply, "and decided I might as well do it now."

In the cold light of early dawn he deliberately got the rifle, aimed at his father's head and fired.

Then he reached in his father's pocket, took out a nickel, put it in his own pocket, and went to do chores.

When he came in, his father was groaning. Carl took up the gun and shot him again. The second shot killed him.

Then he went to a neighbor and said, "A horse kicked Father. I think he is dying."

When the coroner saw the bullet wounds, Carl said, "I did it. I thought if he was gone, I wouldn't be bossed around so much."

He Cried

Carl and I talked very little of the shooting. His eyes filled with tears as he said if he had it to do over again, he wouldn't, then he put his head on my shoulder and sobbed and we both wiped our eyes and blew our noses violently, and that was when we started talking about Tom Sawyer.

Carl has read five books. He is hungry to read, to study.

His father sent him to school only when there was no work to be done, so that he has completed only the Sixth Grade.

Geography is his favorite subject, Indians and cowboys, and distant lands fascinate this lad who before this time had never been more than fifteen miles from home.

Tom Sawyer is his favorite book. We went over to the bookcase to see what there was to read, and Carl reached out eagerly and drew out Richard Harding Davis's *Soldiers of Fortune*.

He was much disappointed when told it was not a book of adventure.

While he is in jail, he has a temporary father and mother in Sheriff Joe Gill and his wife, Grace.

"Moron? Fiddlesticks!" says Mrs. Gill, and for a gentle, motherly soul she manages to look quite fierce about it. "Bless his heart!" she says with a smile, "he needs a mother, that's all."

Saving A Life

Carl will soon have more books than he can read in a lifetime. Distant relatives of his father, all of whom express satisfaction at Mr. Jess's nasty departure from this world, have offered to bring Carl a wagonload of books to read in jail.

After he has appeared before a grand jury, he will probably be sent to school, not a reform school, but a regular school, and then to college, if his lawyer has his way.

He wants to study farming. And perhaps, on the side, aviation.

Then he plans to come home and farm scientifically his four eighties. He has a fortune of $100,000 willed him by his grandfather, if the law should rule that he cannot inherit his father's estate.

And when he has done this, Carl wants a son of his own.

"I'll treat him good, you see if I don't!" he promises, with a quivering chin. "I'll let him play if he wants to, and I'll never, never whip him at all!"

JOHN GLOVER

John had at first liked Augusta's writing style; the short sentences made an impact and were easy to read. His eyes moved quickly from sentence to sentence. Now, given the paper's editorial lead-in, John saw things in a new light. As the editorial suggested, the piece smacked of sensationalism.

Meaty and hard-hitting, Augusta packed a wallop all the way through, slanted in favor of Carl Jess. What must the German community think of that line about German cruelty? The generalization struck John as insulting. Maybe the writer's obvious slant and that particular comment is why the paper decided to preface the story with an editorial. As they said, Claus Jess could not defend himself.

Given the comments about Claus, supposedly from Ocheyedan folks and relatives of the family, John wondered where Augusta had gotten these quotes. And when? She'd been in town only that one day and been busy until she left. When Lyn took her to the train, did she go to Ocheyedan before returning to Des Moines? Where did she get information about the day Mrs. Jess died? Augusta suggested that everyone in the county knew about "little Mrs. Jess's" death. Had Augusta telephoned the town gossip for information? Or did she, as the editorial asked, fabricate details to dramatize the story?

Having completely nitpicked this story, John wished that Augusta hadn't disappeared so hastily. He'd have advised her to do her homework regarding Carl's age when his mother died and the information about the other two children. For a fact, they had not been born dead. When Joe Gill brought Carl from home he'd asked to bring along his mother's Bible, and Joe had seen the entries of names and dates. John was a stickler for statistics. Above all, a journalist should get the facts. If he'd been there the day of the interview, he'd have seen that Augusta got that part of the story correct.

Lou Dwinnell should be happy with this sympathetic portrayal of his client, but the fairy tale ending Augusta suggested was not only unrealistic but absurd. The boy going to college and coming back home to farm? And the closing quote—had Carl actually said that or did Augusta create it? The old word mawkish came to mind. He'd seen the boy only once, in court that first day, but the words simply did not sound like something he'd say.

John imagined a movie screen close up, a wide-eyed child with tears running down his innocent cheeks, his quivering chin, and underneath the caption: "I'll treat him good, you see if I don't! I'll let him play if he wants to, and I'll never, never whip him at all!"

John clucked disapproval. In this enlightened age were they teaching yellow journalism in college? If Augusta had worked for him as a cub reporter he'd have red-penciled this story and sent her back to her desk.

Still, sensational material sells papers. More's the pity.

Grace's picture in the paper pleased John, and she'd been described exactly as he would describe her—motherly. Carl was in good hands with Grace and Joe, if only temporarily and mostly in a jail cell. But, here, too, the quote attributed to Grace did not sound like her. He couldn't imagine her using the words moron and fiddlesticks. Had Augusta put words in her mouth, too?

If so, shame on her.

Having worked both sides of the courtroom, John wondered now, given Augusta's story, if the prosecution would be able to convict this forlorn, orphaned boy whom nearly the whole town of Ocheyedan and much of Sibley, too, had taken under its collective wing.

Charles Dickens could have rendered a novel from this tale of woe. Maybe Augusta Duvall had the stuff that would make her a novelist. Pulp fiction, John thought with dismay.

She had once asked for his opinion on the story. It would take some thought to compose that letter. He might skip it all together; she'd probably asked only to be polite. Her story had been published, all said and done.

LOU DWINNELL

Call it parental pride, but Lou Dwinnell felt certain that his two boys, who were seven and ten, were brighter than Carl Jess at fifteen. All three were similar in the immature manner of boys will be boys, but in intellect, Lou's sons were a notch or two or three above Carl. Again, Lou's opinion. Today he would get an unbiased opinion on Carl from Doctor Donohue, Superintendent at the Cherokee Hospital For The Insane.

Carl had said scarcely a word since Lou picked him up at the jail. He seemed enthralled with the scenery, looking out the side window and then the front and then turning around to look back at something.

"Where are we?" he asked as Lou made a turn.

"We were on Route Nine. Now we'll be on Fifty-Nine all the way to Cherokee."

"So roads have numbers. Are there towns on the way or just farms?"

"Both. Watch for town signs as we go along. Sometimes we don't go right through a town; it might be off to the left or right. You might see a water tower rising into the sky with the name of the town."

"What's a water tower for?"

"Well, it controls pressure." Lou hoped that satisfied the boy because it was more complicated than that.

"There's a sign," Carl said. "Sanborn. Is Cherokee next?"

"No; not for a while yet. There's a road map under the visor." Lou pointed, and Carl dragged down the map and opened its folds.

"Willikers, is this whole thing Iowa?"

"It is. Do you find Cherokee?" Lou pointed to the upper part of the map so Carl wouldn't be looking all over the state.

"I see Ocheyedan. Wait—C-h-e-r-o-k-e-e."

"That's it."

"Are there skyscraper buildings there?"

"I'm afraid not. The main building at the hospital is maybe a story or two taller than the courthouse, but there are lots of connected buildings spread out for maybe a city block or more."

"Is Cherokee a big city?"

"Bigger than Sibley. About double in population."

"What's that?"

"People. There are twice as many people." Lou wasn't sure Carl understood but he didn't explain how to figure what twice as many people would be.

"How long till we get there?"

Lou smiled. "That's what my boys always ask." He checked his watch. "It's about sixty miles to Cherokee so it'll take at least two hours. We've been on the road about a half hour."

Wanting to test Carl, Lou asked, "Can you figure out how much time we have left to go?"

"You mean doing sums?"

"Yeah."

"I'm not good at numbers. Or spelling. I like to read."

"Reading is good."

Carl watched the road for a while. "What will happen when we get there?"

"Well, first we'll eat the sandwiches Grace Gill packed because it might be a long afternoon. Then you'll visit with Doctor Donohue by yourself, and then I'll visit with him alone."

"I ain't been to a doctor. Once I had a bad bellyache but my father said doctors do more harm than good. I've had measles and mumps." He puffed out his cheeks and Lou grinned.

"I heard people say my father wouldn't take my mother to the doctor. That's why she died. When I was little."

Lou let that pass. "Carl, there's something we haven't talked about and, I don't know, but maybe Doctor Donohue will ask about it."

"Jeepers, look at that pretty horse. Oh, there's another."

"Appaloosas. You can tell by the spots on their rumps. Kind of like a polka dot blanket over their backs."

"What's polka dot?"

"A dotted pattern. Ladies like it for the everyday dresses they wear for housework. My wife likes polka dots."

"What's her name?"

"Lucille. Some people call her Lu but that sounds like my name, so we stick to Lucille, or Lucy. We have two boys."

"I hope one of them isn't named Lou." Carl grinned at his joke and Lou laughed. The kid had probably never had much to laugh about but he was fairly quick with humor.

"They're Phil and Henry. Each named for a grandfather."

"Oh, my father had a half-brother named Claus, same as his name. *Oma* named both her sons Claus."

"Do you know what a half-brother is?"

"Someone told me once."

"That means they have one parent the same, like the mother, but different fathers."

"*Oma* had two husbands."

Lou knew that the grandmother's other son, Claus Bohr, had come to get his mother. If Carl were convicted his father's estate would pass to the grandmother, and then she'd leave it to Bohr. The grandfather had left his estate to Carl, so Bohr should have no claim to that.

"How far do we have to go now?" Carl asked.

"Watch for a roadside filling station and we'll get gas and use the facilities."

"What's that?"

"The toilet."

"Do they have pop?"

"I doubt it. Usually gas, oil, water, maybe a few auto supplies."

"Before I was in jail I never had pop. Sheriff Gill gave me some."

"What flavor do you like?"

"Root beer. It's not real beer. I had orange, too."

"I like cream soda."

"How fast are we going?"

Lou checked the speedometer. "Not even thirty miles per hour. This car is two years old so I baby it. I worry about a flat tire."

"What's its name?"

"Name? Oh, you mean what kind of car? It's a Dodge."

Carl ran his hands over the dashboard. "It sure is spiffy. *Opa* had an old car but it's in the barn now. My father doesn't drive much. I sneaked and drove around the farm when I was alone."

Lou noticed the present tense for the father. Sometimes it took people a while to use past tense for a deceased person.

"Did this car cost a lot of money?"

"A good bit; close to eight-hundred dollars."

"My father was rich but he didn't share it."

Rather than comment on that, Lou pretended to check the dashboard gauges and Carl continued sightseeing.

Later, Lou spotted a filling station ahead. "This is outside Primghar; we'll stop for gas." He pulled over alongside a small log cabin with two gas pumps.

"Can I get out and watch?"

"Sure. I'll see if there's a toilet."

The attendant jerked his thumb over his shoulder. "An outhouse is all I can offer. And a pump for washing up."

Lou went around back and when he returned he sent Carl to the facility. When he showed up again Lou had just rolled a cigarette. "When I finish this, we'll eat lunch."

Lou blew a smoke ring at Carl and he said, "Do it again."

Lou did. "My boys like that. You ever smoke?"

"Well . . . one time I got caught smoking' in the barn. First, I got a lickin' for smokin' inside the barn. Fire, and all that. Then my father made a cigarette out of corn husks and tassels and made me smoke it. I puked all over the place. He made me clean that up, even though it was only on the ground. Whoever heard of cleaning dirt?"

"That sounds awful but you know what? If it kept you from smoking again, that might be a good thing. My wife is trying to convince me that tobacco is bad for my health. She says it's even bad for her and the boys."

"How could that be?"

"They breathe the smoke." Lou tossed the cigarette at his feet and ground it into the dirt. "Speaking of health, let's eat."

"There's a table over there with benches," Carl said.

Lou retrieved the basket and they dug in: Ham sandwiches on thick homemade bread, bananas, a dozen cookies, and canning jars filled with milk.

"I never had a banana," Carl said.

"Really?" Lou told himself to stop asking that. There were a lot of things Carl had not seen, eaten, or done. "You need to peel it. Here, like this." Lou zipped the skin almost to the bottom and handed Carl the fruit.

He bit off a third and chewed. His eyes grew wide. "That's good," he said, his mouth filled with mush. He ate the rest and tossed the skin away.

Lou asked, "Did you notice at the Gill's house that cookies grow on trees?"

Carl looked so startled that Lou immediately added, "I'm joking, but she always has cookies. You'd think they grew on trees."

When Carl grinned at the joke, Lou noticed that his teeth were considerably cleaner than when he'd first come to town. Grace had arranged for a dentist to visit him at the jail. He'd cleaned Carl's teeth and given him a toothbrush and a can of cleansing powder. Grace gave Carl orders to brush morning and evening. She told Lou that Carl thought that was a treat because the powder tasted like peppermint. One front tooth had a small chip but the others looked decent for a kid who'd been neglected all his life. Grace had also called in the town's eye doctor, who'd donated glasses for Carl. He wore them today.

But this trip hinged on mental health, not dental or eye problems. And in this case, Lou hoped the boy's mental health was not up to par. Things would go better for him in court.

Back on the road, Lou tried again with what he'd started earlier. "Carl, at the trial, the other attorney might ask questions that don't make sense to you but he'll ask anyway, to show motive."

"Motive?"

"Reasons. For killing your father—"

"Because he beat me and—"

"Listen; pretend I'm the other lawyer."

"And I'm me?"

"You're you. Remember what I told you before; answer the question he asks and stop there. Don't offer information. You might incriminate yourself."

"What's 'criminate'?"

"Never mind that. Answer only the question."

"Okay."

"So, we begin. Carl, you slept with your father the night before you shot him?"

"Yes."

"Did you always sleep with your father?"

"No"

"Could you be more specific?"

"I don't know that word."

"How often did you sleep with your father?"

"I never counted."

Lou bit back a smile. "Did he ask you to sleep with him?"

"I don't remember if he ever did."

"So why did you sleep with him? Was it the only bed?"

"Which question should I answer?"

"Sorry. Was it the only bed?"

"No."
"There were beds in other rooms?"
"Yes."
"Then why did you sleep with your father?"
"In winter to stay warm."
"Did your father ever touch you?"
"We were both asleep but I reckon we touched. He rolled a lot."
"But did he touch you in a way you didn't like?"
"Yessir."
"In bed?"
"No."
"When did he touch you in a way you didn't like?"
"All the time. When he hit me. But hitting isn't touching and he didn't hit me with his hands. He used a whip or switch. Oops, did I tell too much that time?"
"No; you did fine."
"I seen fathers play games with their kids or joke with them. Mine never touched me nice, you know, like if I did my chores good. You pat me on the head sometimes and once you rubbed my shoulders. Nobody ever done that to me before."

Lou couldn't say another word. That had to be one of the saddest comments he'd ever heard.

LOU DWINNELL

Carl fell asleep and that suited Lou. He liked conversing with Carl because it gave him a feeling for the boy's intelligence. But quiet time before arriving at Cherokee would benefit both of them.

Lou mulled over the fact that Claus Jess had likely never touched his son with affection—not so much as a pat on the head or ruffling his hair. For Lou, those motions were as natural as breathing. Carl's responses about his father never touching him with his hands, only a whip or stick, convinced Lou that there hadn't been sexual abuse. Thank God he'd been spared that.

Grace Gill had told Lou details of a story Carl related about his memory of when his mother died. She didn't know if it was relevant, but if it would help in his defense, she wanted Lou to know. Lou wondered now where that reporter from Des Moines got her information about the day Mrs. Jess died. Certainly not from Grace. There were likely a good number of people in Ocheyedan who could verify the story. Or make up a story for the sake of gossip.

Just before reaching the hospital Lou spoke Carl's name a couple of times. He stirred and looked around. "Are we there?"

"Just around this bend."

When Lou approached the winding private road, there stood the main building with turrets and rows of windows. On the adjoining buildings, the hospital itself, some windows were barred. It looked like the kind of building that would have gargoyles perched on ledges.

"Jeepers, it's a castle," Carl yelled, while Lou saw it as a prison.

He had to admit the overall layout was an architectural vision, and the grounds were nicely landscaped. The trees and bushes were budding. The place was twenty-some years old, built to relieve the population at the three other state hospitals: Independence, Clarinda, and Mount Pleasant. The latter seemed an incongruous name to Lou.

He'd visited Mount Pleasant as a child, with his father, to see his father's brother. Uncle Stanley suffered from senility. That was the word Lou's father, a doctor, used, but Lou learned later that Uncle Stanley had a degenerative disorder called Pick's disease. Uncle Stanley died in his late forties, but with the mind of a ninety-year-old man, if any man were to live that long.

Lou remembered the odor; a disinfectant meant to deny all the other smells emanating from hundreds of human beings living in the hellish place. Mostly he remembered the sounds within the building: moaning, groaning, crying, screeching, mewling, yelling, and adults dressed in white uniforms speaking among themselves about lunatics, imbeciles, and morons. Even as a child Lou didn't like the staff using such terms. They were talking about his uncle.

Lou asked his father why he went there when his brother didn't know who he was. His father said, "I know him. He's my big brother."

That didn't make sense to Lou then, but he understood it now. His father went because it was important to him. And who knew, maybe on some level it was important to Uncle Stanley. He always smiled at Lou and said he'd grown two inches, always two inches. If he'd seen Lou every day he'd have said he grew two inches. One time Lou imagined himself growing that much every day and envisioned himself as one of those stretched out figures in amusement park mirrors. The tallest man in the world.

When Lou pulled the car into the parking lot, Carl opened his door and leaped off the running board and stared upward. "Are you sure this isn't a skyscraper?"

"I'm sure." Lou guided Carl toward the administration office, the most impressive of the buildings.

"I heard about elevators," Carl said. "Not the kind with grain in them but the kind people ride in. Can we ride in one?"

"I should think we will."

Carl stared at a man approaching with an attendant. "Why does he have his arms tied around himself?"

"He's a patient and he's a danger to himself and others so they keep him in a straightjacket."

"How does he eat?" Carl looked back as Lou nudged him ahead.

"Maybe they take it off or someone feeds him."

"If I go to this hospital will I have a jacket like that?"

"I'll do everything I can to keep you out of this place."

"I saw a picture of a man tied with chains and he got out of them by himself."

"Probably Houdini," Lou said.

"There's another one," Carl said, pointing at a second man with his arms bound. Then Carl skipped a couple of beats to stay abreast with Lou.

What fifteen-year-old skips? Lou felt certain his boys didn't skip any longer. Run, was more like it. Dashing here and about, helter-skelter.

——————

Inside, Lou and Carl were separated, with a nurse taking charge of Carl to wait for Doctor Donohue. "Can we ride an elevator?" Carl asked.

"We sure will," she said in a tone one might use when addressing a much younger child. Then to Lou, "Make yourself at home. I'll locate you when the exam is finished. Give us an hour and a half."

If there were any place less like home, Lou didn't know where it would be. He hurried out the door, took a deep breath and began a fast-paced walk around the grounds. After a full lap, he returned to the office and read old magazines.

An hour or more later he found himself seated in Doctor Donohue's office, a pleasant enough room given the facility. Cathedral windows allowed light and sunshine and the house plants looked healthy.

Doctor Donohue entered through an inner door and the two men shook hands. They'd met before but it had been a while.

Donohue sat in the chair behind the desk, opened a file and tapped it several times with a pencil. "So," he said, looking at Lou while adjusting a monocle over his eye.

The eyepiece was new. He must need one eye for reading and one for distance. A monocle had to be a nuisance, trying to hold it in place, plus it looked pretentious.

Donohue cleared his throat. "First, our MD gave Carl a physical. He's underweight, malnourished."

"He's being well-fed now. I'd say he's put on a few pounds."

"Keep at it. He's short for his age but that could run in his family. He's gone through puberty."

That word struck fear in Lou; state hospitals were noted for their use of sterilization of the feeble-minded. Cherokee was particularly infamous as the site of lobotomies. Lou let the subject of puberty pass; the doctor would only deny such procedures.

Donohue studied his file and commented as he went along. "The mother was seventeen when she married Claus Jess, who was thirty-five. If she'd had an abusive, drunken father, she was most likely looking to escape him. So she married the first man who asked her, looking for protection."

"She didn't find it with Claus Jess. He fooled her like he did other people. The few who liked him said they never saw the mean side."

"Sometimes women step from one bad situation into another. It's the only way of life they know. But let's look at heredity, defective genes, and innate and predetermined factors such as alcoholism, or insanity."

"I assume you're aware that Carl has an uncle here."

"Yes; the mother's family. Carl fits the heredity factor. His mother's father was alcoholic and abusive. The boy's father was abusive. This passes to the boy, a cycle that isn't broken and he, in turn, when he's had enough, picks up a gun and shoots the abuser. If you've been abused, you will likely abuse."

"Yet, it doesn't seem that way with women. Women who are abused pick abusive men but they don't abuse their kids. They protect them, run away sometimes."

"You're right. But the question is, what we need to determine, is did Carl fully understand what he was doing?"

That didn't seem to call for a response so Lou waited.

"What have Carl's teachers said about his learning, his behavior?"

"There were problems. Truancy and fighting."

"Did his teachers mention signs of abuse, bruises, injuries?"

"No; but it's common for teachers or neighbors to shy away from getting involved. You know, the thinking that it's a father's right to discipline his children, even a man's right to discipline his wife. And, even in this day and age, some teachers use the rod themselves. Carl mentioned getting a licking from a teacher."

"Oh, and what did he say about that?"

"That it was okay because he deserved it."

"Typical. Abused women make excuses for their spouse. I provoked him, or dinner was late, some such reason that she deserved a punch in the face. Same with children; they think everything is their fault. If a parent leaves, they think it's their fault."

"So, what tests did you give Carl?"

"For one, the Binet-Simon test. I trust you're familiar with it."

"Somewhat. I'd like a refresher course."

"I'll get to that. We put Carl through a variety of quizzes and puzzles ranging from simple to difficult. These determine not only mental capacity but concentration, attention span, creativity, hand-eye co-ordination."

Pretty good on that last one, Lou thought. He aimed a gun and hit his target, twice.

"He managed only the simplest math. He wrote two brief sentences on a given topic. We use that more for handwriting analysis than content. I'm trained in handwriting patterns but I'll need to study his penmanship before writing my report. Interestingly, he wrote one sentence in German."

"It was his first language. He spoke it until he started school."

"He was like a boy at Christmas with the puzzles and games. As if he'd never seen any such thing."

"He hasn't."

"Using Lincoln Logs, he put together a small house quickly enough."

"My young boys enjoy those."

"Another facet of our tests is to look at native intelligence. Information that's absorbed as we mature but not acquired by opportunity, such as schooling. For instance, if a child never went to school, he'd still learn certain things from his environment."

"Including violent behavior."

"Behavior, yes, but I was speaking of general information. Before going to school, children normally learn to count and recite the alphabet, maybe read a few words. They learn colors and shapes. On a farm, for instance, they see that crops are planted in spring and harvested in the fall. This is information they simply absorb even if no parent or relative instructs them. That's native intelligence."

"Did Carl test well in that?"

Donohue waved his hand back and forth, indicating so-so. "Now let's look at the IQ results. You wanted a refresher." He tucked his monocle into his lapel pocket and sat back in his chair.

"Two different men claim to have developed the concept of IQ. The German psychologist and philosopher Wilhelm Stern, in nineteen-twelve, and Lewis Terman four years later. It actually dates back to nineteen-four. At that time, psychologist Alfred Binet was commissioned by the French government to create a test which would differentiate normal or above normal children from those who were inferior. Today we call it the Binet Scale or the Simon-Binet Scale, which came a bit later. Terman, mentioned earlier, revised the scale that we use today."

"Got it," Lou said.

"IQ is based largely on the degree of intelligence shown before the age of seventeen. So Carl is at an appropriate age for the test."

Donohue picked up a sheet of paper on which Lou saw a graph showing ups and downs, in blue and red.

"From the top, a score of more than one-forty is genius or almost genius. For instance, Alfred Einstein is said to have an IQ of one-sixty. Before him, Darwin, Kant, Mozart, the number is higher. Of course, we can only guess at theirs in terms of this scale. The next range is one-twenty to one-forty, very superior; one-ten to one-nineteen, superior; ninety to one-hundred-nine, average or normal; eighty to eighty-nine, dullness; seventy to seventy-nine, borderline deficiency, and below seventy, feeble-minded."

"Carl Jess?"

"Sixty-eight."

Lou sighed. He'd thought Carl might be borderline. Lou had no idea what his own test would show. Among his friends and acquaintances, he had no doubt who had the highest IQ. John Glover. And an ego to contain it.

"I'll send my written report to you," Donohue said.

"Are you willing to appear as a witness for the defense?"

"My findings reflect that side of the aisle. But I'd like to visit with him in his home environment."

"You mean take him out to the farm? There's no one there now."

"Perhaps, but at least away from here, a hospital setting. There's another set of tests. I'd like to come right before the trial to make it all one trip."

"Sounds good to me."

"Mind you, the state will have expert witnesses, too. Either side can pay someone to say what will help his case. I suggest you have at least a couple more opinions besides mine. I'm quite certain they'll agree with today's results. When is the trial?"

"Later this month."

"So soon?"

"The judge accelerated the process. No one wants this boy sitting in jail for months. I'll let you know the date."

"Best of luck. Again, in my view, he's a child and won't go beyond his current intelligence. In fact, this experience, the killing and its aftermath, might have caused regression."

Back on the road, Lou slumped against the backrest, weary to the bone. With two hours to go and dusk still coming early, and another stop for gas, he hoped Carl would sleep all the way home. He looked tuckered out.

Carl Jess had in the past, and in his future, a hard row to hoe.

JOHN GLOVER

Much to John's surprise, Augusta Duvall strolled into the hotel lobby one afternoon in mid-April. Her story about Carl Jess had sold a record number of copies of *The Des Moines Register*, not to mention it being reprinted in dozens of papers across the state. Her boss had given her a raise and sent her to cover the trial, after which she would take a few days' vacation in Chicago. John never had written to her about her piece on Carl. Probably a good thing; if her boss liked it enough to reward her and send her back here, it wasn't John's place to criticize.

On the day of her arrival, three days before the trial was set to begin, Augusta joined John and Lyn for supper. The trio picked up where they'd left off and enjoyed a lively conversation on all manner of topics, beginning with current events. The rainy evening brought the subject of the dreadful rash of tornadoes in the southeast, which led to John's reminiscence of a Wisconsin twister in his childhood. "That cyclone picked up a farmer and moved him to the next farm without so much as a scratch on the fella's arm."

"*The Wonderful Wizard of Oz*," Augusta said. "One of my childhood favorites."

"Bring up any subject and Papa has a tale to match it," Lyn said. "Mention boating and he'll tell you about the hunting trip that began on land and ended with him being dumped in Rush Lake and then getting sick on the one brant they shot and he and his fellow pioneers cooked and ate."

"What's a brant?" Augusta asked.

"A goose."

John broke in. "I got dumped in the Ocheyedan River, but the foul fowl came from Rush Lake. Two different hunting trips."

Augusta turned to Lyn. "And you? Have you had adventures, too?"

"Papa is the storyteller but . . . ." He pretended to glance furtively around the hotel lobby. "I worked here as a bellhop when I was fourteen, my first job, and the things I saw and heard." He raised his eyebrows. "Jollification of all kinds."

Augusta laughed. "That's a new word for me." She reached to the floor for her reporter's handbag. "I need to check my dictionary."

Lyn began another story and Augusta forgot about her dictionary.

"Papa, remember the time that guy went on a bender and fired a gun from a buggy? Outside the hotel here. The shot scared the horse and it plowed through downtown, scaring people to death. Both from the runaway horse and the shooting. The visitor said he'd been told by a friend that this was the Wild West and he'd need protection."

"He got protection," John said. "After the sheriff hauled him before me in a manner more emphatic than elegant, I tossed him in jail overnight and fined him a hundred dollars and costs."

"It sounds like a Zane Grey western," Augusta offered.

"Speaking of the Wild West," John said, "there was a time when Lyn fancied performing in the Buffalo Bill shows."

Lyn snickered as John continued. "He let his hair grow past his shoulders, even tied it back in a ponytail."

"Much to your dismay."

John waved off Lyn's comment. "I knew it was a phase." John noted that Lyn could use a haircut now; a bit shaggy on the neck. "It even made the paper when you got it cut. It must have been a slow week."

"Small town papers print just about anything. They wrote about my pet rabbits, and my rooster. Remember Major?"

"I do," John said. "He had a fine military strut."

"A rooster for a pet," Augusta said with a laugh.

John began something but Lyn spoke over him. "When I was a tadpole, well, almost a full-grown frog of sixteen, Papa and I attended Chicago's Columbian Exposition. I had my first box of Cracker Jack there. We toured the city and saw where Missus O'Leary's cow kicked over a lantern and started the fire."

"My hometown, but I wasn't born until two years later. I mean later than the fair, not the fire."

Doing a quick calculation, this was the first that John knew Augusta's actual age: Twenty-five.

Lyn continued. "I had an interesting time going to California years ago, to see my grandfather. I went twice, actually."

"Don't tell me you were there for the earthquake in San Francisco."

"No; San Diego area."

This time John spoke before Lyn could continue. "I believe I told you, Augusta, that Lyn witnessed a murder, five years ago about now."

"I'd love to hear about that. Since the Jess murder, I've become absorbed with murder cases. Maybe that will become my forte. On the train today, two men began discussing a murder but they left the dining car before I could hear the whole story. It had to do with matricide so that piqued my interest. The story happened in San Francisco."

Lyn looked at John. "You read something about that case."

"Yes; at the library in, I believe it was *Collier's Weekly*."

Augusta stopped him with a hand to his arm. "I want to hear about that but first Lyn. How did you come to witness a murder?"

"Oh, that. Well, you might say I was in the wrong place at the wrong time. But I suppose that cliché applies to the victim, not me."

"It's not a nice story," John warned.

"I shouldn't think so. It's murder. Lyn?"

"Well, Papa and I roomed at a house near the depot. It was a Saturday night about eleven. I was awakened by loud voices, argumentative. I looked out the window and saw two men running from the direction of the stockyards. The first one was shorter than the pursuer. The taller man caught up and they began to struggle and fell to the ground, in the snow. I woke Papa and then I threw on some clothes and lit out in that direction. Papa wanted to come, too, but I had to act quickly. Outside, I ran across two fellas and asked them to come with me. The scene we encountered was ghastly, to put it mildly."

Lyn paused. "Shall I continue?"

"Of course."

"The taller man fled and the man on the ground was . . . sorry, Augusta, there's no other word for it, butchered. We learned later there were twenty stab wounds. The knife was left in his hands."

"With the killer's fingerprints, no doubt," Augusta said.

"It was cold; he might have worn gloves. The other men with me left to find the authorities. Sheriff Gill wired towns north and south with my description of the killer, which wasn't all that good. Bloodhounds were brought from Worthington. However, the same train that brought the dogs here headed south with the killer aboard, who got as far as Sheldon and then purchased a ticket for Sioux City. The police nabbed him in Le Mars. Sheriff Gill and Street Marshal Palmer returned here with the prisoner the next day on the noon train."

"Who were the men and why was one killed?"

"They were migrant railroad workers who lived in a boxcar by the depot. The victim was Henry Vasquez from Mexico, and the killer was Frank Martinez. He'd been a soldier in Pancho Villa's army. They'd been drinking and got into an argument and one thing led to another."

"How awful. For the victim, of course, but for you to discover the body."

"One doesn't forget a scene like that." Lyn settled back in his chair. "Papa, the court related part of the story is yours to tell."

"I handled only the preliminary hearing. Charlie Brooks appeared for the defense and Clark and Dwinnell for the State."

"Wait," Augusta said, "Dwinnell is a defense attorney."

"Like me, he works both sides. Along with Lyn, we heard from about a dozen witnesses to the crime or just prior to it. There was enough circumstantial evidence for me to bind Martinez over to a grand jury, without bail."

"Did you testify at the trial, Lyn?"

"Star witness." He patted his chest in mock braggadocio.

"I assume he was found guilty."

"He pleaded guilty by reason of insanity," John said, "but it didn't wash. He got thirty years in the pen at Fort Madison."

"Quite a story for a little town like this."

"Murder has no specific locale. We're not immune to violence."

"Of course not. But sometimes people think that nothing like that happens in small towns. And now you have another murder coming to trial. Tell me, will there be an insanity plea?"

"That's what I hear," John said. "The charge is premeditated murder."

"That reminds me," Augusta said, "what about that matricide in California? You said you'd read about it in a magazine."

"The item was brief. A young woman is alleged to have cut her mother's throat. She claims she'd had nocturnal visions and heard voices commanding her to do this. The voices warned that her mother was a threat and must be eliminated."

"Did Carl ever claim anything like that?"

"Not in his confession in my court. In this California case, a doctor, the superintendent of the nearby state hospital, says he's been monitoring her behavior in the courthouse and considers her insane. But he hasn't issued a formal opinion. Other expert witnesses were being subpoenaed, on both sides. Those close to the case say the defense will present a formal motion to end the trial and empanel a new jury to declare her insane."

"I assume Carl has been tested by experts," Augusta said.

"He has. I'll fill you in on that."

"Actually, John, I'd rather wait and see how the trial plays out. The element of surprise keeps me on my toes."

Lyn grinned. "Surprise can brighten one's day. I sense that Papa is pleased with your surprise visit."

As his face flushed, John felt grateful for the dim lights.

"I'm happy to see you both," Augusta said. "A friend of mine asked, with a laugh, 'You're going to Sibley on vacation?' Partly business, I told him, adding that I have friends here."

Him, John thought. A beau perhaps. And why not? She's twenty-five. Some would consider her an old maid. A spinster.

Lyn broke John's thought when he bounced to his feet and announced, "My chariot awaits."

"Did you buy an automobile?" Augusta asked.

"No; I came on my trusty wheel."

"I enjoy bicycling. Maybe I'll borrow yours and take a spin. The weather is lovely."

"The hotel has a couple of wheels out back. Grab one of those. Well, good night, all. I hope my story won't keep you awake, Miss Augusta."

"Not to worry."

"I like him," Augusta said as Lyn departed.

"I do, too. But you're a pleasant departure. I am pleased to see you again."

"It's good to see you, too. And Lyn."

John waited while Augusta gathered her room key and then they climbed the stairs together; she to the second floor and he to the third, where permanent guests were stored, as he liked to think of it. The attic, the storage room.

JOHN GLOVER

Wide awake, stimulated by coffee and conversation, and Augusta, John thought about the man she mentioned, and his own interest in the fact that she might have a beau. He recalled an article he'd read at the library in what the librarian called "a woman's magazine." He'd learned that the term spinster, in recent years indicating a woman who was unmarried because of shortcomings in beauty or personality, or because she had not found Mr. Right, was originally an honorary term. In the Colonies unmarried women who earned their way by spinning wool, a valuable and necessary skill, were revered as community assets. Massachusetts boasted several well-known single women, among them the suffragette Susan B. Anthony, whom John had met. And Louisa May Alcott, famous for her novel about family life, although the husband and father didn't figure much in the story except for being away serving as a chaplain in the Civil War. The March women, having lost a fortune to the war, were learning to forge their own way and devise ways to support themselves.

The town librarian here, Miss Emily, John called her, approaching thirty, wore the invisible name tag: Old Maid. He'd known her since her childhood so he looked upon her with particular favor. He'd never asked why, when she became an adult, first a teacher and now librarian, she chose to use her middle name, Zenobia, rather than her given name, Emily. Surely the matronly name Zenobia added weight to the image of a spinster librarian.

The term bachelor didn't sound as demeaning as old maid or spinster. Although rightfully a widower, that happened so long ago that John had also been considered a bachelor. Lyn, it appeared, was a confirmed bachelor, but sometimes even men a bit long in the tooth surprised everyone, including themselves, by marrying. John had been thirty-one when he married Mary Frances, and she only twenty.

He and Lyn had been invited to a couple of The Bachelor Maid's Leap Year parties, where parlor games and flirting had been a source of amusement among the guests. Kathleen Barron, the widowed town socialite, enjoyed hosting these entertainments. John called her The Merry Widow, for she particularly liked waltzing, even at wedding receptions where the music tended to be square dances, polkas, schottisches, and jigs, depending on the ethnic group. John had tripped the light fantastic a time or two at such celebrations, having performed the wedding ceremony as judge or justice. He had escorted Kathleen and other single ladies to a movie or play at The Opera House, or been asked to someone's dinner table and bridge game afterward in order to comprise a foursome. Sins of the flesh had been available in the days when he traveled and stayed in hotels or tourist homes. But he'd remained celibate since Mary Frances left him these many years ago.

She came from the Victorian age, with a father in the ministry, which had its own expectations for young ladies. Then she married John, not yet a minister but inclined that way. John had not been as straight-laced as Reverend Upton; in fact, he even favored women in the ministry, but he was a decade older than his bride and with some worldly experience. Mary Frances had been prim by personality and subdued by poor health. Had she been healthy, she would still have eschewed the socialization expected of a politician's wife. It took years after her death for John to admit that he'd accepted speaking engagements to remove himself from a gloomy household. He'd taken Lyn with him when he could, and after Lyn's mother died, John focused on giving him a childhood.

Bless Mary Frances; she'd given him a son. Lord, if there was a higher calling than being father to a son, John couldn't name it.

It struck him now that when Mary Frances died she was only four years older than Augusta. In memory, and in the sepia photo on his desk, taken shortly before they married, Mary Frances looked matronly. Perhaps it was the dark dress. Did women ever wear colors in those days? White in the summertime, but otherwise gray, brown, dark blue, even black.

In that era, one was expected to look dignified in a photograph. But John saw now that Mary Frances had defied that rule of thumb and had managed a hint of a smile, almost a Mona Lisa quality. Quite beautiful overall; full lips, dark eyes, heavily lidded. The term sultry came to mind, but he'd never entertained that notion back then. French-Canadian on her mother's side and John had sometimes wondered if there might be a speck or two of American Indian blood in the line. He noticed traces of those features in both Mary Frances and Lyn. Lyn's hair was like hers, too, abundant, while John's had been only average when young and now had thinned. Mary Frances's hair had truly been her crowning glory; ebony in color and sheen, thick, luxurious, falling to the middle of her back in curls and the sides and top tucked in with combs and pins. When she was dying, and the tresses were tangled and wet from fever and perspiration, her sister wanted to cut it short. Mary Frances would not hear of it. John had been pleased. What difference did it make if her hair matted? After she died, he clipped a curl and held it together with an ivory barrette.

Rummaging in the bureau drawer, John pulled out a small tin box and popped it open. The curl looked and felt the same as it did the day he put it there. He wondered if Lyn had ever seen the hair—he couldn't recall showing it to him. He closed the box and tucked it back in the drawer.

John preferred long hair on women; yet, Augusta's bob looked attractive, and what man wasn't intrigued by today's higher hemlines? Times had changed. Augusta and her colleagues, having the vote, attending college and becoming professionals were a new breed. John admired what he saw. Especially Augusta. He realized now that thinking of her as an old maid because she was twenty-five was as archaic as he himself.

More to the point, should he be thinking about her at all, except as a friend? As the saying went, he was old enough to be her grandfather, which made Lyn old enough to be her father. Quite likely, Augusta had no interest in either of them, other than friendship.

—⁓•◦\◦◯◉◯◉◯◦/•◦⁓—

The Glover men and Augusta were invited to supper the next two nights; the first at Overholser's and tonight at Gill's. While Grace and Augusta were preparing dessert and coffee, and Lyn carried dishes to the kitchen, Joe confided to John. "People are talking about you two."

"Lyn and me? Whatever for?"

Joe lowered his voice. "You and Augusta."

It took John a moment to speak. "Surely you don't mean—"

"Gossip, of course. You know Alma Lundberg."

"Can't say I do. Why would she talk about me? And Augusta."

"Wagging her tongue gives her reason to live. She told Grace that she heard from a friend that you and Augusta were shacked up at the hotel."

John cringed at the crude expression. He balled his napkin and threw it at Joe. "That's highly insulting to both of us. And beneath you to repeat it. For Heaven sake, Joe."

Joe held up his hands, palms out. "Sorry. Don't shoot the messenger. I thought you should know. This friend, whoever the source is, said that you and Augusta went up the stairs together."

"Why . . . what . . . .?" John clenched his jaw so abruptly he could have loosened a tooth. Then he recalled that they had, in fact, gone upstairs at the same time.

"Absurd. There's one set of stairs. How else are we to get to our rooms?"

"Grace and I certainly won't repeat it," Joe said, "but Alma—"

Lyn entered then, balancing a tray as if he were a butler, followed by the ladies. John pulled himself together as best he could. He'd never been easily flummoxed, but this innuendo embarrassed him; it cut to the quick.

Who else had heard this story? While he trusted Joe and Grace, the Lund woman had probably told everyone she knew or met on the street and they repeated it. The over-the-fence communication line buzzed incessantly, as did the indoor party line.

John could hardly bring himself to look at Augusta. With both his pride and dignity wounded, he felt too mortified to tell even Lyn about the gossip. Lyn's work took him all over the county; he'd probably hear it somewhere. Maybe he already had. Surely he would say something.

Lyn and Augusta had their heads together, laughing about something. My goodness, her whole face came alive when she laughed; her eyes sparkled with wit, her nose wrinkled, her mouth . . . .

"John," Grace said, looking first at him and then at Joe, both of them silent. "Is everything all right?"

John caught a breath. "Couldn't be better, my dear. The angel food cake looks delicious."

Feeling a restless night coming on, John added, "If it's not too much trouble, might I have a glass of milk? I sleep better without coffee in the evening." He immediately chided himself for sounding like an old man— in Augusta's company.

"I know what you mean," Grace said. "I'll have milk, too."

Forking a bite of cake while listening to Lyn and Augusta chatter, John counseled himself: See to it that you and she don't go upstairs at the same time tonight. Keep a respectable distance and you won't leave yourself open to gossip. She would be able to leave it all behind, but he lived here.

AUGUSTA DUVALL

Willis Overholser asked Augusta to write about the trial for *The Gazette*. His reporter, Thomas Betts, who'd written the initial story, had found a greener pasture, the bigger market of Mason City, Iowa. Overholser would be out of town during the trial and couldn't cover it himself. Augusta checked with her boss, who had no objection so long as his paper hit the streets before this smaller one.

This morning, John invited Augusta along to the courthouse where he would hear a handful of cases. The first one concerned a dog that followed a woman home and she'd kept it but the original owner had replevined the animal. Augusta needed to consult her dictionary for replevined. In progress now was a dispute about a breeding fee—a stallion owned by the plaintiff. Given the small sum of money owed, it hardly seemed worthwhile to Augusta.

She noted that on the bench John seemed confident, fully in charge. But when the two of them were alone he acted nervous. That hadn't been the case when she first came to town; it began after they'd been at the Gill's last night. Tired, he'd said, back at the hotel and scuttled off to his room while she was picking up her key and trying to get away from the chatterbox desk clerk. His interest in her comings and goings perturbed her.

On her and John's walk to the courthouse this morning, instead of taking a direct route through the business district, where she'd noticed with amusement that John always greeted folks as if he were campaigning for office, he'd led her along the side avenues. A change of scene, he said, but the scene had been alleys and less than attractive store fronts. After two days of light rain, the unpaved road had made a mess of her beige pumps.

Nor had John offered her his arm for support, as he usually did. Might he be attracted to her and didn't want anyone to notice? Surely not, given the age difference. There were plenty of May-December couples, but fifty years difference stretched a gap to a chasm. He'd not been openly flirtatious with her, so why did she even consider that he might be taken with her?

Lyn had made a comment about John being pleased to see her again. And there had been two women talking behind their hands in the hallway when John and she arrived together this morning. Ah, small town gossip. That snoopy hotel desk clerk had to be the behind the scenes reporter. Or the maid. Who else?

It amused her for a moment but then, searching her mind and heart, Augusta found not the faintest urge toward a romance with John. She considered him handsome; one of those men who aged well and might be handsomer now than as a younger man. She admired the life he'd led, his intelligence, his memory for detail, and she enjoyed his company. That was that. She had a habit of touching people on the hand or arm when conversing with women and men. She would strive to avoid that gesture with John.

Augusta regretted that the first night she met John and Lyn she intended to use them as a means of gaining information. She had quickly changed her tune and grown fond of both men. In fact, she thought now, if she were to become attracted to either man, *if* being the word she would underline so the typesetter knew to italicize it, it would more likely be Lyn. There was a lesser age difference. He was, in fact, the age of her two uncles, mid-forties, and her father for that matter. Truthfully, she preferred men closer to her own age. Period.

But her mind didn't let it drop. Lyn was handsome; in a different way than John. She hadn't at first noticed Lyn's good looks; the impression sneaked up on her. Although cut from the same pattern in size and shape: about five-eight and stocky, the two men were set apart by the fabrics of life style: Lyn in denim and whipcord and John in boiled shirts and cravats, and always a suit and hat. John wore polished wing-tip shoes while Lyn's brogans were scuffed. The word dapper came to mind for John; while last night Lyn, wearing a pea coat and knit watch cap, looked like a mariner just in from a sea journey. The attire lent him a rakish but oddly attractive look.

Dark complected, perhaps from outdoor work; his coarse dark hair was not always neatly combed. He had a sensual mouth and his dark eyes looked directly at her when they conversed. He paid attention. But in an avuncular way, she convinced herself now, feeling certain that he had no designs on her, except friendship. She liked him more each day. He'd not gone to college but had evidently absorbed a great deal of knowledge from reading and from a lifetime spent with John. He'd forged a path different from his father's and become his own person. Lyn was, like John, a true gentleman, and Augusta admired his loyalty and love for his father. She found his use of the term Papa endearing.

She couldn't help comparing the difference between the father and son hatred that drove Carl Jess to murder and the loving bond between John and Lyn. She had not before seen such a tight companionship and obvious affection between father and son. Her father, the absent-minded professor, rarely showed affection to his two sons or Augusta. That wasn't to say he didn't love them; he wasn't obvious about it.

A shift in the courtroom scene captured Augusta's attention. When a new cast of characters appeared and began their dialogue, she practiced taking notes with the Gregg Shorthand she'd recently learned. It would come in handy for the Jess trial. The system intrigued John and she had explained the alphabet and symbols to him last night. In turn, he briefed her on court procedures, maneuvers, tactics, and legal terms. In addition, he asked permission to be frank with her about her writing style.

Unsure what to expect, she nodded consent.

He advised that she drop the tabloid style of her earlier piece.

Tabloid? She didn't realize she had screeched the word until other diners looked her way.

In deference to the onlookers, John lowered his voice and added that the piece was a tad yellow. Melodramatic. Leaned toward sensational. A bit of fiction added for drama. The publisher of the *Tribune* had thought so, too.

This was not advice; this was harsh criticism. While she ached to deny the accusation, John added with a fatherly smile, "Try a softer approach."

And then, "Double check details; you had some incorrect last time."

Another jolt. He had taken the wind out of her sails, but she agreed to revisit the story; she had a copy in her handbag.

He'd been right.

Now, while Justice Glover wound up his agenda, Augusta drafted a description of the mural on the wall. Lady Justice would serve as a headline for her Carl Jess story and a description of the painting would lend itself to the story's opening. A writing instructor had advised: Always know the end of your story before you begin. She couldn't know the end of this story—the outcome of the trial—but she hoped her opening would hook readers.

Will Lady Justice Look Kindly On Carl Jess?
By Augusta M. Duvall
August 25, 1920
The Trial: April 19-21, 1920

At high noon on this pleasantly warm spring day, the scene from a second floor window of the Osceola County Courthouse in Sibley, Iowa, appears at first glance to be a patriotic holiday celebration. A mild breeze tosses the Stars and Stripes, saluting the nearby statue of a Civil War soldier. Colorful blankets spread on the lawn create a patchwork quilt design. People dine from picnic baskets or have purchased sandwiches from a man who arrived from Rock Rapids in a truck whose side opens into a serving window. Local merchant Alex Tossini wheeled in a handcart filled with fruit and candy. Two children across the street are dispensing fresh lemonade in paper cups. The mayor strolls among the vendors unconcerned that none of them has a permit to sell here.

The view is misleading; the overall mood is solemn, not celebratory.

Those clustered outside were turned away early this morning when the number of spectators wanting into the courtroom gallery surpassed seating and standing room. They're here for the Carl Jess patricide trial. For some, the fifteen-year-old farm boy's story evokes memories from a decade ago when seventeen-year-old Ernest Groen shot and killed his abusive father on a farm near Ashton. A jury acquitted Groen on the grounds of self-defense.

Seated in the courtroom, awaiting resumption of the proceedings, this reporter is enthralled and soothed by the mural that graces the east wall. Believed to have been added about the time the courthouse was built, in 1902, little is known for certain about its origin. A strikingly similar painting hangs in the Cottonwood County courthouse in Windom, Minnesota. Information on that artwork states it was done by Odin J.

Oyen, from Wisconsin. In Sibley, although it is unproven that Oyen is the artist who executed the mural (the name is obscured), he is given credit on a plaque beneath the picture.

Rendered in Italian Renaissance style, the 11 x 14 foot scene depicts Lady Justice wearing a white robe with gold epaulets. Seated on a marble throne in a courtyard with marble steps, she cradles a sword in her lap. Trees adorn the background and a guard in full armor and holding a spear stands at attention.

On the left of Lady Justice, a robed man holds a book whose title is Common Law. A woman is kneeling, with outstretched arms holding a scroll toward Lady Justice. Another standing figure wears a flowing tan robe with a hood. On the right, a figure clad in red holds a green branch and a book, while another figure holds a book titled Civil Law. One other figure is a man in a red cloak.

The Question Remains

Will Lady Justice be sympathetic to the boy who has now reappeared before the court accompanied by his lawyers, L.F. Dwinnell and I.R. Meltzer?

Carl Jess is the most diminutive figure to have stood before the bench in this room. When brought from his farm home in March, a wretched figure, he might have stepped from the pages of Charles Dickens's *Les Miserable*. Today, bathed and coiffed, dressed in brown corduroy knickers with knee socks, a tan sweater over a white shirt, and a tie tucked into the vee of the sweater, Carl looks every bit the schoolboy he should be.

Sadly, his youthful school days are likely over.

Meet The Jury

Much of the first day comprised jury selection. The jury in the case of Carl Jess, charged with the murder of his father, Claus Jess Jr., on the 7th of March, was empanelled Monday afternoon at 5 o'clock. Judge Hutchinson directed that the question of the sanity of the accused must be tried previous to that of the indictment, as the issue of insanity has been raised.

Selected as jurors were: M. Pettijohn, Harris farmer—M.F. Taylor, Sibley surveyor—August Scharlepp, Sibley section Foreman—George Mohr, Sibley salesman—Edwin Loerts, Sibley farmer—J.C. Frey, Harris farmer—J.E. Vande Putten, Ashton farmer—Chris Schutte, Sibley carpenter—Matt Ellerbroek, Sibley merchant—John Stallman, Ashton merchant—Albert Klosterman, Ashton farmer—J.F. Sellers, Sibley manufacturer.

The Boy's Recollection

Under the direction of his lawyer, Lou Dwinnell, Carl Jess told the court that on Saturday, the day before the killing, his father told him to clean the barn and haul out manure. Instead, he played in the snow all forenoon. His father was provoked and struck him. Carl cleaned the barn in the afternoon, had supper and went to bed, having no further altercation with his father.

Carl said he had been thinking about getting rid of his father for over a year because he wanted to end the lickings. He wanted to rid himself of his father, but he also felt sorry for him. He had thought of poisoning him, but did not know what to give him. He never thought of Rough on Rats.

He first thought of using a rifle while sleeping with his father the Saturday night before the shooting. He said if he had it to do again, he wouldn't kill his father. When asked why, he answered, "Because everyone is making a big thing of it."

Carl said he did not run away because he had no money, and he never fought his father about that. He was frightened after he killed his father and, therefore, he told about the horse kicking him. He said he was not angry with the teacher who licked him, because he deserved it.

A Cloud of Witnesses For The Defense

Dr. George Donohue, Superintendent of the Cherokee Insane Asylum, and Dr. W. P. Crumbacker, Superintendent of the Independence Mental Hospital, testified as expert witnesses for the defense. They presented evidence as to their findings in several examinations of Carl Jess, covering a period of three days last week. The results testified to by each man were practically identical. They regard him as mentally deficient, his intellect and judgment being arrested at age eleven, according to their tests, and they believe he will remain at a standstill at that level.

Dr. Donohue spent considerable time with the boy Thursday and Saturday. He talked to him about his work, his play, and difficulties with his father. Carl said he went hunting and fishing some; did not play baseball or football. His father licked him continually; used a buggy whip or stick. He could not work to suit his father.

Dr. Donohue added that Fred Grabow, an uncle of the boy, has been in the Cherokee hospital for some years. For the past three years he has been mute, refusing to say a word, and he entertains delusions. He is a degenerate of moderate degree. In addition, Carl's maternal grandfather Grabow was a heavy drinker and had a clouded mind.

"Carl is a logical result of ancestry," Donohue said.

Donohue related how he tested Carl using the Yerkes-Bridges System. The twenty tests Carl took gave him a total percentage of 66, when a normal person of his age should test not less than 86. His test result was that of a child of eleven years. Dr. Donohue applied the tests on different days and Carl failed the same tests on both occasions.

"Carl Jess is about as accountable as a child of eleven. An adult, even a boy of fifteen, would have run away. But Carl did not know enough to get away. He could not distinguish the difference between a short and long line, between the weight of two cubes of the same size, and he was a total failure on the ideas of charity, obedience, or justice."

Regarding the supposed motive of greed, that the boy wanted money, Dr. Donohue said that Carl had no concept of money amounts and that he did not understand that land value did not mean cash in the pocket.

In sum, Dr. Donohue concluded, "The boy is mentally deficient and feeble-minded from birth, from heredity. He should be restrained of his liberty and placed in an institution for the feeble-minded."

Further Witnesses

A number of people from Ocheyedan were examined; among them Lee Poole, W.H. Doerr, Mr. and Mrs. J.R. Williams, Frank Hromatko, Mrs. Mary Randall, P.F. Mackel, Rev. E. Fiene, August Arend, August Palenske, and Wm. Hromatko.

Some testified to the utter indifference of the prisoner to the gravity of his situation and the enormity of his deed. The State's evidence showed that Carl apparently acted like other boys. He attended church and Sunday school; ran the tractor and farm machinery, and performed ordinary farm work. He sold milk and collected the money for his own use. He shopped and paid for his own shoes.

Countering the boy's claim that he never had a nickel to spend, various merchants testified that Carl averaged $1.50 per week for candy and ice cream. Other witnesses said he went hunting and fishing; ran his father's auto; had a bicycle, a sled, a baseball outfit, such things as the average boy possesses.

Floyd Kruger of Alpha, Minn., an uncle, told of the boy's relatives who were insane, mentioning Fred Grabow, the uncle in Cherokee. Scott D. Tift, John Gress, and Mrs. John Grabow, confirmed that John Grabow, the grandfather of Carl, was afflicted with alcoholism, many times drunk and abusive.

Dr. Lass of Ocheyedan, called to the home soon after the shooting, told of the circumstances and gave results of an examination of the accused.

Sheriff Joseph Gill and Deputy Chris Wassmann told of their relations with the boy and his general demeanor and disinterested mannerisms concerning the affair.

Dr. Padgham of Ocheyedan, who conducted the coroner's inquest, gave evidence as to the boy's confession on that occasion and the care taken in making him understand the seriousness of same.

Prof. Butson, Superintendent of the Ocheyedan schools, and Miss Froke, Carl's teacher, told of the incorrigibility of the young man. How he had been whipped several weeks after Christmas; that he was mischievous, and absent about forty days each year, always having weak excuses.

During the entire trial Carl Jess sat in a chair, apparently oblivious of what was going on. He sat with his head in his hands or with his eyes cast downward. At times he was sound asleep. Sheriff Joe Gill testified in court Tuesday that the prisoner went to sleep in the courtroom Monday while the judge, the jury, and the lawyers were engaged in an inquiry as to the sanity of the 15-year-old youth who shot and killed his father, Claus Jess, while he was sleeping on Sunday morning, March the seventh.

The Trial Of The Century For Osceola County

Five years ago, on a cold November night, observed by a witness, two men fought on the streets of Sibley and one died, stabbed some twenty times.

Only weeks ago, another murder occurred, this one in the quiet of the countryside on a cold March morning, with no witnesses.

Unlike the murder five years ago, where the two participants were railroad workers practically unknown to most residents, this time the victim and his slayer were well-known in the Ocheyedan community and beyond. Shockingly, the person holding the rifle was a boy, but as we've learned from expert witnesses he is mentally deficient, with the intellect and judgment of no more than an 11-year-old.

This case has been tried solely by local legal talent, who adeptly demonstrated that outside counsel was not needed in cases of the most vital importance to the people of this tightly-knit community. The interests of the State as well as the defense were ably represented. The closing arguments on both sides were concise, conclusive, and masterful efforts. Both the attorneys for the State and the defense acquitted themselves.

Attorneys B.F. Butler and E.H. Koopman appeared for the State, while Attorney's L. A. Dwinnell and I. R. Meltzer represented the defendant.

Jury Deliberated Sixteen Hours.
Received Additional Instructions.

The testimony was concluded at 5 o'clock Tuesday evening; the case going to the jury at 6 o'clock, following counsels' closing arguments.

After considering the case of Carl Jess for 16 hours, the jury returned a verdict Wednesday morning adjudging Carl Jess insane when he murdered his father on the 7th day of March. The jury had taken a number of ballots during the night, but was unable to arrive at any decision up to 3 o'clock Wednesday morning, when they retired for the night. Rumor has it that a number of ballots resulted 6 to 6 and others 5 to 7 in favor of the insanity charge.

At 8:30 Wednesday morning the jurors were called into the courtroom where the judge gave them additional instructions emphasizing the fact that they, the jury, must solely pass on the question of sanity. If they find the evidence of the experts proved partial insanity, they must return a verdict of insanity. The jury returned to the jury room and in a half hour returned a verdict for insanity or mental deficiency. Carl Jess cannot be brought to trial again on the indictment as charged.

The judge complimented the jury on the justice of the finding, which he said was sustained by the uncontroverted evidence of the expert witnesses.

Found irresponsible, Carl Jess will be committed to an institution for the feeble-minded. If his mentality were normal he would stand trial for premeditated murder.

Under the direction of the defense the question at issue was as to the mental responsibility of the boy slayer. It is another Harry Thaw case with the difference that Thaw was said to be emotionally and temporarily unbalanced while Jess is declared abnormally made up mentally, genetically, from heredity, and therefore irresponsible for his acts.

In other words, one (Thaw) had a brain storm and the other (Jess) hasn't the sort of brain that storms. Both victims were equally dead.

At times during this trial, there seemed to be only one side—the defense. John F. Glover, Justice of the Peace before whom Carl Jess first appeared after the heinous act, explained to this reporter that the State's duty is to see that the trial is fair and that justice is served. To a man, no one wanted to see Carl Jess imprisoned with hardened criminals.

Judge Hutchinson will consult with experts on which state facility offers services that are in the best interest of the child. His consultation will include Guardian *ad litem* Frank Hromatko, the neighbor whose aid Carl Jess sought on the morning of the murder.

Looking over the frail boy's shoulders these past three days, Lady Justice treated him as kindly as possible.

JOHN GLOVER

After the trial ended that Thursday afternoon in April, John, Lyn, and Augusta dined at the hotel and discussed the trial, its outcome, and the ramifications for Carl Jess. What were homes for the feeble-minded like and how would he be treated? Would he ever be released?

Finally, Augusta had gathered her handbag and stood. "I can't sit still any longer. I must go write the story and wire it to my editor." She wrapped her head in her hands. "It's all up here, pounding its way to a headache."

Lyn left for home and while Augusta clacked the keys on the hotel typewriter, John chatted with an automobile parts salesman for an hour or more, and then paced the lobby, hoping to see at least a draft of the story. But the hour grew later and later and he nodded off twice in his chair so he dragged himself to his suite and there surrendered to Morpheus.

In the morning, expecting to find Augusta in the dining room, the desk clerk told him she had scurried away to catch the early train instead of her scheduled noon departure.

Instantly despondent that she had once again left without notice, John returned to his room, undressed, and crawled into his unmade bed.

On Sunday after church, John and Lyn took turns reading Augusta's piece in the *Des Moines Register*. Again, it dominated the front page, along with a photo of Carl and Lou Dwinnell outside the courthouse after the trial. For the most part, John put his stamp of approval on the story.

Lyn commented, "I wish she'd used a sidebar explaining who Harry Thaw was to show why she compared his case to Carl's."

Feeling argumentative, John said, "It doesn't hurt to pique interest and let readers who are interested do their own research. We have a lovely library for that purpose."

Lyn scanned the story again while John continued. "I mentioned Thaw to her one day during recess. I didn't realize she would find a use for the information. I also pointed out Carl's resemblance to a Dickens' character.

She painted an illustrative image. And, as you know, I discussed writing style with her."

"She took your mentoring to heart, Papa. It's a good piece of writing."

Two weeks later John held in his hand a picture postcard from Augusta showing an Illinois Civil War monument, and only "Warm regards, Augusta," scrawled on the back. John laughed aloud at the scene. Had she detected his personal interest in her or heard gossip and chosen this subject as a subtle hint that planted his age in the proper era?

Ah, well; they surely did come from two different worlds.

John had occasion to send Augusta a note along with the short piece he wrote for *The Gazette* about the decision on where to place Carl Jess. Overholser added a sidebar explaining the costs of the trial. Residents were entitled to know where their tax dollars were spent, he explained.

Carl Jess Ordered To Home For Feeble Minded

Carl Jess will be sent to The Home For The Feeble-Minded at Glenwood, Iowa. Judge Hutchinson so ordered last Monday afternoon when he held an adjourned session of the district court for that purpose.

Judge Hutchinson believes that the boy ought to go where his mind can be developed so far as possible and where he will not be exposed to criminal influence.

The judge consulted with the parole board and that body had consulted the board of control. All agreed that of the hospitals maintained by the state, Glenwood was best-suited to Carl's age and needs.

No term of limitation of the lad's stay at Glenwood was made by the judge. "I put him in charge of the state of Iowa," Hutchinson said. "The case will be revisited from time to time."

Ambrose Graves of Ocheyedan will serve as legal guardian of the boy's estate.

[Expert witnesses are paid for their time and testimony. The court allowed the experts in the Carl Jess case the following sums: Dr. Crumbacker, $168.35; Dr. Donohue, $140.00; Dr. DeBey, $113.00; and Dr. Lass, $110.00.]

When Willis asked John if he'd like to return to newspaper writing, he replied, "Not a chance. It's time for this old cavalry horse to find a quiet pasture."

He'd enjoyed the camaraderie in the old days, even the rivalry, between newspaper publishers, and the excitement and stress of putting together a weekly paper, but lately he hadn't the stamina for the race to the finish.

So, too, with the law. Despite the nature of the Carl Jess case, spending three days in court had given John a rush. He listened with a trained ear; viewed with a trained eye, explained details to Augusta, longed to be part of the action, not from the bench but before it as a defense attorney. Now, after the fact, the adrenaline had waned. He felt his age.

As a man of the cloth, John accepted that everything that happens is God's plan. Still, it troubled him deeply when terrible things occurred. Why did God give a child to a couple and then snatch it from them a week or a month later? Why did that infant scream with pain from twisted bowels before he died? Why did kindly old Morris Blade stumble into an abandoned well and lie undiscovered until two days later when his son reported him missing? Why was a boy's life filled with unbearable tribulations to the point that immature thinking told him he must kill his father to change the situation?

John knew the answer; such things were tests of faith for the people to whom they happened. He'd been fortunate; no real tragedy had been visited upon him in all his years. But as a pastor he empathized with the afflicted; their troubles brought waves of melancholy that grasped him with a riptide's force.

If there'd ever been a sadder story in county history than Carl Jess and his father, it had receded from John Glover's memory.

JOSEPH GILL

Quiet as a monastery, Joe thought when he returned to his office after dinner on a warm May afternoon. He'd attended a meeting all morning; Chris Wassmann had the day off for a funeral, and the lone prisoner, Carl, Jess, never made noticeable noise. Soon he'd be gone.

On his way to the bathroom, Joe glanced toward the two cells and did a double take. He expected one to be empty, but not Carl's. Well, Grace knew where the keys were; she'd probably taken him home for dinner instead of bringing food here. They'd be back shortly. It might be time for one of Grace's grooming sessions: Carl's twice weekly bath and his once a week hair trim. Joe had the cleanest prisoner in the state.

A half hour passed before Joe called home. No answer. He couldn't recall if Grace had one of her meetings today: garden club, church circle, literary group; he didn't keep track. But if she had a meeting, where was Carl? Had Grace brought his dinner, gone to her meeting and left the door unlocked, and he'd escaped? He'd never shown any indication of wanting to fly the coop. He actually had a comfortable nest here.

But there was a first time for everything. If someone left the door unlocked Carl might have seized the day. *Carpe diem.*

Joe sat down and sorted mail and read what needed attention.

He couldn't concentrate. He called home again. No answer.

Knowing Grace kept an appointment book, he went home and found the calendar. Nothing listed for today. So it made sense that she and Carl were together. But where? And more importantly, why? She had no right to take him anywhere.

Joe climbed in the car and scoured the town, through the park and past the sandpit swimming hole. Too early in the year for swimming. He patrolled east and west and north and south. He watched Lefty Lucas trying to keep his legs on course as he walked toward home. An injury in the war had short-circuited his nervous system and caused a permanent jitter. If moonshine comforted Lefty, and so long as he didn't disturb anyone with his drinking, Joe didn't need the name of his bootleg pharmacy. Veterans had paid their dues.

Back at the office, Joe wondered: Who does the sheriff report to when his prisoner is missing? Judge Hutchinson, who decided Carl belonged in jail instead of living with the Gills? Well, Your Honor, the Gills are looking a tad irresponsible today.

Fuming at Grace, Joe dug into his paper work and watched the clock. About mid-day Hattie Lind came in to complain about the ruffians who used her garden as a shortcut to school and made a tossed salad out of the tender plants sprouting. A spinster, Hattie lived with her parents in a big house along the boulevard. Nice; built before the turn of the century.

Joe stood behind his desk, only a few inches taller than the woman. Mustering his cajoling voice, he said, "Miss Hattie, I appreciate your distress. Grace is coddling her young plants, too. But I can't do anything unless we catch the rascals in the act or you can identify them."

Squinting beneath her straw hat Miss Hattie replied, "Well, if you won't do anything then I'll stand guard before school commences and lets out."

"If you do that, let me know their names and I'll tan their hides."

Hattie turned and huffed out of the office.

In less than a minute Lyn Glover replaced her. "Miss Hattie nearly ran me over in the hall."

"Kids in her garden." Joe sat down again.

"She keeps a neat property."

"Last week it was kids peeping in her basement windows."

Lyn grinned. "Could be something clandestine going on there. Being single is fraught with suspicion, you know."

Joe leaned back in his chair. "Do you have a complaint, too?"

"Only that I can't find your wife. I'm supposed to do a repair but Grace doesn't answer the door."

"Oh, right. I don't know where she's gone. Probably an unexpected errand. Go on in. Do you need me to show you—"

"I know where it is. It won't take more than an hour."

"Leave the bill on the table and I'll square things with you."

At five, Joe left the office unlocked and went home. He checked on the repair in the pantry and found the bill Lyn had written on the tablet where Grace kept her grocery list. He dug in the icebox, reheated beef stew from yesterday, ate, and washed his dishes, with still no sign of the missing persons.

What if someone kidnapped Carl and Grace?

He laughed out loud. That made no sense.

Maybe Carl overcame Grace and knocked her out and stuffed her in a closet? Absurd. That puny kid. Grace was small but always alert around prisoners. Even Carl, Joe hoped.

Still, he roamed through the house, checking all the rooms and closets and feeling silly with every step.

He went out the back door and perched on the stoop. He could see the jail from here; see if Grace showed up with Carl. Damn, where were they?

Across the street, Lou Dwinnell and his two boys were engaged in animated conversation as they walked toward the city park. Lou had the youngest boy on his shoulders, while the other bounced ahead, sometimes walking backward to say something to the others or share a laugh.

What with the Jess patricide, Joe had lately given fatherhood some thought. He never knew his father; never saw a photo of him. Joe and his mother, a seamstress and milliner, had lived in the back of her shop in a small Illinois town. All she'd ever said about his father was, "He left; subject closed." Joe was legitimate; he'd found his birth certificate—father James Gill—and his parents' marriage certificate after his mother died of unknown causes when she was thirty-six and he'd turned sixteen. A family he knew was heading to Iowa to homestead, so Joe offered to help with the trek west.

Lacking knowledge on what a father was supposed to do or be, Joe followed the lead of other men of his generation who had little physical contact with their offspring. Fathers and children, it seemed to Joe, were not supposed to touch. He'd noticed that younger men, his son-in-law and Lou Dwinnell for instance, were more demonstrative with their kids than Joe's generation. Joe would take a bullet for his daughter and her two girls, but when they visited he let them initiate the welcome and goodbye hugs. Other people's children didn't approach him because he didn't encourage it. Or maybe they were put off because he was sheriff. He couldn't be sure. Nevertheless, he preferred it that way. He'd loved one boy, and lost him. Since then, he'd not allowed himself to feel paternal toward another man's son. He'd never addressed boys as Son, like many men did. Now listen, Son, they'd say, and offer manly advice.

Joe kept his distance from Carl, and his pity. The boy had slain his father. And now Grace had usurped Joe's authority and taken Carl somewhere. It boggled his mind how and why she would do such a thing. He glanced down to grind a cigarette butt with his heel and when he looked up there they were, the escapees.

He stormed across the yard and into the office, where he nearly collided with his delinquent wife. "Where the hell—"

She put her finger to her lips. "Let's not talk here."

She was right; he'd deal with them separately. The adult first. The adult who'd pulled a childish truancy. He went into the jail and ascertained that the cell door was locked.

"We'll talk about this tomorrow," he told Carl.

"Sure. G'night, Sheriff Gill."

"I assume you've had supper."

"Yessir."

"I'll check on you later." Joe always did a bed check.

He locked the office and, with his hand on Grace's shoulder, he propelled her out the door.

"Why not handcuff me?" Grace asked as she freed herself and preceded him into the kitchen. The door rattled in its frame when Joe slammed it shut.

Grace sat down and Joe towered over her, as it should be. A big sheriff held more sway than a small one, even when the person being questioned is his wife. "Again, where the hell—"

"Please don't swear, Joe. You know I dislike it."

"Hell is not a swear word; using the Lord's name is swearing."

"Then call it profanity. I don't like it."

Right now Joe didn't care what she liked and didn't like. But he cleared the roughness from his voice and came up with a softer tone. That worked best with her.

"Grace, my dear; where were you and my prisoner?"

"We went to Orange City."

Joe rocked back on his heels. "Orange City? Uh huh. How the . . . how did you get there?"

"On a bus with ladies from the Dutch Reformed Church."

"Why?"

"To see the tulip display."

"And you took my prisoner because?"

"It was Melba's idea. Melba Vanhelsing. Do you know her?"

Joe waved that off. Grace sounded like a child, blaming someone else.

"Why did Melba think this was a good idea?"

"The Christian thing to do."

Joe ran his hands through his hair.

"A day off for the boy," Grace added.

"Prisoners don't get days off."

"Some do, for good behavior."

"Don't make light of this. Did you remind Melba that he's a murderer?"

Grace cringed, as she did whenever Joe called Carl a murderer. "Everyone in town knows who he is."

"So this was a joint Christian effort?"

"We considered it such."

Joe's hernia tightened and he sat down. Grace reached for his hand. "Have you eaten? We had a rest stop on the way home and a bite to eat. A nice little place. I'm not sure where it was."

Grace had an aptness for conciliation, for defusing an unpleasant conversation by injecting ordinary chatter.

"I ate leftovers."

"I'm sorry. I thought we'd be home earlier."

"I don't care about supper. If this gets out it could cost me my job."

"You're not running for re-election anyway."

"That's beside the point. Until Carl leaves here, he's my responsibility. You took him out of my jurisdiction. If he'd have slipped away you'd have been charged with aiding and abetting; you and your Christian cohorts."

Grace said nothing in her defense. Couldn't she at least show concern, and remorse? Not unlike Carl, who sometimes didn't seem to have a clue why he was in jail.

"The judge might have walked in today and wanted to see Carl. And I'd have back pedaled and said: 'Well, Judge, it seems I've misplaced the prisoner, and my wife, too, for that matter.' Or his guardian—"

"But they didn't come in. And no one else will know. The group swore to secrecy."

Joe snorted. "You make it sound like a Girl Scout trip. With one boy in tow."

"Really, Joe; none of the ladies will tell. Carl was well-behaved and it was like he had a dozen mothers or grandmothers."

"Oh, for Chri . . . crying out loud. They were all doting on him? You didn't think to leave me a note? You just spring my prisoner and walk away—"

"I did think about a note but the bus was waiting. And you know, you and I talked about taking Carl outdoors. He could get rickets or muscle atrophy lying around with no sunshine."

"I agreed that it was okay to take him for an hour or two, with my knowledge."

Joe had supervised Carl spading the garden for spring planting and for picking up branches and twigs after a rainstorm. He'd even taken Carl to the park to let him work his arms and legs on the trapeze and monkey bars, and he'd loaned him to Cad Morris, whose back was troubling him and he needed a boy to help deliver ice. Joe had deputized Cad—as a safety mechanism.

"Your taking him today is not the same as letting him outside for fresh air and exercise."

"You're right. Of course, you're right. I assumed you'd know he was with me. But this trip came along and—"

"It couldn't have just come along. It had to have been planned."

"Melba had invited me. I think I told you that. But she had to wait until her cousin let her know that the tulips were in bloom, and then arrange for the bus. She called last night after you were asleep and said it was on for today. That's when she suggested we take Carl along."

"So you did know ahead of time. You should have asked me this morning."

"Would you have let him go?"

"I couldn't have in good conscience allowed it. Certainly not."

"I thought so."

"Grace, sometimes you don't make a lick of sense. You've always understood my job and its duties and responsibilities, and not undermined it. When it comes to that boy, common sense flies out the window."

"He's harmless."

"Really? So it might seem to you and half this town, but he's a prisoner who killed a man. He shot him and when that didn't do the job, he shot him again. He's feeble-minded. That means he doesn't have common sense."

Grace acknowledged with a nod, but then added, "Do you realize he was orphaned at the same age you were?"

"Are you comparing us? He was orphaned because he killed his father. When I was orphaned I pulled up my britches and became a man, pretty much overnight."

Grace touched his hand. "I know. I'm sorry."

A few beats of silence prevailed. Then Grace said, "Carl got some color in his cheeks today."

Joe heaved a sigh. She wasn't about to admit the gravity of this situation. "You got some sun, too," he said. "Didn't you wear your hat?"

"I took it off for a while. The sun felt good. Such a nice day."

"Not so nice for me. I could have been in real trouble."

"I should have left a note for you."

"More to the point, you should not have gone at all. But the paper work is finished and he's leaving the first of June. Frankly, I'll be glad. This town has never had so much commotion. You'd think he's some kind of hero. In fact, half the people in the county think Carl did us a favor."

"Well, I don't know about that. But, Joe, I'm worried about that place he's going."

"You should have seen the place he came from, the squalor."

"I know. You told me. I'm worried about what they do at that hospital. That operation to sterilize."

"You must remember that Carl will become a man, physically, but his mind will remain that of a child."

"So it's okay if they do that to him?"

"If he should father a child that child becomes another ward of the state. And we don't know for sure they even do that procedure."

"Don't be naïve."

"So be it."

Joe had taken this interrogation about as far as it could go. He might as well be nice. "So, were the tulips pretty?"

"Oh, they were stunning. We rode all around town and nearly everyone has tulips in the yard. Some of the bulbs came all the way from Holland. Every possible color. And little windmills, and other yard ornaments. A cute one that looked like the backside of a woman, leaning over in her garden. I bought some bulbs at a roadside stand."

Grace stood and opened the icebox. "Are you hungry? I kind of am."

"I could eat something, with a glass of milk."

"I'll wash up." Grace stepped into the bathroom off the kitchen. When she returned and opened the pantry door she said, "I forgot Lyn was supposed to come today."

"He came. He couldn't find you, of course."

"He cleaned up nicely and put everything back on the shelves. Not in the order I keep them but I'll straighten it out." Grace wrapped on her apron and brought a loaf of bread to the kitchen. Conversation languished while she worked.

"Cheddar cheese for me, liverwurst for you," Grace announced when she brought the plates to the table.

"Just liverwurst? No onion and limburger cheese?"

"Liverwurst will be bad enough on your breath without those other two stinkers. You'd asphyxiate me in my sleep."

They ate in silence for a minute, and then Grace said, "Carl had a good time today."

Joe shook his head with disbelief. "We're not obliged to entertain him. Jesus, Grace, what you did was illegal."

"Language, Joe."

He swallowed the rest of his complaint, along with a bite of liverwurst, which tasted damn good even without the cheese and onion.

"I'm sorry I worried you."

Joe swigged his milk.

"You're not going to punish Carl, are you?"

The woman exasperated him, but all the bad things that might have happened, hadn't. In a few days, Carl would be gone.

Attempting to frame a response to end this conflict, Joe decided to go for humor. "I doubt I can come up with a punishment to top being kidnapped by a busload of Christian grandmothers and spending the day with them."

JOHN GLOVER

With few exceptions, John had delivered the Decoration Day speech since the town's founding in 1871. Come to that, he'd given speeches at more celebrations than he remembered. He never used notes; his repertoire of comments and jokes and lines from scripture or literature or life experience lay stored in his mind, whatever the occasion.

He particularly liked patriotic events and this morning he felt energetic, aided by his walking stick. An old trapper had given him the cane, artfully carved from a diamond willow branch, as payment for legal services. Until this past year, John had used the stick more for effect than support. Even so, he liked its look of adornment and its feel of authority.

At the podium, John stood in front of the Civil War Memorial he'd christened two years before. He opened his speech back then and today with the words inscribed on the base below the soldier.

"Soldiers, Sailors, Citizens—May the memory of their valor and patriotism be perpetuated."

People often asked if the sculpted soldier was General Sibley, for whom the town had been named. It wasn't. The generic figure represented all who fought for the Union Blue. Memorialized on the base was the local post of the Grand Army of the Republic, G. A. R. 118.

John and his pioneer friends used to laugh about their naming the town for General Henry Hastings Sibley. For the town's first Fourth of July celebration, the general had sent a flag, which he was supposed to present to John, mayor at the time. The general didn't show up, and the depot agent later reported that Sibley had arrived and stepped onto the train platform at the caboose, took one look around, snorted, and got back on the train. John and his cronies wondered if they should have reverted to the original name for the town: Cleghorn. It had no particular significance, but then again, neither did Sibley.

This morning John related to the crowd his experience at a Civil War encampment last fall at Cedar Rapids. Some 8,000 veterans registered and most of them had marched in review.

"It's nearly sixty years since the day Fort Sumter was fired upon," John now told the group basking in the sunshine, "and I remember the day as well as yesterday. Those were stormy times in the history of our country and it's still a raw memory."

Stirred by emotion, John placed his hand on his heart. Seeing Joe and Grace Gill, he added, "And the loss of boys from our community in the Great War, fourteen from this county, and also those taken quickly by the Spanish flu, we remember them today, and we miss them." He choked on his words; truly feeling the loss.

John's speech was followed by one from a veteran of the recent war, Ralph Overholser, who announced that *The Gazette* had just published a book, an Honor Roll with photos and information about all those from the county who served. Plans were underway for a permanent memorial to be placed on the courthouse lawn.

There stood Willis Overholser with his arms draped around the shoulders of his other veteran son. Seeing other fathers and sons in the crowd, and Lyn out there somewhere, and families together for the day, John's mind drifted to Claus and Carl Jess. Maybe there were other families like them; people hiding deep secrets that caused great stress. But why did most of them hold together and only now and then violence erupt? Thank God it was rare.

John turned back to the ceremony, where the valedictorian of the current graduating class had begun introducing the poem he would recite. "This verse was scribbled on a scrap of paper by Lieutenant John McCrae, a Canadian doctor who later died of wounds suffered in France during the Great War."

Placing his hand on his heart he spoke loud and clear, from memory:

In Flanders fields the poppies blow
Between the crosses, row on row
That mark our place; and in the sky
The larks, still bravely singing, fly
Scarce heard amid the guns below.

We are the Dead. Short days ago
We lived, felt dawn, saw sunset glow,
Loved and were loved, and now we lie
In Flanders fields.

> Take up our quarrel with the foe:
> To you from failing hands we throw
> The torch; be yours to hold it high.
> If ye break faith with us who die
> We shall not sleep, though poppies grow
> In Flanders fields.

The recitation brought John to an audible sob when he realized that the poem's locale was Ypres, France, where Fred Gill had fallen. John had read that a movement had begun to make poppies the symbol for Decoration Day.

The program ended with the Pledge of Allegiance led by Boy Scouts. John and Lyn rode to the cemetery with Lou Dwinnell, where a chorus of grade school girls in white dresses handed flags and flowers to the throng of people entering through the scrolled metal gate. The girls' arms held clumps of red and pink peonies with heads as big as cabbages, whispers of white spirea, and boughs of lilac whose heady fragrance would not be denied. Mary Frances had loved lilacs. A bouquet from the yard had been by her bedside when she died. John scolded himself for not bringing lilacs today. They were ubiquitous all over town.

He limited his stroll to the section where his wartime comrades lay and then to Mary Frances's gravesite. On the way he stooped to retrieve a sprig of lilac someone had dropped, and offered it to Mary Frances. Next to her grave lay plots and headstones awaiting her husband and son. Only the date of death would need to be inscribed.

———

Lyn walked home from the cemetery and John caught a ride to the hotel with Lou, whose wife and sons were away visiting relatives. John invited him to dinner; he'd wanted to talk with Lou about the Jess case.

They chose the holiday special: fried chicken, potato salad, and baked beans. With that settled, John said, "I don't know if I've seen you since the trial. You and Ivan did a stellar job."

"I appreciate your support. The expert witnesses sold the case. Even the State's witnesses couldn't disagree with Carl's degree of retardation."

Unfolding his napkin in his lap, John said, "The whole situation these past few months has prompted me to ruminate, as old men are wont to do, on the subject of fathers and sons. My father was as kind as Jesus himself, so it's difficult for me to identify with the Jess household."

"It's something most of us can't comprehend. John, that kid had never had a pat on the head or a shoulder rub. He shied away one time when I patted him. I guess he thought I was going to hit him."

"Sad, sad. There but for the grace of God."

"I didn't know the father but some said they never saw the cruel side of him."

"Me among them. And I consider myself astute. I'm a judge for crying out loud. But you know, within this shell we call a body we carry both good and bad traits. Sometimes we take pains to not reveal one facet of personality to the general public. Case in point, I once had a neighbor who barely spoke to me; his face as sour as a cut lemon."

John leaned back while the waiter set a plate in front of him and then Lou and moved on. "One day when the neighbor had a visitor I heard great laughter and nonstop conversation coming from there. I was outside when the visitor left and I said hello to the young man. Turned out it was the sour man's nephew. We got to talking and from what he said about his uncle, who'd been like a father to him, he almost had me believing that the old man had created the universe."

Lou laughed. "My grandfather was a grump to my grandmother but he spoiled me rotten."

John signaled the waiter and asked for a glass of water.

"I'm the first to admit my failings as a father, and a husband, for that matter. I took that to the Lord long ago, but I expect it'll come up again when I meet my maker."

"None of us is a perfect father, or son, or husband, certainly not me. But in my estimation you and Lyn are both fine fellas."

"I thank you for that. I wasn't fishing for a compliment. You know, I wouldn't change a thing about Lyn. I really wouldn't. For a motherless boy, he's done all right. He's a gentle soul, like my father."

John paused to recall something. "There's a minister I admire, Ralph Sockman, of Christ Church in New York City. In one of his speeches he said, 'Nothing is so strong as gentleness. Nothing is so gentle as real strength.' That speaks of Lyn. He's gentle and strong. He'd make a good father, but he didn't choose that path."

"Did you hope he'd follow in your footsteps?"

John smiled. "He might have been confused. My footsteps zigzagged in many directions. A rival newspaperman once wrote in his column that if John Glover were to apply himself to one thing he might be successful. Another one said I wouldn't be satisfied until I'd held every office in the county."

Again Lou laughed. "I was thinking of the law. As to Lyn."

"It occurred to me a time or two. A father and son law firm. But like I said, I wouldn't change a thing about him."

"My youngest boy wants to be a lawyer. The older one, since the war, has been fascinated with soldiers. He wants to be a general."

"There's nothing wrong with lofty ambitions. But, I pray every day that we have no more war. That might be naïve but pray I shall. I wondered at the ceremony how many more war memorials might be erected on the courthouse lawn."

"I'm afraid it's inevitable," Lou said.

John waved at a man who'd entered the dining room; a salesman he'd met recently. Then he continued. "As you know, I was a member of the Four Minute Men and on the draft board for this past war. I shuddered every time we saw off a train load of boys. And worse yet, met them coming home in coffins. Fred Gill was a hard one. I knew him since he was born, rocked his cradle and walked the floor with him when he had colic. Joe never talks about Fred. He keeps his feelings close to the vest."

"I doubt I could speak if I lost one of my boys. I simply can't think of anything worse."

"Agreed. I'm grateful Lyn was too old for the war. He wouldn't have been cut out for soldiering. Of course, none of us is until we're called. War is . . . well, there's no single word to describe it."

John shook his head, dispensing with images from long ago. They often came unbidden, even when he wasn't talking about the war. He could be walking down the street and a dreadful scene might assault him.

"At the encampments I attend, we veterans swap war stories. There are always some who claim they never killed a man. I don't see how that's possible in a bloody skirmish. People sometimes ask veterans if they'd ever killed a man. I use an evasive reply. 'Shooting on the battlefield is like being one of a dozen men shooting from a firing line at an execution. You don't know for sure if your gun was the one that brought down the prisoner or the enemy.' These many years, that thought has saved my sanity."

"I can't imagine being in a war."

"No; I expect one can't. As for murder, who among us is capable and who isn't? Would I, or you, had we lived with what Carl Jess did for fifteen years, put an end to it?"

"That's a tough one," Lou said. "We can't know until faced with a situation. But I've come to believe that anyone who commits premeditated murder has a mental defect. Or suicide, for that matter. Something must be wrong with the brain in order to commit that act. For that matter, Claus

Jess, who bullied and abused his family—there has to be something wrong with the mind to behave that way. To practice cruelty every day."

"I'm certainly no expert, but the mind is an intricate system of wiring and impulses, and things go haywire. But, does that mean every murderer should be found not guilty by reason of insanity? That Mexican five years ago pled insanity but it didn't wash."

"Well, that presented as a clear case of pre-med. He was carrying a butcher knife."

"Some said he wasn't; that he went home to get the knife."

"Same thing. He had time to think about and return and do the deed."

The waiter brought dessert. In keeping with the day, he served red gelatin topped with whipped cream and blueberries. Admiring the creation before tucking in, John said, "Change of subject, who is taking Carl to Glenwood?"

"Willa Eddy, the new County Welfare director."

"I haven't met her. I don't envy her the job. It would truly break my spirit to accompany that boy, any child, to an institution. Even though this was the best option. I did some research. Did you know the town was founded by Mormons?"

"I did some reading about it, too."

"It interests me because of the Civil War connection. After the war, a Veteran's Orphans Home was located there. Evangelist Billy Sunday spent time there as a child. It later became the Iowa Asylum for Feeble-Minded Children. The facility was set up as an educational center for children ages five to eighteen who could not otherwise be educated in normal schools due to low intellect. The program included music, domestic sciences, physical education, and manual labor. Of course, that was long ago and it sounds good on paper. You and I both know that Glenwood practices eugenics, at least on women."

John failed to stifle a yawn and Lou caught him in the act. John grinned and said, "Looks as if I've managed to bore even myself."

Lou obliged with, "It's always interesting chatting with you, Judge. And thanks for the meal."

"The pleasure was mine."

As the men shook hands, John added, "I'd like to visit Carl before he leaves. My duty as a pastor. It will likely mean more to me than it will to him."

"My father used to say that about visiting his brother who had early onset dementia. He was in a home for the feeble-minded."

Although it was long ago, John offered the usual sentiment. "Sorry to hear that."

Then, before Lou left, "Say, you have youngsters. What can I take Carl as a gift?"

Lou grinned like a boy with his hand in the cookie jar. "The boys' mother would skin me—she doesn't approve—but I'd say comic books. Some doctor she read about is convinced that comic books cause children to become anti-social, perverts, drug addicts, even murderers."

"If he's serious he has answered the questions we posed earlier. Why do people kill? Get rid of comic books and our woes are cured."

"I suggest skipping those called Action this or that, or super heroes. Choose something funny like Popeye or Felix The Cat, or even Tarzan. That should be safe."

"This is a literary format in which I'm not well-versed," John admitted. "Maybe I'll read them beforehand. Mind you, only so that I can converse intelligently with a child."

LOU DWINNELL

At home, cocooned in a backyard hammock after dinner with John, Lou ran through their conversation. John claimed he wasn't disappointed that Lyn hadn't followed him into the law. Lou hadn't been convinced.

On the other hand, given John's ego, Lou wondered if, subconsciously, John didn't want Lyn competing with him, maybe even outshining him. The old man did enjoy the spotlight. At any function where the two appeared together, Lyn stood in the shadow of the older man, as quiet as John was gregarious. While John's devotion to Lyn since childhood was no doubt well-intentioned and genuine, had John overdone it? Had he never let go of Lyn the child? Lou guessed that if John said, "Jump," Lyn asked, "How high?"

Still, they were thick as thieves.

Far different than Lou and his father.

Lou entered the world in Iowa City while his father was still in college. Then came medical school, internship, residency, and finally on staff at the new University of Iowa hospital. So for the first ten or so years of Lou's life he'd had, for the most part, an absentee father. When Dad was home, he needed to catch up on sleep, so Mom took Lou to a movie, a museum, the library, a trolley ride to a picnic by a river. Having his mother's undivided attention was great until he grew older and found it stifling. He later heard the term "only child/doting parent syndrome."

Mom never directly criticized Dad; instead she took out her frustration over his absence with a repetitious query: "Where is Phil when I need him?" Even when it was something like using the dust mop to clean cobwebs off the porch ceiling. How would he have done it any differently than she did? Besides, she didn't need to do the task at all. A doctor's salary allowed her the luxury of a weekly cleaning girl.

Lou's most vivid memory of time spent with his father was their trips to see Uncle Stanley in the State Hospital. They left on the train early in the morning and returned late at night. Lou didn't know if the reason for the clear memory had to do with the train ride, the nature of the trip, or the fact that it was he and his father alone. Maybe all three.

Lou's mother died when he was a Freshman at the University. It happened to be an actual case of "Where is Phil when I need him?" She'd fallen down the cellar stairs and hit her head. Might she have been saved if her doctor husband had been there? Lou had never asked that question of his father.

After his mother's death, Lou chose to live in a dormitory, and the only time he saw his father was on school vacations. Even then, they went their separate ways—Dad to work and Lou to cavort with his fraternity brothers and attending to a summer job.

With a law degree in one hand and a bride in the other, Lou opted for a small-town practice rather than one in the city. Here, he rarely had work that pulled him away from evenings and weekends with the family. He could enjoy Henry and Phil without ignoring them or spoiling them. There needed to be balance. While he did not brook bad behavior, he would never put his hands on his sons in anger. Look at what extreme anger did to Claus and Carl Jess.

Lou felt ready to nod off, and most likely would give in to the urge. He'd rather that Lucille and the boys were here. They'd take a picnic to the park and stay for the band concert.

Well, he'd drop by the band concert anyway. He hoped John Glover wouldn't be on hand with one of his impromptu orations. Lou smiled now at the memory of one affair he'd attended where he overheard a woman ask her husband if there wasn't someone else in town capable of giving a speech.

JOHN GLOVER

John had no idea what conversation he would have with Carl Jess. He hadn't spent time with young boys for decades. He asked Lyn to accompany him, but Lyn said he had no experience along that line either. On the job, children hung around and watched him work and asked questions. He advised John to ask questions of his own to keep the boy talking. Any topic—it didn't matter what.

John arrived at the jail with a packet of comic books and a bag of cookies that Grace Gill had given John for himself.

Joe brought Carl into his office and before stepping out for a walk, he introduced the two. "Carl, this is John Glover come to visit you."

Carl showed no sign of recognizing John from the court appearance on the day of the shooting or from John having been at the trial.

"Are you a doctor?"

"I'm a lawyer and a minister. Today I'm Reverend Glover."

"Are you gonna preach to me?"

"No, just talk." John laid his packages on Joe's desk. "I brought you cookies and comic books."

Carl reached for the comic books. "I've never had these."

"I'm told that boys collect them, and then they swap—"

"What's swap?"

"Trade. Let's say I had a Tarzan comic you'd never read and you had something I'd never read. We'd trade."

"For keeps?"

"It could be, or just borrow."

Carl flipped through the pages of the Tarzan booklet. "I ain't never seen a jungle."

"Nor have I."

"Or a monkey."

"That I've seen. In the Chicago zoo. The one in the book is a chimp. Actually, it's a chimpanzee."

"Naked people live in jungles." Carl picked up another book and paged through, not reading, only looking at pictures.

"Carl," John said to gain attention. The boy didn't look up.

"Did you attend Sunday School?"

Carl glanced at John. "I went to Sunday church."

"Yes; and some churches have Sunday school, to teach children about God and Jesus. There are good stories in the Bible. Real adventures you'd like. Noah and the ark, Joseph's Coat of Many Colors, and Jonah and—"

"David and Goliath."

The darkness in Carl's eyes chilled John. One minute a mere child and the next he made an adult observation, connecting himself and his act to a Bible story.

"When my father went to church he acted nice to people, like he never done nothin' mean. Some people liked him. I liked him when he was nice like that."

Another mature observation. If Claus had been even the slightest bit kind to Carl, the boy might have been forgiving enough to spare his life. Did he feel remorse now; think about his father at all? John couldn't ask that question of him.

"I brought you booklets from the Sunday School at my church. They have Bible stories with pictures. You can color them. Oh, I should have picked up a box of crayons."

Then John thought that surely boys his age didn't still color. Even boys of his mental age.

"I have a Bible. It doesn't have pictures but my name is in it. My mother wrote that I weighed nine pounds when I was born."

"My, that's a big baby."

"My sister's names are there. They died. Like my mother."

"Yes; a long time ago."

Carl's attention diverted as he moved around the room. A minute or two passed. He paused at a table where Joe had left a hand of Solitaire in progress.

"Do you know how to play Solitaire?" John asked.

"Nah. *Oma* said playing cards is sinful."

"I could show you how to play. Or teach you a game called Rummy."

"I wonder where *Oma* is. She never comes to visit me."

"I heard she went to live with her son. Out of town."

"His name is Claus. Like my father's. I think I met him once."

"Yes; I believe he came for the trial."

"He could have brought *Oma*."

"I understand she's very old. It's hard for her to travel."

"I saw you at the trial with that pretty girl."

"Miss Duvall."

"Is she your wife?"

"No, she's a friend."

"Why were you there?"

"At the trial? I'm a lawyer, and a judge. I'm interested in law."

"I went to Cherokee to see a doctor. Someone said in court that I have an uncle who lives there 'cause he's crazy. I could have visited him that day I went. Maybe when I go there to live."

"You're not going there, Carl. You're going to Glenwood. I hear it's quite nice. You'll have classes, and other activities."

"I'm tired of school. How will I get to this place?"

Lyn had been right; boys ask a lot of questions.

"A woman will take you, on the train. It's down at the bottom of the state. Here, look at this map on the wall. Glenwood is in this southwest corner. You'll probably spend one night on the train."

"Really? Sleep on it? I like trains. I rode one once."

"I like trains, too. I like sleeping on them."

Sheriff Gill came into the office. "How's everything going?"

"Quite well," John said, thinking: Better than expected, but he realized it had been tiring, stressful. Even just these few minutes.

"Grace will bring supper soon so I should take Carl back to his room."

John extended his hand to the boy and they shook. "Good luck to you, Carl. I'll pray for you."

Carl pulled something from underneath his shirt. "I have this to bless me. The lady who gave it to me called it a. . . ."

"Scapular," John offered.

"That's it." Carl gathered his belongings and Joe led the way through the hall to the jail.

Watching the boy retreat, John saw another image—Carl walking through the door of the red brick building in Glenwood. He'd seen the hospital pictured in a reference book at the library.

Abruptly, the boy in the image became Lyn, age nine, walking into the house alone after they'd buried his mother.

John wondered now if he'd been a comfort to Lyn at that time and in the days that followed, or had he been caught in the web of his own grief and left Lyn to his own devices? The boy had run freely on the streets of Ashton. Nothing to harm him. Everyone looked out for him.

John had long shouldered guilt regarding Mary Frances. The doctors had advised a move to a warmer climate, Florida or California. He'd done some research, but he simply hadn't the means to relocate the family and his law practice, which had barely sustained them most of the time. He'd taken on other occupations for extra income. Mary Frances had been cheerful about it; telling friends they had indeed moved south, that Ashton was south of Sibley.

"John," Joe said, "are you okay?"

"Oh, sure. Just wool-gathering. The boy reminded me of someone."

"Grace is going to miss him."

"Mother to the world, your Grace. And how are you? That hernia still bothering?"

"Ah, sometimes. Say, why don't you come have supper with us?"

John had a mind to decline, but quickly decided that the company of good friends might be just what the doctor ordered.

"I'd like that. It's a well-known fact that it's a sin to turn down one of Grace Gill's meals."

JOSEPH GILL

Grace said no to Joe's invitation to go along to the depot when he took Carl this morning. She'd said goodbye to Carl last night and Joe reckoned that, given her attachment to the boy, the depot would be a grim reminder of seeing Fred off on the troop train, and then later retrieving his flag-draped coffin there. She had, of course, packed a basket of food and a canvas knapsack of—Joe didn't know what. She'd wanted to buy Carl a new wardrobe and toiletries, but Joe assured her the facility would provide whatever he needed. He belonged to the State now.

Rummaging through the knapsack, he found an index card with their name and post office box number, along with stationary and envelopes, six sharpened pencils, and a sheet of two cent postage stamps. Evidently she expected to be pen pals with Carl. There were two books: *The Ransom Of Red Chief*, by O. Henry, and *South Sea Tales*, by Jack London, and the latest issue of *Boy's Life: The Boy Scouts' Magazine*, a bag of hard candy, and a half dozen packages of Black Jack gum. Carl had one time covered his top teeth with the black gum and smiled at Joe. He had to have learned that from Grace; she used to do that with Mildred and Fred.

From the bottom of the bag Joe fished out a cap. Stitched to the lining, alongside a manufacturer's label, Grace had added a name tag: Fred Gill. Seeing the name in print still jolted Joe. Mildred had given the green twill cap with a snap brim to her brother for his birthday, maybe his thirteenth. He'd worn it on a canoe trip with a church group. Joe placed the cap over his nose, trying to detect a familiar scent. He did, but it wasn't Fred. Grace had washed the cap and it smelled of homemade soap. Joe began to stuff the cap in the knapsack, then changed his mind and tucked it inside his jacket.

The train had already arrived when Joe parked at the depot. He'd expected only Willa Eddy from Welfare, but she and Lou Dwinnell and John Glover were in a circle of conversation. John wore his clerical collar.

There followed a recital of greetings, one to the other, and then Carl spoke to John, "I remember you. You brung me comic books."

"That's right, Son. I've come to say farewell and Godspeed."

Carl didn't seem to know those words so Joe covered the moment by handing him his knapsack and food basket. Addressing Willa, he asked, "Shall I give the suitcase to the porter or will you put it in the overhead?"

"I'll handle it. I have only a small overnight bag."

As the train commenced its departure racket, John addressed Joe. "May we have a moment of prayer?"

Joe nodded. If ever a boy needed prayers, this one did.

Reverend Glover placed his hands on Carl's shoulders and spoke above the din. "Lord, heavenly Father, whose glory fills the whole creation and whose presence we find wherever we go, watch over Carl Jess as he makes this journey. Surround him with your loving care; protect him from danger, and bring him safely to his destination, and bring him peace in his new home, through Jesus Christ our Lord. Amen."

"Amen," the group chorused at the same time the white-jacketed Negro porter called, "All aboard."

Joe felt satisfied that the hefty Willa Eddy, dressed in a tailored business suit and her gray hair wrapped in a turban, looked formidable enough to handle Carl. Her handbag alone would make a good weapon. Carl seemed chipper as a meadowlark, winging away on a new adventure. He waved and called, "Bye, everyone. Bye, Sheriff Gill."

"Do you have your glasses?" Joe asked.

Carl patted his shirt pocket. "I'll be able to see things on the way."

Joe shook hands with Carl before the porter helped first Willa and then Carl up the steps. When Carl stared at the man who retracted the metal steps onto the train platform, Joe realized Carl had never seen a Negro in person.

The travelers soon appeared in a window, waving through the dusty panes. "Back to the office," Lou said, and sauntered off. Joe and John stayed while the train steamed and huffed and heaved and ground its gears and lumbered south trailing gray scarves of smoke.

"Well; that's it," Joe said when he could be heard and the ground had stopped shaking.

Donning his Panama hat, John said, "We began this together and now we've seen him on his way. We've done our duty."

"Need a ride?"

"Thanks. I feel like walking."

"Come on by sometime. Bring Lyn. We'll play Whist. Grace will be feeling blue for a while."

"We'll do that." John grasped the knob of his walking stick in his fist, stepped carefully over the tracks and followed the gravel path toward the business district.

———

In his car, Joe opened the door and sat sideways on the seat to light a cigarette. While smoking, he placed his free hand inside his jacket, beneath his badge, next to his heart, and clutched Fred's cap.

Suddenly, his sympathy for Grace's feelings turned to anger. What was she thinking giving Fred's cap to Carl?

The two boys had no common ground.

Or did they?

Both had faced an enemy on the battlefield; Fred thousands of miles from home and Carl in his own home.

Joe paused, giving this thought.

That's where the commonality ended. Any further comparison was like Grace comparing Carl's circumstance of being an orphan with Joe's.

Fred gave his life for his country.

Carl took a life.

Recalling the scene in the farmhouse, Joe realized that only three months had passed since the shooting. It seemed longer. The prisoner himself hadn't been any trouble. The fact was, although Grace meant well, her mothering of Carl had more than once created problems for Joe, legally and personally. Now his responsibility in this story had been accomplished.

He dragged on his cigarette and tossed the rest onto the parking area. He pulled his legs into the car, positioned himself behind the wheel, but didn't start the car. He opened the window and gulped a breath of fresh air. The tobacco taste on his tongue caused him to wonder why he smoked.

Leaning forward, he gained access to his wallet in his back pocket. Opening the worn leather folder he drew out a photo that always hit him below the belt—Fred's army Doughboy picture. An enlargement hung in the hallway at home, alongside the Gold Star flag that had adorned the parlor window during the war. The flag announced to passersby that this home had suffered a great loss.

Joe didn't begrudge Grace the Gold Star Mother pin she wore daily, but it riled him that only mothers and wives of men killed in the war were honored with a gold star. He'd read that 100,000 women had lost a loved one in the war. Grace belonged to the national organization of Gold Star Mothers.

What about fathers? Didn't fathers suffer an equal loss?

When Joe allowed truth to conquer denial he recognized that Fred had always been Grace's boy. Before Fred climbed aboard a troop train, Grace had pulled him into an embrace that almost toppled both of them. Fred said something to Grace that brought a smile to her tear-stained face. Joe and Fred shook hands to say goodbye. When the War Department asked whether to bury Fred overseas or send his body home, Joe let Grace decide. She wanted him home. So did he, but he'd have done whatever Grace wanted. The man of the family shouldered the pain and looked after the women—Grace and Mildred and her two girls. Joe's gold star was actually brass, with six points and the word Sheriff on it. He'd sworn to honor and protect, and that meant his family as well as everyone else in the county.

Sully, the depot agent, interrupted Joe's thoughts when he stepped outside and called, "Car trouble, Sheriff?"

"No, no; just mulling over some things." He waved a notebook to indicate his concentration.

"So the boy is off to the home."

"That's right."

"Ah, I hear a telegram coming in. See ya around."

Joe intended to leave, but his mind wouldn't shut off the subject of Fred. It dawned on him that he had bottled his grief for two years and never allowed himself to mourn. Grace had been shattered into such a fragile state that he had all he could do to keep her going through the motions of daily life. He'd been a soldier; stalwart while hiding his wounds. The sheriff's badge became a shield behind which he hid his feelings in order to support Grace.

Joe had wanted to rage and rant but held his tongue when people tried to comfort him by saying that Fred was in a better place. Joe couldn't agree more. Fred did not belong on that battlefield a million miles away. But neither did he belong in Heaven, which is what these people meant. Heaven was for later, after a person had lived a full life. He knew his Bible—not as well as John Glover or Grace—but the verse came to him now: *The days of our years are threescore years and ten; and if by reason of strength they be fourscore years, yet is their strength labor and sorrow; for it is soon cut off and we fly away.*

Fred flew away all too soon. This should be his better place, with his mother, with his family.

Now, it seemed as if Grace had let go her fierce hold on Fred and was able to transfer love and caring to others, to a boy orphaned by his own terrible act. Today she'd had to release him, too. No doubt she'd had a good cry after Joe left with Carl.

Aching with too many feelings surfacing at once, Joe's eyes stung and an actual sob burst from within. Just one, but God; it felt good. He heaved an anxious sigh, and another, letting tears flow.

Something told him his time had come to experience the emotions that went with mourning: Despair, depression, sorrow, loss . . . righteous anger at whomever he damned well pleased: the Germans, the government, even Fred, who'd enlisted when his parents, his mother in particular, asked him to wait to be recruited. He might curse and swear, too, and Grace could just bear with it. There shall be weeping and gnashing of teeth, the Bible stated somewhere. John had offered to counsel Joe. Maybe he'd take him up on that. So long as John didn't get too preachy. He had that tendency.

Joe winced as his hernia writhed. Did pent up feelings have an effect on his twisted gut? He developed this condition since Fred died. Ulcers supposedly came from worry, maybe hernias did, too. He needed to release his tension now, not next January when he would retire. By then maybe he'd be free of the mourning bonds and he and Grace would spend time together, take a trip somewhere. If she wanted to go visit Carl, he could manage that.

Joe shook his shoulders, vigorously, and felt less burdened—for a moment, at least. His plan was well and good in theory, but reality told him to return to the office and play sheriff. Duty first.

Stuffing Fred's cap in the glove box where Grace wouldn't see it, Joe started the car and drove through downtown. A quiet June morning. He hoped for a quiet summer; when he might be called on only to free a cat from a drainpipe, run off teenagers necking at the sandpit, or kids tipping outhouses or smashing watermelons in the middle of main street. Maybe he'd nab those hoodlums who taunted Hattie Lind.

Summer would be a time for Joe Gill to heal and rehabilitate.

Come January, he would shed not only the sheriff's badge but the figurative personal shield of armor he'd worn.

JOHN GLOVER

Come the dog days of summer, a cream-colored envelope arrived in John's mail slot at the hotel. As he entered one afternoon the desk clerk waved the envelope. "It's from Chicago. There's one for Lyn, too. Do you want to take it or should I give it to him?"

"He'll stop by later; I'll give it to him."

John carried the mail to the reading table. The oversized square envelope had an embossed return address but no name. The address wasn't familiar but then John didn't know anyone in Chicago anyway.

Inside that envelope was another, plain, unsealed. It held a wedding invitation, an RSVP card, and a stamped return envelope to the sender: Mr. and Mrs. Harris Duvall.

The invitation read: Mr. and Mrs. Harris J. Duvall request the honor of your presence at the marriage of their daughter, Augusta Mary, to Mr. Paul William Radford . . . .

Augusta? Living in Chicago again? Was Paul Radford the "him" she'd mentioned the last time she was here?

She might have let him know she was getting married. Where were her manners?

Annoyed, John stuffed the envelopes and card and Lyn's envelope into his jacket pocket and went upstairs. Suddenly weary, he lay down on the bed.

The next thing he knew Lyn came through the door. "Caught you napping," he said.

John came upright and sat on the edge of the bed while he came fully awake. "I didn't know I'd fallen asleep."

"We usually don't," Lyn said. "I go out like a flick of a switch."

"The humidity takes the starch out of me." Standing, John tried to smooth the wrinkles from his clothing. "Speaking of taking the starch out, I don't know if I like this fabric or not. It's wrinkly."

"Prunes are wrinkled and you like them."

John cast him a look. "You're witty today."

"Your new suit is seersucker. It's supposed to look that way, so you don't need to worry about wrinkles."

"I'm not worried. But why make material that's already wrinkled? That's like jackets with patches on the elbow when you buy them. And, when did you become a fashion expert?" John recognized a cranky tone in his voice.

"I read, too, you know. The library has all manner of magazines. Seersucker was created to be worn by the poor. It's cheap to manufacture. Now that college boys have begun wearing it, it's trendy. And probably more expensive."

"So, folks won't know if I'm poor or fashionable."

"You're always dressed to the nines, Papa."

"And I've mostly been poor."

John glanced at the clock on his desk. "Let's have a bite to eat."

"I brought you tomatoes from my garden. I told the cook I'd bring a bushel of sweet corn tomorrow. They can serve it as long as it lasts."

"That won't be for long. I'll be in line."

John picked up his summer hat; he might want a stroll after supper. Maybe to the park for the weekly band concert. On his way out the door he grabbed his jacket with the mail in the pocket.

In the dining room, John handed Lyn his envelope.

"What's this?"

"A wedding invitation. Augusta."

"Augusta Duvall?"

"Do you know another?"

"And I'm invited? Did you get one?"

"Well, of course. How else would I know what's in your mail?"

Lyn glanced at the invitation. "Well I'll be a monkey's uncle. I don't recall her mentioning she had a fella."

"I haven't heard from her for months. And suddenly—"

"She was here in, what was it? April. That's not so long ago."

They ordered the special and while they waited for supper to arrive Lyn read the entire message on the card. "This is high-falutin'. The reception is at the Palmer House."

"Is it now? I didn't read that far."

"You didn't read it?"

"I got distracted. I fell asleep."

"And wait, it's on your birthday."

"On my birthday? The wedding? Let me see that."

Lyn handed over the card. "Would you like to go, Papa?"

John scoffed. "I'm not up for that."

Their plates came and Lyn continued, "Come on. The Glover men dining at the Palmer House. When have you had dinner on your birthday at the Palmer House? Or anytime, for that matter. Were you ever there, on one of your many trips hither and yon?"

"Never," John said. "I doubt I'd spend that kind of money for a place to sleep even if I had a bankroll in my pocket."

Lyn forked into a baked potato and took a bite. "I'd need to buy a suit and a white shirt, and a tie, and shoes, and—"

"Wouldn't you think she'd have let me, us, know, and not leave it to her parents to announce it?" John tossed the invitation back at Lyn.

"I'm the last person to know about wedding etiquette."

"But the first to know about clothing fashion."

"Possibly it's the parents who make the announcement. They're the ones inviting us. It came from their address."

John pushed string beans around on his plate. "I'm certainly not up on the rules, but my word—"

"You seem unduly indignant."

"I'm not indignant." John stabbed his potato. "Well, maybe I am. I've been peevish lately."

Lyn grinned. "Not that anyone would notice." He waited a beat and then, "Shall we plan a trip to Chicago?"

"Not me. You go if you wish."

"Only if you'll go. Think about it."

"I have. I'm not going."

They ate in silence. At least Lyn ate; John pushed his food around and nibbled a bite or two. Finally Lyn summoned the waiter for a dish of vanilla ice cream. "Two scoops," he said.

"None for me," John told the waiter.

"So, have you thought about it?" Lyn asked.

"About dessert. I said none for me."

"No; the trip to Chicago."

"I told you I'd thought about it. I'm not going."

For a fact, John couldn't afford a trip. He lived on a small military pension, fees for serving as Justice of the Peace, and the occasional probate or claiming a widow's pension, or a land settlement. He doubted if Lyn could afford a trip either. "I'll ask Grace to pick out a gift. I have no idea what's appropriate."

"That's only one reason to be grateful we have Grace," Lyn said, delving into his ice cream.

John reached over and spooned a dab of vanilla cream. Sometimes it soothed his stomach after a meal. Lyn pushed the bowl closer and John nabbed another spoonful. "I'm sorely disappointed that Augusta didn't tell us."

"Papa; it's not as if we're family."

"But I thought we were friends."

Two days later John received a note from Augusta. It rambled, with dashes instead of complete sentences, which annoyed John. She'd been terribly busy, sorry—but she had wonderful news—on her vacation in Chicago she'd been reacquainted with an old family friend, Paul Radford—they'd had a whirlwind courtship—and decided why wait? She'd taken a position with *The Chicago Tribune* and loved it. Remember when I told you I was the first female on the *Register* staff? Well, I'm first on the *Trib* staff, too. Paul is a lawyer—by the way—you'd like him John and he'd adore discussing the law with you—I would be honored if you both came to my wedding. Warm regards, Augusta—

John tossed the note at Lyn. "She sounds like a giddy schoolgirl."

"She's young, Papa, and in love."

"Even if she knew him before, she met up with him in April and already she's marrying him. Is that the way it's done now?"

Lyn read the note. "Are you satisfied now?"

"About what?"

"You thought she should have told you. Now she has."

"After the fact. After the invitation arrived."

Lyn laughed. "I think we should go to the wedding."

"This doesn't change my mind."

"Palmer House dinner? Your last chance. I read in the paper that it's no longer big enough for the business it attracts. In a year or so they'll be razing it to build a new one."

"Really? I hadn't heard that."

"Then you'll go?"

John crossed his arms and leaned back. "You seem to have forgotten what the word no means."

"Peevish old man."

"You heard it first from me."

LYN GLOVER

Winter blustered in with a vengeance and as the season progressed into a new year, Lyn became increasingly concerned that Papa wasn't up to snuff. He'd turned seventy-five on the day Augusta got married, and he'd said nothing more about that event. It had amused Lyn how persnickety Papa got over what he considered a belated invitation. If he'd had a late-in-life schoolboy crush on the much younger woman, he'd moved past it. Last November Augusta had sent a clipping from a Chicago paper showing a photograph of her exiting a voting booth for the first time. Thank you for supporting women's suffrage, she wrote across the photo. She also sent an article she'd written about the first national election in which women had voted. Papa had liked Augusta's writing style. And at Christmas there had been a wedding photograph and a thank you for the gift.

Lyn detected no mental lapses, but Papa admitted that he couldn't keep up the usual physical pace. Annoying as that was, he said, he'd rather lose mobility than his mind.

The desk clerk told Lyn that John seemed feeble. Lyn disliked that term—given the Carl Jess case. But that had to do with feeble-minded, not the body. Slowing down was a more apt description. Everyone's activity slowed in winter; folks hibernated, avoiding the cold, raw temperatures. Right now, Lyn had no outdoor work and not much inside either, so he kept company with Papa in the hotel lobby, which was better heated than Lyn's cottage.

Papa retained his enthusiasm when engaged in conversation with the traveling men who frequented the hotel. Lyn once wondered why, of Papa's many professions, he hadn't been a teacher. Formally, that is. He had, of course, taught Lyn to read, to research, to ask questions. He'd taken Lyn into the wilderness and taught him to read a compass and build a fire using flint. They'd camped out, and fished and hunted, but Lyn didn't like killing animals, and Papa didn't either. He'd done it to survive, but they no longer needed to get their meals that way—not when they had a can opener, a summer garden, and a market basket.

A handful of local men had read law with Papa, among them, long ago, William Harding, the recent past governor of Iowa who'd been raised here. In the newspaper business, Papa had taught would-be journalists to write succinctly. He'd tutored Augusta, hoping to make her a better writer. And he believed he had. In typical John Glover fashion, he'd taken credit for what he saw of her recent writing.

Lyn enjoyed watching Papa take center stage at the hotel like he had on the debate or speech podium, on the pulpit, in the court room, at Chautauqua, and on the soapbox when he stumped for political office or when he supported prohibition and women's suffrage. Lyn hadn't the charisma for that, but he'd attended Papa's performances since he'd been knee high to a grasshopper. Lyn tucked that expression away these days or it would set Papa off and running with grasshopper stories of the eighteen-seventies, or whenever it was. Lyn had heard the stories so often he'd forgotten when it actually happened. Here at the hotel, Papa had a new audience. And the stories were entertaining. Over the years they were not rubbed smooth as a stone from the retelling but instead gathered bits and pieces of embellishment and changes in detail. Lyn used to correct Papa, but he'd stopped doing that. What did it matter? Storytelling made Papa happy. Lyn didn't remember much about his mother—most of what he knew came from other people's reminiscences, their praise for her. His mother's sister, Addie, and his Upton grandparents kept her alive for him when he was a boy. When it came to fathers, Lyn didn't need anyone to tell him, or need a case such as the Jess family for comparison, to realize that he'd hit the jackpot with John Glover. Sure, Papa could be demanding, pushy, but that was his nature, his personality.

Tonight, after a light supper, Lyn and Papa retired to the pair of Morris chairs in the reading nook, with a steam radiator just beyond for warmth. All the same, Lyn tucked his coat around Papa's legs and he didn't object. They read; they discussed what they were reading; they moved about to stretch their legs, sometimes chatting with people who came into the hotel. It being Sunday night, several salesmen had checked in, ready to peddle their wares on unsuspecting merchants. One fella told Lyn that sales were better in cold weather because merchants had less business and more time to stand around listening to a spiel.

When the hour grew late, and Lyn prepared to leave, Papa said he'd stay up a while longer. "I can't seem to get comfortable in bed," he complained, rubbing his neck.

"Shall I call a doctor?"

"No, no; you go home. I'll go on up soon."

"I'm not tired. I'll hang around. I don't relish a walk in the cold."

They tried a game of chess but Papa couldn't keep his mind on it and they abandoned the board. As it turned out, neither of them went to bed that night. They dozed in their chairs, and woke now and then, disoriented at not being in bed, and when morning came they had breakfast in the dining room. Neither was talkative, being groggy from lack of decent sleep.

Later, Lyn noticed that in discussing current events with a salesman at the next table, that Papa became unusually excited. From time to time he massaged the back of his neck. Lyn lingered, pretending he had nowhere to go, when in fact he used the hotel phone to call a customer and say he'd be delayed. Soon enough Papa would be exhausted enough to be talked into going upstairs. Maybe he'd sleep through the day, but that meant he'd not sleep tonight. What to do?

At one point the manager asked Lyn if he'd take a look at a wall in the office, where moisture had developed. Lyn said he could easily fix that and would bring his tools tomorrow. He thought about going after them now, but an inner voice nagged at him to stay.

Along about eleven-thirty, Chris Wassmann came in looking for John. "I think he's napping," Lyn said. "He didn't sleep much last night. Can it wait?"

"Well, it's Joe Gill. He had surgery this morning for the hernia."

Anticipating more, Lyn waited.

"He didn't make it. Died on the table." Chris's voice broke on the word died.

Lyn reeled backward and nearly collided with a hotel guest. "I don't think Papa knew about the surgery. He would have mentioned it."

"He wouldn't have known. Joe did some heavy lifting the day before, moving boxes from the office to home. He got bad pain and went to the hospital. The intestines were strangulated. He actually had two operations and died during the second."

Lyn shivered and wrapped his arms around himself.

"The first person I thought to tell was John," Chris said.

"He'll want to be with Grace. If it's okay, I'll tell him. He's been up all night himself; maybe coming down with the grippe. I'll get someone to drive us over to the Gill's."

"I hope he'll be okay. I should get back and spread the word."

With Chris gone, Lyn paused to collect himself before going to the nook, where he'd last seen Papa. He looked old and weary; his unshaven chin showed five o'clock shadow, as did Lyn's when he'd glanced in the mirror in the men's room.

"I smell dinner," Papa said, his voice weak, "but I'm not hungry."

"Barley soup on the menu. You should eat something."

"Soup might hit the spot." He leaned forward for his walking stick.

Lyn held out his arm to stay him. "I need to tell you something."

Papa inclined his head toward Lyn, his good ear, he called it.

"Chris stopped by. Chris Wassmann." Lyn paused but decided to go all the way. "Joe Gill went to the hospital. His hernia was strangulated and he died during the operation."

Papa's eyes roamed wildly and he grabbed at his chest as if to hold his heart in place. "That can't be right. He's years younger than I am. He just retired."

He hoisted himself to his feet by holding the arms of the chair, and then fell back into the seat, dropping the walking stick. "I need to go to the hospital."

For a second Lyn thought Papa meant for himself.

"Joe's probably not there anymore. This happened about eleven o'clock." Lyn retrieved the walking stick and put it in Papa's hand.

"Then I need to be with Grace." He put his hand to his brow as if he had a headache and then lowered the hand and covered his left eye.

"Sit still. I'll find someone to drive us."

"I need air." The words came in a pulmonary wheeze.

Lyn grabbed his own coat, still on the chair from last night, and threw it around Papa's shoulders. He seemed to have shrunk. "We'll step onto the veranda. But it's cold."

"My vis . . . shun ish blurry."

Lyn supported Papa to the front porch, where he complained, "I feel faint," and crumpled to the floor before Lyn could grab him.

Lyn yelled for help and the manager appeared. "Call a doctor," the manager called to the desk clerk. Lyn and the manager carried Papa inside, where the manager nodded toward the Ladies' Room. "There's a settee in there." Someone in the hall saw the situation and opened the door to the room.

Dr. Winkler arrived within what seemed only minutes. It occurred to Lyn that the doctor had just lost a patient during surgery and now he'd rushed to attend that man's friend.

After examining the patient, Winkler spoke solemnly, "He had a stroke, Lyn," and then used the old term, "apoplexy."

Leaning against the wall for support, Lyn viewed himself in the mirror, his face pewter gray, his frame shaking. "Will he recover?"

"I can't say for sure but—"

"He might?"

"It's not likely."

Lyn closed his eyes and then opened them. "Is he in pain?"

"No; he's unconscious." Winkler covered his mouth and coughed. "Joe Gill died this morning. Did John know that?"

"That's what brought this on. I told him and he fell apart. But he hadn't felt well last night and this morning."

"This could have been coming on since then and shock pushed him over the edge."

Winkler placed his hand on Lyn's shoulder. "Sit with him. It's possible he'll try to speak or know you're there. Talk to him if you wish. I'll be in the lobby if you need me."

"Please call Reverend Parsons. Papa would want him here."

"I will. I'm sorry, Lyn. I greatly admire your father."

Lyn appreciated the doctor's use of present tense. Papa was still here.

Seated in a dainty chair, in a room with pink flowered wallpaper, Lyn spoke four words, "I love you, Papa."

When the pastor arrived, Lyn sat between him and Papa, holding one of his hands and one of the pastor's. Together they prayed and bore witness to John Glover's life slipping away.

Doctor Winkler came into the room now and then, laid his stethoscope against the patient's heart and held his wrist for a pulse check. "Slowing," he said. "It won't be long."

Lyn leaned close to Papa's good ear and whispered, "Go in peace."

He reached into Papa's vest pocket, withdrew his timepiece, loosened the chain and fob, and held the watch in his hand. Papa had carried the watch as a soldier under General Grant in Virginia; the watch had been Lyn's grandfather's, whom Lyn had never met. The man Papa referred to as the patriarch, as kind and gentle as Jesus. The man's initials were on the watch case: WLG. William Lyndale Glover. Lyn's full name was not Lyndale, only Lyn. His middle name was Fisher, Papa's mother's maiden name. He had spoken lovingly of her, too. That's about all Lyn knew of his paternal genealogy, and not much more of his maternal side.

Later, it might have been minutes or an hour, when Winkler nodded, and Lyn's fingers could no longer detect Papa's pulse, he looked at the watch cupped in his hand and murmured, "Time of death, two thirty-eight p.m., January seventeenth, the year of our Lord nineteen and twenty-one."

As Papa grew cold, so did Lyn.

He shuddered as all energy and spirit drained from his body.

Instead of his heart thrumming with emotion, it seemed to cease beating.

LYN GLOVER

When Lyn reached his cottage in early evening, nearly paralyzed with fatigue, he stumbled over the baskets of food, covered bowls, and cake and pie tins on his threshold. The food brigade had been set in motion. The donors could have put them inside; Lyn didn't know anyone who used a door lock. Scavenger animals might have gotten into the parcels.

He'd never had so much food at one time, and never so little appetite. After bringing in the donations, he lit the three kerosene lamps throughout the room. He kindled a fire in the fireplace he'd built onto the cottage, and another fire in the cook stove. Together, they quickly warmed the room even on this bitter night.

Unwrapping a baked ham, Lyn's stomach churned with nausea, evoking one of Papa's stories; a tale about a hunting trip for ducks or maybe it was geese. The three men bagged one and took it home to cook it. The oily smell sickened one man. Then Papa and the other ate the roasted bird and fell onto their beds. The way Papa told the story had always brought a laugh from his audience, but it now brought only sadness to Lyn.

Someone had left a dozen oranges, shipped from Florida to the person whose address was on the sticker. Lyn didn't recognize the name. The covered bowls and cake tins and a wire egg holder had names attached with white adhesive first aid tape, and the baskets and boxes contained cards. He would need to write thank you notes—Papa had long ago taught him that courtesy.

A knock on the door startled Lyn; he rarely had visitors, but when he opened the door there was only a brown paper grocery bag on the doorstep. He pulled out a warm tray of frosted cinnamon rolls and a sympathy card with the signature: Mr. and Mrs. Lowe, your neighbors. They were an elderly couple for whom he'd done small jobs, gratis, except for a meal as payment.

Lyn left the covered, non-perishable foods on the table. The ham, a slab of bacon, a round chunk of butter wrapped in cheesecloth and tied with a black ribbon, a chunk of cheese in paraffin paper, and a jug of milk he stored in the discarded washing machine outside the back door. It served as an icebox in winter, and with its lid closed, the food was safe from creatures. While he was outside he went to the outhouse, which sat directly under a city streetlight that shone on the path.

Back in the house, Lyn sipped the glass of milk he'd held back from the jug. With it, he forced down a handful of saltine crackers and then washed away the dryness with milk. The cinnamon rolls did not tempt him as they usually did. None of the food looked appealing.

By rote, Lyn stoked the two fires and shut off the wicks on the lamps. Then, by firelight, still in his clothes from the day before, having slept at the hotel last night, he staggered to his cot, fell onto it, and closed his eyes.

The adrenaline that had propelled him through the day still surged. His body and mind remained active as he tossed about, reliving the events, beginning with watching Papa's body being removed from the hotel where he'd lived these past few years. Word had spread and a handful of people clustered outside the hotel, their heads bowed.

At the funeral home Lyn had been surprised to learn that not only had Papa paid for his own casket and service, he'd done the same for Lyn. Papa had never passed along this information, although Lyn knew a cemetery plot awaited him. He dreaded the next few days when he would be required to serve as host for the throng of residents remembering his father, eulogizing him, and mourning his sudden and unexpected death.

Even when death is imminent, Lyn thought now, as it had been today after the stroke, the final second is unexpected. Shocking. A stab to the heart.

"You're a good soldier," Papa used to say to the boy Lyn, along with a pat on the head.

Papa had been the officer; Lieutenant Glover, Company F, 38th Wisc., and Lyn the foot soldier. Now the officer had gone down and left the soldier in charge. He would do his duty; be a comrade; and then, when Papa had been laid to rest, Lyn would retire the position he neither sought nor desired.

LYN GLOVER

The weekly paper carried front page stories about Papa and Joseph Gill, the circumstances of their births, the details of their professional and personal lives, and their deaths. Two prominent men, friends, gone on the same day made for dramatic news.

Papa's photo appeared on the left under the headline: Apoplexy Closes Life of John F. Glover. On the right, Joe Gill's photo appeared along with a smaller font headline: Death Calls Ex-Sheriff Joseph Gill. He had, on January first, finished eight years as sheriff and had not run for re-election.

John Glover's funeral was said to be the largest ever held in Sibley, making Lyn wonder who kept such statistics. Perhaps the funeral home. The language describing Papa wrought Lyn with both grief and pride: loyal, brave, widow's advocate, generous, a private and public servant, a clear head and warm heart, forceful, gifted with faith, hope, and charity, and a philanthropist with his knowledge. One speaker among the many who took the church pulpit where Papa had often stood said, "John F. Glover has been transferred to a world fairer than this, and this earthly abode is better for his having lived."

Outside the church, Lyn overheard a man comment that Joe Gill had been short-changed, that it was his misfortune to die on the same day as John Glover. Lyn hoped that no one had made such a crass comment to Grace and her family. At the cemetery, the hotel manager placed his hand over Lyn's and pressed into it Papa's walking stick, which had been left behind the day he died. It afforded mental strength as Lyn stepped toward the funeral director's waiting car.

Lyn and Grace Gill had leaned on each other more than once these past days. On the evening after Joe's funeral Lyn had dinner at Grace's and spent the night. Her daughter and family had returned to their home and Grace insisted that Lyn stay rather than walk home on a night that had grown frigid. He hadn't the words or energy to refuse her. Neither of them wanted to be alone.

In the morning, over breakfast, they picked up their reminiscing. "I still wake up thinking Joe is here," Grace said. "I was just getting used to him being home instead of at the office."

"I know what you mean. I think about walking to the hotel to see Papa. The fact is, I need to go there and strip his room."

"I'm not ready to sort Joe's things."

"No rush for you, but the hotel will want the room vacated."

Grace smoothed a wrinkle from the flowered tablecloth. "It comforts me that Joe found peace with Fred's death. Not that one ever does, completely. He struggled, but he'd come to accept it. He'd even gone back to church."

"I noticed that," Lyn said. "It pleased Papa."

"John counseled him, you know. They had discussions about death and the hereafter."

Although Lyn hadn't smiled lately, he did now. "Papa had plenty to say about the hereafter. He pontificated on the subject as if he'd been there and knew its secrets."

Grace returned a smile. "One time when he was here, sitting on the porch with Joe, two Jehovah's Witnesses came up the walk. Joe would have sent them away but John invited them to sit down and they had quite a conversation, an hour or more."

"That sounds like Papa."

"Another time when John was here, I overheard Joe say he resented my attention to Carl Jess, as if I'd forgotten Fred. I felt terrible. John told him that we must each look after all God's children, not only our own. That sometimes others need us more than our own. I agree with that."

Grace reached into a drawer and drew out a cap. "When Carl Jess left here, I packed a bag of reading material and candy and such. I put this cap in, too. It was Fred's and I thought Carl could use it. After Joe retired and brought things home from the office, I saw the cap in a box. I never told him I saw it. If he wanted to keep it, that was fine. I won't part with it again." She wiped her eye with the corner of her apron.

"I shouldn't tell this, but I suppose it's okay now," Grace said. "A week or so before Carl left, I took him on a trip to Orange City to see a tulip display. We went without Joe's permission. Oh, my, I've never seen him so angry."

"You absconded with the prisoner?"

"On a bus with the ladies from the Dutch church."

"Actually, Grace; I heard about this."

"You heard about it? Well, I swan. Joe swore me to secrecy. He said if it ever got out it would cost him his job."

"He told Papa about it, and Papa told me. You know how it goes."

"Yes; well, I told Mildred. We had a laugh over it."

Lyn shifted position on his chair, thinking he should go home. "You mentioned Carl. Have you heard from him?"

"Only a Christmas card. It looked like one the home purchased in bulk and handed out. It was a picture of the hospital there in wintertime. Just his name signed on it. We were planning a trip to visit him when the weather warms."

"Lying in bed last night, I thought about all the homeless boys who've spent time here. Who was that Bohemian boy who stole items from Dr. Hill's house?"

"Anton Ziek."

"He was about Carl's age, and said he'd gone to the house looking for work, not with the intent to steal. Papa got him acquitted and then he stayed here with you and Joe for a few days."

"Anyone who spent time around Anton knew he wasn't a bad boy. He could barely speak English and found himself in unfortunate circumstances. He worked while he was here. He helped Fred take off the storm windows, wash all the windows inside and out, and put on screens. We'd liked for him to stay longer but he had Gypsy in his blood."

"Papa and Joe were quite a pair."

"Joe admired John, but I believe he envied his success at so many things."

"Oh, that. He stepped into many careers but if money is the gauge of success, that didn't happen. I often had more money than he did."

"He once said his most important work was gaining pensions for war veterans and their widows." Grace pulled a newspaper off the buffet and scanned it for a moment.

"I like what one person said in his eulogy. 'Measured by worldly standards, John Glover was hardly a successful man. He came here when land could be had for the taking, but with all his varied attainments he died with little worldly gear. But he had the satisfaction of unselfishly serving his fellows, of always seeing the best in them and of being respected and loved by them. He possessed unbounded faith, hope, and charity, met every obligation of manhood bravely, and so far as possible in this life was a happy man.' Here . . . ." She passed the paper to Lyn, who had his own copy at home.

"His failure was my mother."

Grace seemed surprised. "His words, not mine," Lyn said. "He didn't have the money to move to a warmer climate when she was ill."

"Mary Frances was already compromised by consumption by the time that prescription for a warmer climate came. I remember looking up the definition of scrofula—I'd never heard the term—and finding it was tuberculosis of the bones and lymph glands. She must have suffered terribly."

"I remember her cries and moaning. When I was allowed to see her, they warned me to not touch her; that her bones might break. I had to wear a mask over my mouth and nose. The nurse tried to cover the open lesions on her neck but the bandages slipped away. It made me think of the leprosy I'd heard about in Sunday school."

"It must have been frightening at your age. But you see, moving to a warmer climate might have made her more comfortable, or perhaps not, but it wouldn't have been a cure. And imagine how physically painful it would have been for her to travel from here to some far off place."

"I suppose so. Still, it bothered Papa that he hadn't the means to follow doctor's orders."

"I can see how it would. Of course it would. Joe resisted going to the doctor even though he was in horrible pain. I spoke harsh words to him. I nagged until he went, and then he died in surgery. But he'd have died without the operation, too. We can create detours, but the outcome won't change if it's your time to go."

Lyn nodded and added, *"Alea iacta est."*

"The die is cast," Grace said, as if responding Amen to a prayer.

"When I was a teenager I stayed with Aunt Addie for some reason. I picked up a book and found a letter from Mother to Aunt Addie. Mother thanked her sister for staying with her while Papa was away somewhere. She added that she believed Papa took unnecessary trips for respite, to get away from her illness. But she did not begrudge him the time away. For one thing, it brought her dear sister for a visit."

Grace patted Lyn's hand. "We all have weaknesses."

"Even John Glover," Lyn murmured and immediately hoped Grace hadn't heard him. It sounded harsh. But over the years it did seem as if people thought John Glover could do no wrong.

"Of course," Grace said. "It took Joe two years to muster the strength to accept Fred's death. I believe Carl's situation somehow prompted him. It brought him to discussing father and son relationships with John."

"One more story and then I must go. When I was seventeen I wanted to get away for the summer. Just go somewhere and be on my own. Truth is, Papa was getting on my nerves. I told him I wanted to work and save money for college. He said he could send me to college. Well, the way I saw it, he didn't have the money but I didn't broach that subject. I didn't want to hurt his pride. I just said that this job would help pay expenses and I'd heard about a construction job in Le Mars. I went there and worked for Nicoli DiBaggio, a stonecutter and brick mason. He was old-school, and amazing to watch. He was one of a crew building a church."

Lyn stopped to wet his whistle with coffee. "Anyway, I liked the work so much I decided I didn't want to go to college. I wanted to work with my hands. I was good at it. Nicoli said so. He told me, in broken English, 'The mark of a man is not what kind of work he does, but that he works—honest work.' I finished high school and then went back and apprenticed with Nicoli. Papa wasn't thrilled but he got over it."

"Well, you're a fine craftsman. John was proud of you. That much I know."

During a moment of silence, Lyn could think of nothing to add to this conversation. He rose and carried his dishes to the sink. "May I help with these?"

"Certainly not; it will give me something to do."

"Then I leave with many thanks for your kindness. I slept well for the first time since Papa died."

"I'm happy you stayed. Don't be a stranger. Drop by anytime, like you and John always did. You know me; I need someone to fuss over."

With nothing more than a tearful embrace between them, Lyn left.

LYN GLOVER

After the tidiness of Grace Gill's sunlit home, Lyn surveyed the disorder at his cottage. He'd returned all the dishes and pans in which food had arrived, and he'd written thank you notes. Willis Overholser had brought extra copies of the paper carrying the obituary and other stories about Papa. "You'll want to send these to relatives and friends," the publisher said.

Lyn had to think about who he might send the papers to: Aunt Addie and her husband had copies. Papa's sister in Waterloo died years ago. Lyn had telephoned her son, who'd come to the funeral and had read the papers while here. Papa had a couple of male cousins in Wisconsin who had visited a time or two; they would want to know. And maybe Augusta Duvall Radford. She had disappointed Papa a few months ago, but, yes; Lyn would send the papers to her, along with the *Sioux City Journal*'s tribute to John Glover. He'd been a contributor to their paper for many years.

Lyn had one more duty; moving Papa's things from the hotel room. He borrowed a delivery truck from Brunson Hardware and parked it in the alley behind the hotel. Upstairs, he entered Papa's unlocked door. Leaving it ajar, he ran his hand over the metal G on the door. The four rooms on this level had once been A, B, C, D, but Papa removed the C from his door and added a G. Rather, Lyn had switched it. Papa had never been handy with a screwdriver, or any tool, for that matter. Well, writing instruments; yes. But put a hammer in his hand and he'd use it as a gavel. How had he managed to build a settler's shack when he arrived on the prairie? Lyn recalled him saying the house didn't need to be fancy, only a certain size to prove that you meant to stay with the claim.

Lyn removed the screws from the G and pocketed the letter. The hotel would want to revert to a C. Papa had what the hotel called a suite, which amounted to a sitting room with a desk and chair, a reading chair with an upholstered cushion and matching hassock, and a floor lamp. Two steps up put one into an alcove bedroom with an adjoining bathroom. Lyn had used the shower on occasion but preferred his washtub at home. Actually, it was a horse watering trough he confiscated when the town pulled up some of the hitching posts to make room for automobile parking. He could stretch out in the tub and read while bathing.

Lyn noticed a smell; not offensive, but a blend of toiletries and garments with that chemical odor of dry cleaning, and . . . what was that on the bedside table? A half-eaten apple that had turned to mushy cider. He detected the inky smell of newspapers and magazines, and book binding paste, the same smell as the library. Papa had helped found the public library opened just three years ago. He loved the Carnegie style building and all it stood for, but he had a private library here at his fingertips.

His collection included law books, atlases, histories, philosophy, theology, astronomy, archaeology, anthropology, world religions, a couple of volumes published in Greek, classic novels, and even pulp fiction. If a subject came up, Papa could discuss it.

The desk held papers and files and folders and stationary in the pigeon-holes. The drawers were crammed with writing instruments and check stubs, slide rulers, ink bottles whose contents had long since evaporated, a tray of alphabetized letters for typesetting a newspaper, and items whose purpose Lyn could not discern. Without looking at what everything was, he dumped the contents of the desk into a box. The desk he would leave for the hotel. He had no room at his place and the desk did not have family provenance. Papa acquired it a farm sale. Or maybe a client gave it to him as payment for legal work. No matter. If the hotel didn't want the desk, they would dispose of it.

In a small, flat drawer Lyn had not noticed before, he found a triple folded sheet of paper with Papa's handwriting on the top fold.

The Last Will and Testament of John Franklin Glover.

Startled, Lyn knew that reading this now would likely overwhelm him for the rest of the day. He would take it to Lou Dwinnell.

The closet held summer shirts and winter shirts, three suits, two for summer and one for winter—Papa had been wearing the other winter suit—a handful of ties, sweaters, a flannel bathrobe, four pair of shoes on the floor in boxes, and even a pair of spats tucked in one box. And cartons of photographs and diplomas and certificates and papers of all kinds. Most of the photographs bore no names identifying the subjects, and many of the paper materials had turned brittle and showed evidence of silverfish damage. A small jewelry box held two rings bearing college insignias, a fancy stick pin with a red stone, and a G.A.R. lapel button.

Papa had been wearing his wedding ring and Lyn buried him with that token and his glasses.

The dresser drawers revealed underwear, socks, belts, suspenders, pajamas, and a summer robe of seersucker, the fabric Papa had grumbled about being wrinkled. In one drawer lay a tin box, which Lyn opened and found within a curl of dark hair—his mother's, he imagined, as he ran his finger across its softness. He recalled seeing the curl as a child, when he'd snooped through the house while alone one rainy day. He closed the box and stuffed it in his pocket.

He couldn't remember moving all this when Papa began boarding at the hotel. The two of them had moved several times and he'd hauled their belongings from one place to the next. Many a time they'd not had two dimes to rub together but they'd accumulated plenty of stuff. Papa always got a laugh from others when he joked that if he found money in his pocket the garment must belong to someone else. He'd had only a few dollars in his pocket when he died.

Now Lyn remembered—he hadn't moved Papa into the hotel; he'd been in California visiting Grandfather Upton at the time. A funny scene from then emerged. He'd come home from his trip and stopped at the house Papa rented. He walked through the back door and a man at the kitchen table looked up and said, "Who are you?" The man didn't know where Papa had moved and Lyn had to inquire of Joe Gill.

Today he had brought empty cartons and as he filled them, he carried each down the back stairs to the truck. When he had finished packing every piece of Papa's life, he stripped the bed and left the soiled bedding in the middle, and a dollar, which he found on the closet floor, on the dresser for the maid.

———wwooe̶ro̶o̶ro̶oooww———

At home, knowing that he would not have room for everything in his cottage, Lyn moved what amounted to Papa's estate into the front and back seats of the automobile someone had abandoned here several months ago. He'd heard of people who detested horseless carriages, as they were first called, but to just leave one somewhere seemed peculiar. It wasn't an old heap; it was a black 1917 Hall Touring car. He'd reported the vehicle to Sheriff Gill, thinking it might be stolen goods, but Joe had no reports of missing autos and there was no way to trace the owner. Lyn's neighbor, who had a three stall barn, what used to be part of Gill's livery, let Lyn stow the car inside, away from the elements. With the car doors and windows shut tight, Papa's belongings were almost hermetically sealed.

For supper, although he still hadn't much appetite, Lyn ate a piece of cake that had gone dry. He threw the rest of the cake in the garbage pail and then cut a chunk of ham and ate it sandwiched between two slices of cheese. Papa always chided him for eating dessert before his meal. Why did everything he did now bring a memory of Papa?

Sorting through the accumulation of food, he tossed much of it in the pail. There had simply been too much for him to eat.

Exhausted, Lyn collapsed into a chair in front of the fireplace. He longed for his boon companion, as the paper had called his and Papa's relationship—boon companions.

Lyn had a couple of close friends from his youth, but his favorite person to spend time with had been the inimitable John Glover. Not even the few girls Lyn courted long ago could compare. Bess over-compensated for a slight lisp by being incessantly merry; a habit that wore on his nerves. Clara was smart and bookish, but boring, and Sophie clearly liked Papa better than she liked Lyn. Well, he liked Papa better than he did her. Oh, and there was Abigail, whom Lyn had quite fancied. Papa said she was rude. Or was it crude? No matter; nothing had come of it. Abigail had spurned Lyn.

He pulled out Papa's pocket watch, not because he cared what time it was but because it felt comforting in his hand. The watch had a history of Glover men: the patriarch to his son, and to the next son; and now it was the timepiece from which Lyn had recorded Papa's death. He didn't know how long his grandfather had the watch before giving it to Papa, but it had to be more than a hundred years old.

Lyn rose and took from the mantel the compass Papa had given him as a boy. In one hand he cupped the watch; its second hand moving silently while the bigger hand waited its turn to sweep away another minute. In Lyn's other hand, the compass needle wavered as he tried to still his tremble. Until the needle steadied again, he wouldn't know which direction to go.

He'd been too young when his mother died to miss her for very long. But it would be a struggle to find his way without the guiding hand that Papa had always provided.

LOU DWINNELL

Lou Dwinnell arrived at his office at nine. Lyn Glover had called last night and asked to stop by first thing. It would take only a few minutes, he said.

Lou had seen Lyn on Sunday, walking toward the hotel. Then he stopped, as if remembering that John wasn't there, and turned around and shuffled back the other way. Lou recalled sometimes forgetting that his mother had died. Home from college, he'd come in the door and expect to see her in the kitchen or reading in the parlor. It takes a while to get used to someone not being where you expect them.

Lyn had been two grades ahead of Lou in school. From what Lou recalled, Lyn had been a good student but that didn't satisfy one teacher who said he should do better; he was John Glover's son. She called him lackadaisical, an underachiever, a boy who should go to college but probably wouldn't. The coach of the summer baseball team, on which Lou played, too, said Lyn had a good pitching arm, but Lyn preferred the outfield. At town festivals when there were foot or bicycle races, Lyn invariably came in second. One of the kids commented that Lyn was a dedicated also-ran. "It's as if he tries to not excel." Some of the kids considered Lyn an odd duck, but kids had opinions and names for each other that usually weren't based on anything substantial.

Lyn had excelled, though. He'd apprenticed to a stoneworker from Italy and as the years passed he earned a reputation of being the best mason in the state of Iowa. His handiwork appeared around town and he'd headed the masonry crew that built the library.

In Lou's view, Lyn's personality bordered on . . . maybe, aloof. He sometimes seemed to be listening and, at the same time, staring right at you but with his mind on something else. On the other hand, shyness was often mistaken for aloofness. But they were something of a piece, weren't they? Both could be worked to advantage. An uneducated person might be reluctant to speak out of not knowing what to say on a particular subject.

That wasn't Lyn, though; with John Glover for a father he'd absorbed information of all kinds since birth. Lou had heard Lyn expound on any number of topics if the occasion presented itself and if John were not there to speak first.

Lou's wife didn't like Lyn when she first encountered him, but now she sang his praises. Lucille had hired him to lay a brick pathway through her rose garden, but when he arrived he paced off the footage and looked things over and said, "No; no, this calls for a *petite alle*," in what Lucille described as a phony French accent. He added, "Flagstone, not brick, and the *petite alle* will meander through the garden and end with a bench where you will sit and enjoy the view."

Lucille had been speechless. She'd set her mind on brick, but she'd been persuaded on flagstone. Then Lyn suggested a fence along the property line for privacy and to conceal the actual alley than ran between residential blocks and where homeowners kept their trash cans and other unsightly personal items. Lyn made the bench from scrap metal and lumber, no charge; it was his pleasure. The whole project cost Lou far more than the original idea but Lucille loved inviting friends to walk with her in the *petite alle*. Lou observed that she used a tad of phony accent of her own when she spoke of her garden path.

Lou had considered John more an acquaintance than a close friend; with the law as a connection. He respected John as a jurist but, not to speak ill of the newly-departed, John often leaned toward overbearing.

Lyn, too, was more of an acquaintance and, right now, a client. He had soundlessly appeared in the doorway. Lou rose and extended his hand across the desk. "Good morning."

Lyn shook the hand. "Morning, Lou."

"How's everything going?"

"Well enough."

Lou considered small talk: the cold weather, the long winter, but mundane chatter did not fit the circumstances of this visit. The poor guy looked worn out and dejected.

"Have a seat," Lou offered at the same time Lyn took the client's chair. He didn't remove his coat and Lou didn't suggest it. He did drag a stocking cap off his head and brush back his hair. He pulled a document from his coat pocket and passed it across the desk. "Papa never mentioned he had a will."

"Oddly enough, many lawyers don't even make a will."

"He wrote this twenty years ago. As I said over the telephone, there's not much to this it."

Unfolding the paper, Lou saw two handwritten paragraphs followed by a long list of dates.

"We usually read a will aloud to those persons cited therein." Lou chided himself for the legal term, but this was a business meeting.

"That would be me," Lyn said.

Lou read from the paper:

I, John Franklin Glover, being of sound mind and body, but bereft of worldly goods of value, do bequeath to my only heir, Lyn Fisher Glover, the family name, which to the best of my knowledge I ne'er besmirched. In addition, I have defended said name when a newspaper publisher, whose name I will not cite, attempted to smear the name and my reputation.

I also leave to my son, Lyn Fisher Glover, all belongings at my place of residence and on my person at the time of my death. This includes cash, of which there is likely to be little, as I've spent what I acquired. I have no bank deposit box, no checking or savings account, and no cash hidden in the mattress or elsewhere.

John Franklin Glover
January 1, 1900
January 1, 1901
January 1, 1902

Lou glanced up. "Do you want me to read all the annual updates, including this year?"

"No need. He signed it the first year so I guess that's it. Does this need to go through the courts?"

"No, but I'd like to formalize it for public record. That's called summary administration. I think John would like it being stored in the courthouse he watched being built and where he spent a good bit of time."

"Whatever you say. Let me know the fees and for your time today."

Lou waved that off but then, knowing that Lyn always paid his way, said, "I'll be in touch on that."

Lou detected that the strain of the past week had settled on Lyn's face and his slumped shoulders. When he hesitated for a moment, Lou asked, "Anything else I can help with?"

"Don't think so."

"If there is anything, let me know. Oh, he got a pension of some kind. They'll need to be notified of his death."

"I'll take care of that. I have the address."

As Lyn turned to leave, Lou said, "I'm curious. You didn't find a stash, did you?" Sensing Lyn's sadness, Lou smiled to indicate jest.

"A dollar on the closet floor," Lyn said. "I left it for the maid."

"It wasn't a Confederate Dollar, was it?"

Lyn laughed. "Might have been."

WILLIS W. OVERHOLSER

Last night's snow settled a downy blanket of cotton batting atop every shrub in sight. A lacy fringe adorned the spines of tree branches, and chimneys in the neighborhood wore white haloes. Judging by the snow cap on the birdfeeder Willis guessed there to be about nine inches. If it were a weekday the whistle at the light plant would have been implemented about seven o'clock, telling students and mothers that school wouldn't be held today. Or maybe not; it took a blizzard to bring things to a halt. A nice snow like this brought people outdoors. It being Saturday Willis didn't need to be at the shop, but he'd venture out later anyway. He'd take photographs and talk to those who didn't mind a cold nose and wet feet. Snow begat gaiety: sledding, snowmen, snow angels, snowball fights, and tobogganing. In the early years, there'd been a toboggan slide, paid for by English immigrants. The slide began across the street from the courthouse and ended several blocks away at the depot. Willis had taken the ride a few times and found it exhilarating, in addition to the panoramic view from the top. With the advent of automobiles filling the streets, the structure had to be taken down. Too, there'd long been complaints about it being unsightly, and concern about children climbing the structure and falling off.

Through the window, Willis saw two neighbor boys, each with a shovel over his shoulder. He'd hire them later to clear the walkway in front of the office and here at home. This storm would be front page news for Thursday's edition, unless something urgent usurped the space before then.

This year's important news had come less than three weeks into January, when the town lost two well-regarded men on the same day. A staggering blow. At fifty-three, Willis was younger than John Glover and Joe Gill, but their deaths aroused anxiety about his own mortality. All three men had been tight friends and already Willis missed seeing Joe and John around town.

He lit a fire in the fireplace, sat next to it in his favorite chair and propped his slippered feet on the hassock covered with Bea's crewel work design. In an hour of so he'd make coffee and breakfast. He'd never been able to stomach food or drink first thing in the morning. If Bea were here she'd already have consumed a pot of tea. She'd taken the train yesterday to visit her sister in Mankato. They shared a Valentine's Day birthday and rarely missed spending the holiday together. They'd probably been hit by this same weather system. No matter, they'd be snug in the Victorian family home.

Willis's tortoise shell cat leaped from the windowsill to his lap. Twister had no interest in going outside, ever again. As a kitten, she'd hobbled to the backdoor with a fractured leg after a small tornado touched down outside of town. No telling where she'd originated and she never showed a sign of wanting to return to wherever it had been. She still had a hitch in her git-along since weathering that storm. Willis wouldn't part with Twister for all the cash in the First National Bank. He rewarded her now with a vigorous rub between the shoulder blades. The massage relaxed both of them and Willis laid back his head and lapsed into reverie.

From his vantage point at the newspaper, he had his finger on the pulse of the town and he kept his eyes and ears open. He strove to be observant without being obtrusive. He gleaned, without trying, the general genealogy of folks; who married into which family and that sort of thing. He had chronicled the lives of hundreds, maybe thousands, of residents from birth to cemetery. He tried to figure out what made people tick; how events, large or small, affect people in either a positive or negative way.

Case in point, the Jess homicide that dominated the collective conversation last year. The anniversary of that tragic event would be in March, and quite likely there'd be folks reliving it. Maybe he'd mention the anniversary in his column, *Don't Read This*. Bea had given him the title for his weekly commentary. "How could anyone resist reading it?" she asked. "It's like telling a boy to not walk through a mud puddle."

She'd been right; dozens of people over the years had told him they turned first to his column. On second thought, he wouldn't mention the murder anniversary. Why bring that horrific deed and that poor boy to the forefront again?

What interested Willis about the case, even now, was how it had men in town considering their own father and son relationships; men who ordinarily didn't talk about private matters of the heart. Willis and his three sons discussed the topic at dinner one Sunday. The boys each claimed, playfully, that he was his dad's favorite, while his daughter gloated that she had no rival. She was Daddy's favorite daughter and her mother's, too. Willis told them that he had a favorite son but he wouldn't reveal it if they tortured him. Of course, he had no favorite, but let them think so.

The topic of fathers and sons had arisen after a Rotary meeting last summer after Carl Jess had been sent away. Willis couldn't say now who started the conversation but it immediately became apparent that the topic touched a nerve with Benton Stark. He stood and said, "Most of you know that I'm estranged from my son and that I will not discuss the matter." Benton couldn't leave the room fast enough. Willis knew, and suspected others did, too, that young Stark had been found in a compromising situation with another male. They'd both moved to California.

Two or three other men straggled out, too. They either had no interest in the conversation or wanted no part of it. A couple of them didn't have sons. Douglas Cahill wiped his eyes and excused himself. He needed to get back to the office. A couple of years ago his son in college dove into a swimming pool and hit bottom. He lived at home now, paralyzed from the waist down.

Three generations of the Rockwell family were in attendance. They operated an insurance business. The oldest spoke for the trio. "We have our differences on how to run things but when I crack the whip the others listen."

The remark cut too close to the Jess story, but no one remarked on it.

Ross Meader said he gets along fine with his two sons but he'd had a distant upbringing from his father. Lou Dwinnell nodded as if his situation matched that one.

Joe Gill listened but said nothing. Willis knew that John Glover had begun counseling Joe about his loss. As for John—everyone knew about his bond with Lyn.

Bob Johnson offered, "My youngest quit college and went to work on a dude ranch but I expect he'll be back. I'm biding my time. That works with my kids."

Questions were raised.

Did anyone think his son would kill him?

Audible gasps. Certainly not.

What if the circumstances were like those at the Jess home?

Silence followed. What would one do?

Reverend Glover covered the religious angle with a mention of Cain and Abel, the first homicide. Fratricide, actually.

"Are there more patricides than matricides?" someone wondered aloud.

"Probably," another man said. "It's a patriarchal society so men are more likely to get into disagreements with one another."

"But women are coming on strong," someone said. "They're not as meek as they were."

Joe Gill spoke to that. "I've seen my share of domestic situations that get out of hand. Disagreements are one thing; killing is another. Most people settle their arguments without violence."

Heads bobbed in agreement.

Someone—Willis couldn't recall who said what—wondered if mother and daughter connections were as complicated as father and son. And other family relationships. Sons and mothers? Daughters and fathers?

"Lizzie Borden took an axe and gave her father forty whacks," offered Jay Summers.

That brought a laugh to the somber subject, and an end. Time to return to work.

Lyn Glover was a Rotarian but he hadn't been there that day. What would he have said about himself and John? Now that extremely close tie had been severed. Lyn watched his father die. That had to have been a gripping and intense experience. How might it change a person?

Although Willis was only a decade older than Lyn, he'd always felt sort of paternal toward him. When Bea returned they'd have him over for dinner. Keep him involved; try to fill in the gaps on Sundays and holidays. Bea wanted the upstairs bedrooms repapered. They would chat while he worked. They always got on well.

Willis would keep an eye on Lyn.

This, too, shall pass. With time on his side, Lyn would be all right.

Last year began with a jolt—a brutal murder. This year brought a shocker; two good men gone to their reward. God rest their souls; the town history would record their contributions.

This county seat town had a vitality that Willis admired. And its people, as well. Salt of the earth. He would continue to bear witness to the happenings, big and small.

"We'll soldier on," he told Twister. "Things will play out according to God's plan. Right now, He's telling me it's time for breakfast. How about a scrambled egg?"

Twister's perky black face with a brown nose brightened Willis's mood and dissolved the gloomy thoughts he'd been considering.

GRACE GILL

For want of a moat, the Iowa Institute for Feeble-Minded Children might have once served as a medieval fortress. Isolated from the town of Glenwood, and comprised of several buildings with varying architectural styles, the largest structure soared five stories and boasted a triangular spire seen from miles away. The next building had a boxy rectangular addition capped by a minaret. What looked to Grace like dormitories had simple roofs with ordinary chimneys. Away from those, down a slope at what might be a utility building, a massive chimney rose many feet—she couldn't guess how high it reached. Exhaling gray vapor, the smokestack dwarfed a cluster of small outbuildings; equipment sheds probably.

Grace had done her homework at the library in anticipation of a visit with Carl Jess. Ironically, today, March 7, 1921, marked the one year anniversary of the day he killed his father. The date of this visit had been coincidental; the occasion presented itself when her son-in-law needed to attend a relative's funeral in a town near Glenwood and invited her to ride along and keep him company. She and Vince left yesterday and spent the night in a hotel en route.

An eight foot high wrought iron fence surrounded the buildings, beyond which lay about a thousand acres belonging to the hospital. Vince idled the car at the gate, rolled down the window, and waited for the attendant to come forward.

"Name, please," he requested.

"Grace Gill," she called, leaning toward Vince to be seen.

"Your name?" he asked the driver.

"I won't be staying. Just drop off and pick up."

The gatekeeper checked a list on his clipboard and then handed Vince a Visitor card. "Keep the permit for when you return. Ma'am, you'll want to check in at the building with the steeple." He swung open the gate and allowed the automobile through.

Ascending a hill, the grounds looked shabby to Grace; overgrown and unattended. But this hospital had been around more than fifty years, and in addition, the extended winter had taken a toll everywhere.

Vince pulled in front of the spired building onto a flat surface. He put the car in neutral, engaged the handbrake and then got out and went around to assist Grace from the passenger seat.

"Many thanks," she said. "Give my regards to your family."

"I will. Not sure how long I'll be."

"Don't rush. I'll be fine."

She waved Vince on his way and then snugged her Persian lamb coat around herself. Joe had surprised her with this luxury at Christmas and since his death it had warmed her beyond what she expected of a winter wrap.

She stepped to the door, where a sign requested: Please Ring Buzzer. She did so, and waited, a slight cough erupting into the cold air and ending with a visible puff of moisture.

"Good morning," a cheerful woman called as she opened the door.

"Good morning. Grace Gill to see Carl Jess."

"He's waiting. Right this way." She has kind of a waddle, Grace thought as she followed the woman.

Led into an expansive room, there stood a smiling boy alongside a stone fireplace with a roaring fire. Had he put on a few pounds and grown an inch or two? Grace couldn't be sure.

Holding back tears, she steeled herself, smiled, and greeted him. She refrained from hugging and instead squeezed his upper arm, a gentle show of affection

"Hi, Missus Gill."

He wore what amounted to a two-piece uniform in a medium blue twill fabric. Other boys in the room wore the same and the one girl Grace saw wore a blue jumper and a white blouse.

"Did you come on the train?" Carl asked while Grace took off her hat and coat. "I came here on the train."

"My son-in-law drove me. He had business here and will pick me up later."

Carl seated himself and Grace took the chair opposite him, close enough for visiting.

"Did Sheriff Gill come?" Carl asked.

Grace knew that Joe would come up but not this quickly. Might as well get the topic over with and move along. "Sheriff Gill passed away."

"He died?"

"In January. He had a hernia problem. He died in surgery."

"That's too bad. I like him."

Present tense, but that was fine. Grace often thought of Joe in present tense. "Thank you. He was a good man. Do you remember John Glover?" Grace regretted the question; she didn't intend to dwell on death today.

"He gave me comic books."

"He died, too. The same day as Sheriff Gill."

"Did he have a surgery?"

"No; a stroke."

"What's that?"

"It's a . . . sickness."

"Oh."

Grace handed Carl a reused Whitman's chocolate box. He tore off the cover. "Gee willikers, fudge." He bit into a piece. "What's this white stuff?"

"Divinity. I think you'll like it."

He took a piece and consumed the whole thing, shaking his head all the while. "Ya, that's good." He ate another piece of fudge. "We ain't supposed to eat between meals."

"It'll be our secret. The woman at the front desk said I could bring it."

Carl put the lid on the box. "I'm saving the rest."

"Good idea."

Grace settled back, thinking about what to say next. Then a boy approached; big and muscular, with a mass of curly hair.

"Hey, Carl," he said in a husky voice.

"Hey, Roger," Carl responded without enthusiasm.

When Roger moved on, Grace asked, "A friend?"

"Nah; he's a bully. Loony." Carl twirled his finger beside his head.

Grace kept a serious face. "So, do you like it here?"

"You bet. I have my own room with two other boys. We each have a bed and a desk."

"How's school?"

"Better than country school. But I'm sixteen and we don't have much now. Just a few classes. And PE."

"What is that?"

"Umm . . . exercise."

"Oh, yes. That's important for any age."

"We play basketball."

"It's Monday. Are you supposed to be in school?"

"I don't know." Carl wrinkled his brow and seemed to think about it. "They told me to come here for a visitor. Oh, do you know what?"

Grace leaned forward. "Tell me."

"I have a job. Important."

"Really?"

"I work for the govmint."

"The . . . government?"

"I sort mail and deliver it to offices and people."

"Ah, yes; the mail is government business."

"You betcha. Do you know it's against the law to mess with mail?"

"I do know that."

"I'll bet Sheriff Gill knows, too."

Grace paused. "Yes; he knows about that law."

"It's against the law to open someone's mail or even read a postcard that doesn't have your name on it. I had to do a promise. Like in court. What's that called?"

"Do you mean an oath?"

"That's it. I had to do the oath that I wouldn't snoop and I would . . . respect . . . privacy."

"They must trust you to let you help with the mail."

Carl stared out the window. "I'm trying to remember something." He turned back. "I know. When you sent me a Christmas card I delivered it to myself."

Grace didn't realize she'd been tense until she laughed. "That's funny, Carl."

"I know. We all have mail slots so I delivered the card to mine and then read it later. I sort envelopes by ABC."

"Alphabetical order."

Yes. Like . . . Gill would come before Jess."

"That's right."

"Because G comes before J."

"Uh, huh."

"Charlie said I do good work. He's the boss."

"And you like him?"

"Yes. Not everyone gets mail. Some people never do."

"That's too bad. It's nice to receive mail."

Roger approached again and this time he punched Carl on the shoulder and moved quickly on.

Carl lurched to his feet, both hands fisted. "I'll get you back," he yelled.

Roger swiveled around. "I'm shaking in my long johns, Prissy Boy."

An orderly appeared seemingly out of nowhere and stood between the boys. Roger kept going and Carl remained standing, his eyes following Roger.

Grace reached toward Carl and he unfurled his hands and sat down. Wide-eyed, he stared at Grace as if trying to place her. His face and eyes gradually relaxed and he said, "Where's *Oma?*"

This scuffle had taken him back to the farm.

"I believe your grandmother is with her other son."

Carl seemed to weigh that. "His name is Claus. Same as my father's."

Attempting to remove him from the past, Grace glanced at her watch. "What else should we talk about?"

The question became moot when someone across the room played Chopsticks on the piano.

"That means dinner time," Carl said.

"It does? It seems like I just got here."

"They don't use a loud bell 'cause it scares some people."

"What a good idea. I like that."

"But you know what? Peg knows how to play the song and she does it sometimes during the day, for a joke."

"That's a good one," Grace said, happy that the patients had a sense of humor.

Carl stood by his chair. "Are you eating dinner with us?"

"They told me it wasn't allowed, but I can use the staff cafeteria."

"Carl," an orderly called, "you heard the signal."

He darted off and before Grace left she saw him join a line where a nurse dropped a pill into each open hand, gave the patient a paper cup of water and watched to see the pill swallowed. Did they all take the same medication, a tranquilizer, perhaps?

On her way to the cafeteria Grace noticed a little girl of six or seven, seated with a woman, probably her mother. The child jerked now and then and shouted words Grace could not decipher. She wondered if the girl had Tourette syndrome. Did she have another affliction as well, a diminished mental ability, or did her tic and speech problem alone make her a candidate for living in this place? Did every family have a sad story?

Grace answered her question. Yes; we're surrounded by tragedy. No one escapes it. She had thought the world ended when Fred died. Certainly, life as she knew it ended. Her faith had been seriously challenged, but she believed there was a reason Fred died and that reason might never be clear. Accept it. Stop asking: Why me? *Why not me* is more appropriate to one who believes in God's plan. Somewhere in the Bible it promises that

God will make something good out of devastating storms. Oh, but in the interim, they are difficult to weather, unbearable.

"May I help you?" a voice asked, and Grace realized she'd come to a halt in the corridor.

"Oh, thanks. I see the cafeteria is just ahead."

In the food line, Grace recalled reading that this facility housed about 1100 residents and 175 staff, give or take a few. It must be pandemonium feeding that many people. How many shifts would it take? She chose a bowl of potato soup, a baking powder biscuit, a pat of butter, and a bowl of tapioca pudding, one of Joe's favorites. She hadn't made it since he died.

The tables were mostly filled but as she looked around, a nurse sitting alone motioned to her. "Better grab this seat; they go fast."

"Thanks," Grace said, setting her tray and handbag on the table. She'd left her coat and hat in the visitor's room. And Carl's candy. Would it be there when she returned? "I'm Grace Gill," she told the woman.

"Meg O'Brien. You're visiting, I assume." She swabbed her soup bowl with a half slice of bread, folded it, and ate it.

"Yes; Carl Jess."

"Our little mailman. He's a dear. Your son, grandson?"

"A friend."

"They need friends here. Don't you know some of them never have a visitor. It might as well be an orphanage like it was when it first opened. The poor souls."

Having now spent time with Carl, Grace wasn't sure he fit the label poor soul. He seemed happy. But maybe she could gain some insight from Meg. "How long have you worked here?"

"Umm, let's see. Coming on twelve years."

"I wondered, are boys and girls segregated?"

"Well, for sleeping, yes, indeed. Separate dorms, locked for the night. During the day they come together for their jobs, activities, movies, sports, school classes, dances."

"Are there problems with . . . you know, romance maybe?"

Meg laughed. "They're teenagers, some of them. Hormones. Cuddling, kissing, but we discourage it when we catch them."

"Do you have runaways?"

"It happens, when they're beyond the fenced area in the garden and such. But they don't know where to go and it doesn't take long to find them. The townsfolk panic when there's an escape. We try to keep it quiet but word travels. They're not dangerous, these kids."

"None of them? There are hundreds of patients here."

"Well, sure, but those are in lock-up. They go out only with guards."

"Carl isn't considered dangerous?"

"That little guy? He's about twelve, up here." Meg tapped her temple.

Grace hardened herself to speak the next words. "He killed his father. Shot him in the head. Twice."

"I know his story. His father was a real bastard, I hear. Excuse my language."

"What if someone here threatened Carl? An orderly, or he mentioned one boy who's a bully."

"Who's that?"

"I don't recall his name," Grace fibbed.

"Well, you know, we are a hospital for the feeble-minded. That means they're not very bright."

"I understand the term."

"And we now and then get an orderly who has more on his mind than looking after these kids. If you get my drift. But like you said, we have hundreds of patients. There's no end to potential for trouble. We're trained to handle it."

Grace had no doubt they handled it: pills, restraints, lock-up, shock treatment, sterilization. This woman would never own up to any of that.

"Well, back to work for me," Meg said. "No rest for the wicked or those who work in the state hospital."

At least she didn't call it the loony bin or crazy house; terms even educated people tossed into conversation.

"I enjoyed talking to you," Grace said.

"Nice meeting you. Where do you live?"

"Up north, near the Minnesota border."

"My, you have a ways to go. Did you come by train?"

"I motored with my son-in-law."

"Safe travels to you."

"Thanks, Meg."

———·~∞·o·≎∙o≎∙o∙o∞~·———

Carl had resumed his place, where Grace had left him. "I have sixteen minutes before my job." He pointed to a wall clock. "We have to know the schedule."

"All right. I had a good dinner. Did you?"

"Yep. I sat by Leo. He told a story."

"Do you want to share it?"

"Well . . . ." With his finger on his chin, Carl thought about it. "He said that this girl, Belle, played with boys in the tool shed."

Oh, dear, Grace thought.

"One of the boys was Roger."

"The bully?"

Carl nodded. "Leo said that Belle is eighteen now so she went to another place." He paused. "Before she went there she had the operation."

Grace held her breath.

"Roger is almost eighteen and he's going to have the operation before he moves to the place for older kids."

Keep calm, Grace told herself, wondering where the children heard this information. And quite likely they didn't always get it straight or only part of the story. The staff was supposed to be professional, but they were human beings who naturally talked about their work.

Carl yawned. He seemed lethargic since dinner. Since the medication.

"I'm glad Roger is going away," Carl said. Again his eyes glinted with what Grace identified as anger.

"He does sound like a trouble-maker."

Carl watched the clock; its hand ticking off seconds and minutes.

"Carl, I enjoyed visiting with you," Grace said to catch his attention.

"Okay, bye, then." He stood, ready to report for duty.

"Don't forget your fudge."

"Oh, yeah. I'll share it with Charlie, my boss."

"That's nice of you."

"Are you coming here again?"

"I'll try my best."

"And Sheriff Joe, too."

Grace bit her lip, and as the clock clicked at the hour, Carl walked away.

With tears flooding her eyes, Grace couldn't move a muscle.

When she recovered, she took measure of this visit. Carl seemed virtually unchanged since last summer. Did that mean the experts had been correct, that his mental growth had ceased at age eleven? The child in him hadn't grasped that Joe died. When did a child begin to understand death? Surely at eleven or twelve the concept became clear.

Grace leaned back in her armchair and closed her eyes, remembering again that today marked a year since Carl killed his father. That awful Sunday when Joe answered a call for assistance out in the country and then spent the day in court, and ended up bringing home a small, frightened boy. A child who confessed to killing his father and wore the man's blood on his clothing. Things moved quickly from that day to the end of April, when a jury decided that Carl was a mere boy who didn't understand the consequence of his act. And in June, he'd been delivered here.

Coming upright in her chair, Grace recalled Carl's quick flare of anger at Roger, and she asked herself a disturbing question: Was Carl, whatever his chronological or mental age, a one-time killer or, given extreme provocation, might he repeat his crime?

There was no way to be sure, and Grace gave way to profound sadness.

By the time Vincent arrived, she'd composed herself and found comfort that for a while today, Joe had been present tense. Carl had given her that.

LOU DWINNELL

Lou had occasion one day to take Grace Gill the documents finalizing Joe's estate. He owned two pieces of rental property that should provide Grace enough income—if she practiced frugality. He suspected she always had.

He'd told Grace he couldn't stay but she had a pot of coffee ready and cups on the table. "I wanted to tell you about my visit with Carl Jess," she explained. "My son-in-law had to go down that way so he dropped me off."

Lou sat while she brought over a plate of cookies and joined him at the kitchen table. Her house always smelled of baking.

"It happened to be the anniversary of the shooting," Grace continued. "Of course, I didn't mention that to Carl."

"How are things with him?"

Grace settled her hands in her lap but then withdrew one to hold her cup. "In general, I'm optimistic about his placement. What I saw was clean and comfortable. He seems happy and busy. He works at sorting mail."

"That sounds positive."

Grace smiled. "He said it's an important job; that he works for the gov-mint."

It took Lou a second to understand the word. "Oh, I see."

"I got a kick out of that. He was so serious, and proud."

Like a child, Lou thought, like his boys when they were praised for doing a good job. "Did you see any intellectual growth since a year ago?"

"He seemed about the same."

"Then you're satisfied with the opinion that he's stuck in adolescence?"

"Well, of course I'm not satisfied, but yes; he's still a child. He might have grown an inch or two and put on a few pounds. Still very small. His attention span flits about like it always did. After I told him that Joe died, he still spoke of him in present tense."

Grace rose to refill their cups and sat down again. "I was disturbed to see signs of raw anger. Even when a boy who punched Carl on the shoulder was twice his size. Carl would have gone after him if an orderly hadn't stepped in."

Lou snapped a cookie apart and ate half. "Of course he had no gun handy like at home. It would have been fisticuffs."

"That time; yes. I assume it wouldn't take much to get a kitchen knife if a patient wanted one."

"We could paint all sorts of scenarios, but do you believe he's a danger to anyone? That he'd plan ahead and find a knife and go after someone?"

Lou immediately knew that was a dumb question.

"He did once before. Not a knife, but a gun." Grace fingered her Gold Star Mother pin. "But there are orderlies close at hand. And the patients take a pill before dinner. I saw them handed out. Carl seemed calmer by the time he came back after dinner."

"I know you can't help worrying, Grace, but we have to trust they'll do their best by him. Joe and you, we all did what we could. For the most part, the town was on his side. None of us wanted to see him in prison with adult criminals."

"Oh; no, that would be dreadful. My goodness."

Grace nudged the cookies closer to Lou. "I am concerned about the surgeries performed there. The kids know and talk about it."

Lou nodded, indicating he knew what she meant. He'd rather avoid the subject.

"Joe and I discussed it and he fell on the side of caution. He said it's a necessary evil; that feeble-minded children having children is detrimental to their health. And it puts a burden on society."

"All good points, of course. I'll visit Carl sometime soon."

"That would be nice."

Lou stood, preparing his exit. "How are you doing, Grace?"

"Oh, I'm muddling through, you know. It's a change without Joe."

"I miss seeing him around the courthouse."

"Others have said that. How's your family?"

"Doing well."

"Tell Lucille to come by and bring the boys."

"I will."

"It's too quiet around here."

"Those two rascals would take care of that problem in short order."

Grace glanced toward the hallway. "I have chores your oldest boy could handle. I need to put boxes in the attic. Joe's things."

"I could do it now."

"No, no; I could do it myself but kids need their own money to learn how to handle it and understand the cost of things. Joe didn't approve when I gave Fred a nickel for doing chores. He said kids shouldn't be paid for household work. That's being part of the family. He was right, of course. I paid Fred only for extra chores."

She had to be thinking about Carl having no concept of money.

"Henry would be glad to help. Don't overpay him, though."

"The little one, too. I'll find something for him to do. I might need help baking cookies."

Lou laughed. "That's better than money. How's Saturday morning?"

"Send them over. Saint Patrick's Day is coming and I have a shamrock cookie cutter."

LOU DWINNELL

In late April, on the one-year anniversary of Carl's commitment to the state hospital in Glenwood, there appeared on the District Court docket the Notice of Guardianship Annual Report and Application for Court Orders. The notice was filed by Lou's partner, attorney for Carl's guardian, A. J. Graves.

In sum, the document, written in the usual legalese of herein, therein, heretofore, hereinbefore, thereby, and aforesaid, asked for approval of the guardian's past year's expenses and reimbursements, approval to do the same in the coming year, to continue to lease said lands, collect rents, make repairs on the buildings, pay the taxes and insurance and do all things in relation thereto as it may seem for the best interest of his ward. The bank holding the estate also presented its report. The notice appeared in the paper and was mailed to Carl Jess, now sixteen, to George Mogridge, Superintendent at Glenwood, and To Whom It May Concern.

Lou knew one man with concern. Claus Bohr, the half-brother of Carl's father, had come to Lou about filing a claim against the estate to provide financial aid for his mother.

"She's senile and deaf and in a wheelchair," he explained. "My wife can't handle taking care of her and I'll never commit Mother to a state hospital. With all that money sitting in a bank, some of it should go to Carl's grandmother for private nursing."

"I understand," Lou said. It made sense, but he was able to wash his hands of the proposed suit, citing a conflict of interest for his law firm.

Then an odd thing happened. While Bohr had been in Lou's office, Mrs. Jess passed away in her sleep.

Sometime later, Lou heard, but had no personal knowledge until he read it in the paper, that the court had authorized an order for a reappraisement in the case of Claus Bohr vs Carl Jess, *et al.* Apparently

Bohr still felt entitled to some of the estate, although he was not a blood relative of Carl Jess.

In June, another surprising thing happened. Lou's neighbor, whose reading taste ran to dime novels, penny dreadfuls, pulp fiction, sawdust prose, and detective magazines whose cover models' cleavage rivaled Vaudeville's Mae West, gave Lou a copy of a magazine called: *Malice Aforethought.*

Lou had seen other editions and this one did not display a buxom beauty or a grisly crime scene; it featured a picture of Carl Jess, the one that had been in the *Des Moines Register* at the time of the shooting. The headline streamed beneath the boyish face read:

Patricide Pays
Teenaged Killer The Richest Boy In Iowa

Inside were photos of Carl's parents and the farmhouse where Claus Jess had been shot to death in the bedroom. The window of that room had a big X across it. The headline read:

Greed Was The Motive
By Donald A. Hirsch

Carl Jess, aged 16, has a comfortable room at the Iowa Institute For Feeble-Minded Children. The facility is located in Glenwood, which sits in a hollow of the scenic Loess Hills along the Missouri River. Here at this self-contained community of some 1000 residents and 175 staff members, Carl attends classes, academic and recreational, and is assigned jobs: weeding the garden, busing tables in the cafeteria, shelving books in the library, and sorting mail.

Does Carl belong in this peaceful setting; this state-funded boarding school, or should he be incarcerated in state prison with like-minded criminals?

Don't let the innocent-looking youth dupe you.

Consider this: In March of 1920, on a farm near Ocheyedan, Iowa, while his elderly and sickly paternal grandmother slept in another room, the motherless teenager shouldered a rifle and shot his sleeping father in the head. Then he casually went about his business of an ordinary day, making and eating breakfast, and milking the cows.

Back in the house, he was surprised to hear his father groan. He'd not killed him. Carl shot Claus Jess, Jr. in the head a second time. This time the deed was done.

Carl's stone-deaf grandmother did not hear either disturbance.

After making an attempt to clean up the blood, without success, Carl walked to a neighboring farm and told the owner, "Pa got kicked in the head by a horse last night and this morning I found him dead in bed."

The startled neighbor went home with the boy, whom he described as unconcerned. The neighbor was quickly suspicious. If the man had been kicked in the head the night before, the evidence had been destroyed by two gunshot wounds. The coroner confirmed the cause of death. A horse was not the culprit.

Carl broke down and admitted he shot his father whom he said "licked me with switches and whips and made me work like a slave and never gave me even a nickel to spend."

His father had plenty of nickels. He had recently sold his farm for more than $100,000. In addition to a thousand dollars cash found in the dilapidated house, Claus Jess had a deposit box filled with gold coins and stocks and bonds, and several bank accounts, all combined, worth a fortune. Carl, the only grandchild of his paternal grandfather, had inherited his estate, worth another $100,000, which is being held until he comes of age.

There's the rub—his age. Chronological or mental?

At the trial held in Osceola County last year, Carl was found not responsible for the murder—due to his being feeble-minded with the intellect and judgment of no more than a child of eleven.

Consider this: Fifteen-year-old Carl Jess premeditated (for some time, he said) shooting his father. He concocted an alibi (a horse kicked him in the head), and executed both the plan and his father.

Is an eleven-year-old capable of that?

Perhaps Carl's mind is developed far beyond even teenaged.

What about remorse? When asked if he regretted killing his father, Carl said yes—because everyone had made a big deal about it.

The experts have spoken; they say his intellect will remain at a standstill. Although the prosecution called witnesses to counter Carl's claims about not having spending money, that only served to establish that he had no concept of money; again like a child. The entire county rallied around the defense that this is a feeble-minded boy.

As reported last year in the *Des Moines Register*, ". . . his dream is to study farming. And perhaps, on the side, aviation. Then he plans to come home and farm scientifically his four eighties. He has a fortune of $100,000 willed him by his grandfather, if the law should rule that he cannot inherit his father's estate. And when he has done this, Carl wants a son of his own."

According to the *Register*, Carl said, with a quivering chin, "I'll treat him good, you see if I don't! I'll let him play if he wants to, and I'll never, never whip him at all!"

That will remain a dream; a fantasy. Because Glenwood houses only children age five to eighteen, Carl will be moved to an adult facility when he comes of age, his chronological age.

Because he was not convicted of murder, his massive estate is in the hands of a guardian. When he dies, it will go to the State of Iowa.

Carl Jess is rich beyond his dreams, but he will never get his hands on even the nickel in spending money he desired when he murdered his father, and which he took from the dead man's pocket.

Greed came to naught.

Lou tossed the magazine on his desk. The writer had obviously not visited Carl; he had simply taken information from other sources, even the quotes. He'd spiced up some of the quotes with changes—putting the word "Pa" in Carl's mouth. Lou had never heard Carl use the term Pa; he always said "my father." The author's addition injected rural folksiness and suggested a comfortable relationship between the boy and his father.

Reading the story reminded Lou that he should visit Carl. One of these days he'd get around to it. He currently had a case that would take time and energy—a faulty part on a threshing machine that might have led to a young father of three losing his lower arm. It would be a negligence case, Lou against a city lawyer for Allis-Chalmers Manufacturing.

Visiting Carl would have to wait for now.

LOU DWINNELL

The negligence suit dragged on for months. The defense finally found a witness who claimed the plaintiff had been fooling around and not watching what he was doing around the threshing machine. Lou lost the case.

Carl Jess slipped his mind, except for the annual guardianship report. And the Clerk of Courts notified Lou that the court had denied Claus Bohr any funds from Carl's estate.

Lou's practice grew and what free time he had, he spent with his boys. It kept him young while they grew like tadpoles; slender and lanky, like Lucille's family.

Lou became president of the state bar association, which meant time away from home now and then.

His widowed father moved into the house and died within a year. While there, the two men attempted to become reacquainted and, Lou felt, they succeeded. The old man had enjoyed his grandsons; particularly the younger one who carried his name.

The boys and Lou were involved in Boy Scouts; the oldest eventually completed Eagle, like Dad, but now, at sixteen, Henry had more interest in girls. And learning to drive, which tried Lou's patience but he enjoyed seeing the determined kid behind the wheel. Henry and Phil played high school sports, music, drama, the whole experience. It pleased Lou that they still spent time with him, a movie now and then, early morning fishing, listening to his long-winded stories about the old days or his current cases. The three of them enjoyed huddling around the radio, trying to tune in "This is Station WNAX, Voice of the House of Gurney in Yankton, South Dakota." The boys relished picking up music or news from a place ninety miles away.

After Lucille felt poorly for far too long with no explanation from local doctors, Lou took her to Mayo Clinic. They detected a disease called lupus, which sapped her strength and could be life threatening. Lou did what he could at home to help out, and brought in an after school hired girl.

One summer Lucille hired Lyn Glover to repair the *petite alle.* "Have you seen Lyn lately?" she asked Lou that evening.

"We say hello on the street. I doubt I've had a real conversation with him since I probated John's will. Why?"

"He looks different. His hair is down to his shoulders."

"Hmm."

"Actually, it looks attractive. When it got in his way, he braided it."

"Really? Were you out in the sun too long today?"

"No, but I sent your oldest son out to pull weeds while Lyn was working. He said Lyn was interesting."

"Oh, yeah? What did they discuss?"

"Theology, Henry said."

"Well, he is Reverend Glover's son."

"People always say that. He's also Lyn Glover."

Lou lifted the lid on a pot. "Smells good."

"He came on a motorcycle."

"It's a motor scooter."

"What's the difference?"

"Well, size for one thing. I don't know."

"Henry said Lyn looks good with long hair. He added that he might grow long hair when he goes to college this fall."

"Not while I'm paying his bills."

"He's eighteen, Lou. He also mentioned wanting one of those raccoon coats that were popular a few years ago."

"He wants old clothes instead of new? That's a twist. Are we eating soon? I have to go back to the office and work."

Henry going to college this fall? How could that be?

More and more, Lou had moments where he asked himself: Where has the time gone? The answer smacked him in the face one morning in 1928. He'd started out the door, headed for court, when his secretary motioned him back and passed him the telephone.

"Long distance," Clara whispered. "Independence, Iowa."

Lou wrinkled his brow. "Who do I know . . . . ?" He took the phone; said, "Lou Dwinnell speaking," and listened.

He nodded, still listening. "I understand."

Clara hovered.

"Thank you for calling. I'll notify the appropriate people."

"What was that?" Clara asked, removing the phone from his hand.

Lou caught a breath, cleared a lump from his throat. "Carl Jess died."

Clara covered her mouth and spoke through her fingers. "No; when, what—"

Flustered, Lou checked his watch. "I'm already late. I'll tell you later. But don't mention it to anyone until I notify those who should know first."

Clara nodded. He trusted her.

Driving to the courthouse Lou made a mental list. He'd need to call Grace Gill's daughter. Grace now lived in Spencer with Mildred and Vince. And Carl's guardian, Ambrose Graves, and get the legal papers rolling on closing that arrangement. Then he'd stop by the newspaper and give Willis the details. Let him handle it. That way, anyone still interested in Carl Jess would hear the details instead of gossip.

THE SIBLEY GAZETTE

MAY 6, 1928

Lou Dwinnell and I.R. Meltzer, attorneys for Carl Jess at his 1920 trial for killing his father, and A.J. Graves, guardian of Carl Jess, received word that Carl passed away at age 23, the result of smoke inhalation during a fire at the Iowa Home For The Insane, Independence, Iowa. He was buried at Independence.

Officials confirm that Carl left the dormitory but dashed back inside to rescue a cat he had acquired without permission. He became overcome with fumes. The cat escaped out a window.

Readers will recall that 15-year-old Carl, of Ocheyedan, was found irresponsible of the crime of patricide because experts testified that his intellect had come to a standstill at age 11. He was committed to Glenwood Home For Feeble-Minded Children, where he remained until the age of eighteen, at which time he was moved to Independence.

As the only heir to his father's and grandfather's estate, those accounts had been held by the Bank of Ocheyedan. Carl's guardian was in charge of Carl's extensive farmland, which has been rented out these past years. Carl Jess's considerable estate reverts to the State of Iowa.

———〜〜～๑∖℮↻⊙⊙↻℮∕๑～〜〜———

It turned out the townsfolk *were* interested in the boy who stirred things up eight years ago. There being no shortage of opinion, one need only eavesdrop on the street.

Oh, yes; I remember that awful day he killed his father.

In cold blood.

Dying in the fire was his come-uppance; his punishment.

We mustn't judge. Vengeance is mine, sayeth the Lord.

He got away with murder.

Do you call being locked in an asylum getting away with it?

Thou shalt not indulge in virtuous condemnation.

He couldn't have been feeble-minded if he knew enough to go in to rescue a cat.

That shows he *was* feeble-minded. A smart person wouldn't go back into a burning building for a cat.

He loved that cat more than he did his own father.

Maybe the cat was easier to love. I remember that man.

I do, too. He wasn't so bad. The kid exaggerated.

Carl is a hero for saving that animal. I'd do the same for mine.

He had no respect for the law, ever. He killed his father and he kept an illegal cat.

Well, those two acts are hardly basis for comparison.

My heart broke for him back then for all he went through and now this sad end.

And so it went, until next week's paper showed photos of a violent wind storm out in the country that uprooted a dozen trees, and captured everyone's attention.

In time, Lou put Carl Jess's file in storage.

Case closed for his part.

LYN GLOVER

There were those five kids again. Stirring the scrap pile with a stick until a rat appeared and then the one with the B-B gun popped off a shot and the kids cheered. One boy used a slingshot as a weapon and another had a homemade gun that used a snap clothes pin as the launcher for a wide rubber band cut from an automobile inner tube. The ammunition would smart plenty if a person were the victim.

As Lyn stepped out the back door one of the kids called, "Hey, Glover." They called him that—just Glover. Papa would have boxed Lyn's ears for calling an adult by his last name without Mister or Missus in front of it. Well, Papa wouldn't actually have boxed his ears; he never laid an angry hand on his son. But he'd made it clear that children should respect their elders.

Lyn waved but didn't encourage the kids by going over to talk. He didn't mind their digging for treasures, maybe a pair of bedsprings that could be attached to the shoes for a bouncy walk, whatever interested kids that age, probably twelve or thereabouts, but he'd rather they didn't rile the rodent population. He had enough trouble with neighbors about that.

The kids wandered off, which suited him fine. But one of these days he could use their help with a moving project.

His cottage had been part of what used to be Joe Gill's livery in the early days of the town. Some twenty years ago, when Lyn moved in, the house had been a step up from the boxcars along the railroad track where migrant railroad workers and their families lived. Papa had once compared Lyn's cottage to the settler's shack he'd constructed on the prairie when he landed here from Wisconsin.

Papa had no neighbors, no obstructions, not even trees, as he looked out his one window at a rolling sea of uncut grass and wild flowers. He'd kept a lighted lantern in the window at night, a welcome signal to anyone who might come that way. Lyn remembered the open prairie. When Papa bought and sold land, he took Lyn along and let him run through the grass. The boy imagined Indians skulking about, and when the image in his mind turned to scalping, he ran to Papa for protection.

Now Lyn's house and property had been declared an eyesore. Having been in the salvage business since forty-two, shortly after the country entered the Second World War, his inventory piled in the backyard was not exactly the grand view others in the Grandview addition anticipated when they moved here. One woman kept the shades drawn on the side of her house that faced his yard. A man complained, "There's already a city dump east of town. We don't need another one here." When Lyn used rat poison, they complained about the death smell. He couldn't please everyone, or even anyone, it seemed. A couple of kids had asked if there were bodies under the pile. "It's a midden," he replied, "so there's no telling whose bones are there." Let them look up that word if they didn't know it. That's what Papa always told him: "Look up the word. Use the library."

The late thirties had been an economically rough time for everyone. But Lyn's neighbors, whose slogan became "being poor doesn't mean trashy" went on a cleaning spree in their yards and spruced up the outside of the houses, too. He cleaned his front yard but did nothing to the back, so they took him to court for maintaining a nuisance. Lou Dwinnell suggested, in a polite way, that a suit and tie would be appropriate attire for court. Lyn managed to pull together a presentable outfit, in his opinion; still, he drew looks from people in the courthouse. They'd not been around during Papa's bailiwick, but quite likely they'd heard of John Glover, and of Lyn Glover, the eccentric son; eccentric being the nicest term used. He'd heard people talk, even when they thought they were being discreet.

At the trial in Justice Court, the city attorney pointed out that if the defendant were acquitted, that would mean people could locate unsightly nuisances in other parts of town, anywhere they pleased. The city would then be in a fine mess, wouldn't it? Dwinnell argued that the case had originally been started as an equity proceeding, but that it had changed to a criminal proceeding because those who signed the complaint did not wish an equity suit, since they would have to employ counsel and undergo the risk of suit themselves. Lou won the case. It appeared that the plaintiffs didn't care enough about the problem if they had to spend their own money. Well, who had money to spare these days, anyway?

Papa would have been on Lyn's side, even if he agreed that Lyn should rid himself of the junk. To be fair, and to heed Papa's voice in his ear, Lyn promised his neighbors he'd clean his property. He had no desire to antagonize anyone. But he put it off, one reason or another, and suddenly the war came along. Part of the Home Front effort was for folks to recycle materials of all kinds:

paper, leather, tin, metal, aluminum, rubber, silk stockings, even bacon grease. States and towns were given a quota to meet. Lyn asked himself: Where are people going to store the stuff until the government folks can pick it up? There could be piles of junk in every yard, like that city attorney suggested during Lyn's trial. Why not have the junk all in one place, and make his collection legal? He spread the word via the weekly paper that Lyn's Salvage For The War Effort paid by the pound. He'd pick up the material if it wasn't too large for his handcart. He'd made a small profit during the war.

The kids who'd been here this morning had been sellers. They collected junk around town and brought it in their coaster wagons. They lived east of downtown, along the far end of the Ninth Street boulevard, and Lyn lived west, across the tracks. He didn't know their names but had dubbed them The Ninth Street Gang because they reminded him of The Dead End Kids in the movie posters at the Royal Theatre. The red-haired and freckled-faced boy had a Mickey Rooney look, so Lyn thought of him as Red. He'd heard someone call the girl, Gwen. She had red hair, too, but for some reason Lyn thought the two kids weren't related. He figured her for the daughter of the family who owned The Barracks Tavern, a rowdy place on Saturday nights. Two of the boys he named for their hair: Curly, and Hank, whose blondish hair was short in back and on the sides with a wavy hank over the forehead. The last boy was taller than the others, so he became Legs.

The war had officially ended in August, and Lyn, pushing seventy, wanted rid of the salvage business. He could still find odd jobs around town, enough to keep him in groceries.

The city had bought his property so they could expand the fairgrounds. He gained only a few bucks because of unpaid back taxes. They would haul away the junk, raze his cottage, standing by only a wing and a prayer, as the war slogan went, and bulldoze the whole area.

First, he had personal belongings to move elsewhere, his and Papa's. Papa's things were still in the neighbor's barn in that old car. Lyn never had gotten it running. The barn would be torn down, too.

Lyn had made an arrangement with an acquaintance, a schoolmate—that's how long they went back—for a place to live. Ross Meader owned a building in the business district and Lyn would live rent free in the upstairs rooms and would in turn provide as-needed upkeep on Meader's various rental properties. Bartering had been a good system in Papa's day, and it still worked now.

That's where the kids with their wagons would come in. Lyn needed help moving. Figuring they were roaming the neighborhood somewhere, he set off to find them.

LYN GLOVER

On moving day, just before school commenced for the term, here came The Gang, the boys in dungarees and white sleeveless undershirts, their arms suntanned and boyishly muscular. Gwen wore her usual bibbed overall over a tee-shirt and held the tongue of a Radio Flyer wagon in each hand. They were the kind with the sides built up, and looked fairly new. Where she'd gotten them was anyone's guess. "I've got two hands," she said. "I can pull both."

Her red hair and attitude reminded Lyn of that girl reporter years ago. What was her name? With women's suffrage a success, she'd been eager to prove she could keep up with the boys. Gwen, too, aimed to show her friends she could hold her own; she could pull two wagons at a time.

Curly brought a handmade flatbed carrier about twice the size of a sled but on roller skate wheels. Hank had added slats to the side of his wagon so it would hold more material. Lyn laughed out loud when Legs rode into the yard in a cart pulled by a harnessed goat.

"PopPop loaned him to me," Legs said. "His name is Adolf." The black and white goat had a black patch of hair above his mouth that resembled a Hitler moustache. "PopPop said Adolf is frisky and needs a workout."

Lyn had already filled his pushcart, and now he instructed the kids on what was to be moved and what was to be left on the scrap heap. "Pile 'em high; there's plenty of rope to secure your load. Everything in the car goes with us. Start with that."

He'd caught two of the boys by the car this summer, reaching through the windows, pulling out papers and books and tossing them back in. "Run along," he'd told them back then and they'd scattered.

Today, while loading their vehicles, they asked, "Who's this?" as they held up a photo or diploma or certificate.

"He was the mayor," Lyn said, or, "That's Judge Glover," whatever the case might be. Papa had worn a variety of professional hats.

Gwen studied a daguerreotype of a soldier. "What war is this?"

"Civil War," Lyn answered.

"Is it you?" Red asked.

"A little before my time."

Hank, who must have thought Lyn was deaf, said to Curly, "He looks old enough."

"Squirrely old guy, ain't he?"

Lyn stifled a laugh. He did have a mess of stuff squirreled away. He was leaving a heap of it here to become ground fill.

Red found a rusted wheelbarrow and yelled, "Hey, should we fill this?" He tried pushing it and the wheel wobbled and fell off. They all laughed and he tossed the whole thing onto the junk heap.

"Glover, can I have this compass?" Curly yelled, startling Lyn for a moment. But he had the compass Papa had given him so it was all right. "If it has your name on it," he yelled back.

Curly looked it over as if he thought he'd actually find his name.

Gwen pocketed something but Lyn didn't care; it was from the junk pile, not from the car. Those things were Papa's.

Then she picked up what looked like a velvet box from a jeweler. Lyn sidled over and watched as she pulled out an oval locket, about two inches in diameter.

Lyn held out his hand. The front of the jewelry had a filigree pattern while the back was smooth, with 14 carat gold printed in miniature letters and the initials MFG in a larger font. When opened, one side had a wisp of fine dark hair held in place by a thin horizontal bar. The other side featured a photo of a baby with dark hair.

"Who is that?" Gwen asked.

"I reckon it's me," Lyn replied.

"It's really old, huh?"

"For a fact, young lady." He'd never seen it before but it looked familiar. Maybe he remembered it from childhood, or his mother wore it in a photograph. He put the locket in the box and thrust it deep into his pocket. He'd put it with that curl of his mother's hair in a tin box.

When all the wagons were loaded, Lyn led the way, like the Pied Piper. Chances were good they might be carrying vermin within this cargo. Lyn waved Papa's walking stick, a drum major leading the band. People stopped and watched as if this were the Decoration Day parade. Some laughed and some shook their heads with dismay. Lyn had long ago grown used to people gawking at him, and the kids enjoyed the attention.

In the first block of the business district, Lyn halted his workers in front of The Palace Café and the Post Office, where a doorway between the two led to a set of rickety stairs whose pitch looked to Lyn like a difficult climb.

He told the kids, "You carry everything up. My legs aren't what they used to be. And no sense dawdling. I'm paying you a flat fee, not by the hour. The faster you work, the sooner you'll have your money."

Up and down they scurried, with people stopping for a minute to see what was going on. Several greeted Lyn, but most kept their distance.

When the wagons were empty, the six of them promenaded back to Lyn's place and reloaded. This time he was reminded of the prairie schooners Papa used to talk about. One in the lead and the others behind.

Nearing the apartment again, Legs called out, "Oh, crap."

Lyn looked back to see if the boy's cart had tipped over. But it was literally crap; the goat had dumped a steaming, stinking pile on the sidewalk.

"Pee yew," the kids behind Legs chorused, and skirted around him.

Lyn held up his hand to halt everyone. "Circle the wagons. Legs, you can't leave that."

"What thould I do?" he asked, his nose pinched tight.

Hop Chambers answered the call. He came out of his barber shop and handed Lyn a dustpan and a waste basket and then retreated.

Lyn gave Legs the dustpan. "Scoop the poop into the gutter."

"He's a poet and don't-know-it," Gwen said and the kids laughed.

Legs held his nose and scooped the mess forward while Adolf bleated and scraped his hooves on the sidewalk, ready to move on.

"Shee-it," Hank said. "It smells like he had rotten eggs for breakfast."

When the offending pile lay in the gutter, Lyn poured the content of the waste basket, a multi-colored wad of hair clippings, over it. "That'll keep the flies off and it'll all dry up and blow away."

"Morning, Lyn," a voice called from the middle of the street.

Lyn looked up. "Willis."

"A little problem?"

"Not anymore."

Overholser grinned as he came forward.

"You don't need to write this up in the paper," Lyn said.

"I wouldn't know how to word this donnybrook without offending the womenfolk."

Lyn wiped his brow with a red bandana. "Reminds me of a story. Bess Truman was asked by her ladies group if she could do something about

Harry using the word manure. She said it had taken her forty years to get him to use that word."

The men laughed and Willis said, "Good one; I'll use that in my column," and went on his way.

"What should I do with this dustpan?" Legs asked, holding it in his outstretched arm.

"Leave it by the barber shop door with the waste basket. They can wash it or throw it away."

"Can we get moving?" Hank called. "I've been holding my breath for ten minutes. I'm gonna croak if I don't breathe."

"Lead the way," Lyn said. "You're the head wagon. Legs, you and Adolf bring up the rear."

"They already did," Gwen said, and the group zigzagged along the sidewalk in gales of laughter. Kids were a laugh a minute.

———

Lyn lost count of how many trips they made, but around noon a teenaged boy stepped out of the café carrying a tray of hamburgers with the works, French fries, and glasses of Coke. Lyn tried to pay for the lunch, but the kid waved it off. "Dad said it's on the house. Welcome to the neighborhood."

In late afternoon, when the kids were carrying the last load upstairs, Lyn shuffled into the bank on the corner to change three twenties for fives.

"Don't spend it all in one place," he advised as he distributed the payroll.

"Thanks, Glover," they said almost in unison, and they all looked at the crisp five dollar bill as if they'd never held one before. He remembered seeing kids, probably these same kids, during the war, waiting at the depot for the troop trains coming through. The soldiers hung out the window waving money, yelling for milk or chocolate milk or ice cream, and the kids grabbed the bills and scooted across the street to the creamery to fill the requests. Lyn figured on a good day they each made ten bucks. He could've used that kind of money. Half the men in town could've used that kind of money.

Now he told the gang, "I want your word you'll stay away from what's left at my place. It belongs to the government. You might get arrested if they find you there."

"Jeepers, you mean the F.B.I.?" Legs asked. "J. Edgar Hoover?"

"The city government, and you don't want to mess with them. I've tangled with them." Lyn patted Adolf on the head and he released a bleat. Better that than what he'd released earlier.

The kids straggled off, leaving Lyn to wonder what their first stop would be: Candy, ice cream, comic books? They'd spend the money before it burned a hole in their pockets.

Looking at his empty handcart, he realized he had nowhere to stow it like he had at the old place.

Stepping through the doorway, he landed in a narrow foyer. If he set the cart on end it shouldn't be in the way. Who would use these stairs, anyway, besides him? He bumped the cart over the threshold and tilted it against the wall.

Tired from the day's work, he scaled the stairs, at the top of which a window looked out on the alley behind the stores. Above, a light fixture with a chain hung within reach. He pulled the chain but the bulb did not light. He'd buy a new bulb tomorrow.

One door led to a bathroom, and the other to his new digs. He could barely get inside for all the stuff piled in the two small rooms. The scene revealed a maximum of both today's industry and abandonment—the kids had pretty much dropped their parcels and gone down for another.

One of these days he'd get rid of most of this; some of it, at least; sort and straighten, piece by piece. No rush, though. Those old books might be interesting to read when winter set in. County history. No one knew that better than Papa had. He should have written his stories in a book. There probably was a journal or two around here.

Lyn opened the front and back windows for cross ventilation and then lowered himself across a stack of quilts and blankets. He didn't wake until the sun had flared its rainbow of colors over his old residence across the tracks.

Most of the businesses were closed for the day, and traffic noise had waned. Supper aromas from the café wafted up through the heat registers in the floor. This place would be cozy in winter; he would have no fireplace or stove to keep lit. Right now a pleasant summer breeze swayed the thin curtains on the windows.

Somewhere in this muddle Lyn had a canvas army cot that made for good sleeping if padded with quilts. He had a two burner hotplate, a toaster, a coffee pot, a fry pan, a can opener, and eating utensils. A refrigerator with a compressor on top purred over there between two windows.

Lyn closed his eyes and before drifting off again, he heard Papa's voice blessing each place they'd lived over the years.

"All the comforts of home," he always said.

And together they said, "Amen."

AUGUSTA DUVALL RADFORD

Augusta Radford tooled out of The Windy City in her vintage Packard, a deep green 1937 convertible coupe. On the open road she let the breeze play havoc with her still auburn hair, by virtue of her hairdresser. This would likely be her last trip on these particular roads, what with the recently authorized Dwight D. Eisenhower National System of Interstate and Defense Highways, already abbreviated to "The Interstate." She'd seen pictures of the plans and couldn't imagine driving through that twisted maze. The proposed plan would skirt many of the towns and villages she enjoyed driving through or stopping for refreshments at a Mom and Pop café. Since her time in Sibley years ago she'd found small towns and their people fascinating. She would stop in Sibley on this trip—for auld lang syne. She hoped Lyn Glover might be there. He'd be close to eighty, but maybe.

The countryside felt therapeutic: the green rolling hills, the tidy farms with silos towering over the trees, the red barns, many of them suggesting Chew Mail Pouch Tobacco or with those decorative hex signs used by the Amish. She didn't even mind the manure smell that wafted toward her. It represented life; manure replenished the already rich topsoil. And the crops. What did farmers say—corn should be knee high by the Fourth of July? She couldn't be sure which of those fields held corn, but everything looked promising.

To stave off boredom and fatigue, Augusta read road signs, watching for Burma-Shave jingles, the lines separated by miles. Sometimes, distracted, she missed a line, but this one she caught in full:

> Unless your face
> Is tingle free
> You'd better let
> Your honey be
> Burma-Shave

When her granddaughters were passengers, they sang the verses but then complained, "I don't get it," or "What does that mean?"

Augusta's destination was the Black Hills of South Dakota. She and Paul had spent their honeymoon there thirty-six years ago, staying at the new but rustic Custer State Park Lodge. Each morning they awoke to a herd of buffalo silently descending, like a mirage, out of the trees onto the lawn of the lodge. The newlyweds had done all the touristy things; the Badlands, panning for gold in Lead, and visiting saloons in Deadwood where real life Wild West characters lived and died. Calamity Jane, Wild Bill Hickok, Wyatt Earp, and Sheriff Seth Bullock. Now widowed, Augusta would this time view Mount Rushmore and glimpse what was being touted as the beginning of another immense carving—this one of Crazy Horse, an Indian Chief.

Since Paul's death, Augusta sometimes talked to herself; comments she would have made to him. She did that the next day when she wheeled into Sibley and didn't know which way to turn. "Did you expect it to look like it did in nineteen-twenty?"

Back then, some people still used a horse and buggy, and many walked wherever they needed to go. Now, based on the number of cars parked in the business district, no one walked. The cars ranged from jalopies to fairly new models. Although many original buildings still stood, Augusta did not see one familiar business name.

Wait; make that one—the newspaper office, just the place to find out if Lyn were still around. Willis Overholser, too. He was older than Lyn, if memory served, so they both might be gone.

Augusta pulled into the Texaco filling station, where a man with the name Sammy initialed on his shirt filled the gas tank, checked the oil and washed the bug-splattered windshield, all the while admiring the car from every angle. "You should have a screen for that grille," he said. "You'll need a chisel to get the bugs off."

Augusta laughed. "That's like putting an apron over a prom formal, isn't it?"

Sammy laughed, too. "I hadn't thought of it that way."

Augusta pulled away, randomly turning corners, not knowing where she might end up. The library oriented her and she found her way to the courthouse. There sat the Gill's house, where Augusta had met that mistreated boy, Carl Jess. What had become of him? She planned to find out today. And Grace Gill; a truly nice lady.

The residential areas were lined with nicely-kept homes and manicured yards shaded by lofty trees. Motoring along the boulevard, her Packard drew attention from a trio of children. They yelled something and she waved. When she parked downtown and two men gawked at the Packard, she recalled when men looked at *her* that way. They had in nineteen-twenty, both men and women. They'd gossiped, too. John Glover, that dear man, did he have crush on her? She'd fretted about it at the time but never had been certain.

Augusta slid from under the steering wheel, opened and closed the door gently, and ambled a few doors down to *The Gazette* office. In Chicago she'd have locked the car, but not here in broad daylight.

───────❧───────

Inside the office, with no one seemingly around, Augusta inhaled the familiar smell of printer's ink and newsprint, but heard no rumble and rattle and clank of machinery. The presses were idle. Oh, the commotion those beasts made as they ground and twisted and turned and chopped newsprint into sections and folded the papers. She'd taken to wearing ear plugs but that didn't begin to muffle the roar.

"Help you?" a woman asked from behind Augusta.

Startled, she turned. "Oh; hello. I was caught in a time warp. I used to work in a place like this. A lot of years ago."

"I've been here since Guttenberg invented the press. Or so it seems. Actually, it was late nineteen-twenty."

"I was here in early-twenty, covering the Carl Jess trial."

"Really? I arrived shortly after that business. I'm Levon Woodward, social editor, obits, rodeos, whatever needs writing."

"Augusta Radford. I was Augusta Duvall then. With the *Des Moines Register* and later the *Chi-Trib*."

"Big time."

Augusta could have told her about a trial she covered years ago, big time indeed, but the woman appeared ready to go out the door. She didn't ask Augusta to sit down.

"Is Willis still around?"

"He's on this planet, eighty-seven years and change, but he retired long ago. He still writes his column. He should be dropping it off today. Stick around and you'll catch him. So, how does the village look?"

"It's changed—a lot."

"We rearrange and redecorate store fronts now and then to confuse visitors."

"I hoped I might find Lyn Glover, too."

"Aww, Lyn. I'm sorry; he passed away. Bless his heart. Let's see, in March, I think. It was still cold. He had a heart attack; rallied for a month or so but then passed on."

"Oh, I'm disappointed but I half expected it. When I knew him and his father, Lyn was in his mid-forties, I'd say."

"He was seventy-eight when he died. A sad case, really."

Augusta cocked her reporter's ear. "What do you mean?"

"Ah, here comes W.W. now."

The old newspaperman stepped inside, took one look at Augusta and said, "You're a sight for sore eyes."

"You know who I am?"

"Prettiest redhead I ever met."

She hugged him, gently, for he seemed frail.

Levon said, "Time for coffee and gossip at The Palace. I have space to fill for my column."

Willis laid a sheet of paper on her desk. "Here's mine. Probably lots of mistakes. Miss Smith-Corona never won the spelling bee."

"That's why you hired me."

"Nice meeting you," Augusta said as Levon departed.

"You, too. Don't wait thirty years for your next visit."

Watching Levon cross the street, Augusta smiled as the word *skittered* came to mind. Willis must have read her mind. "Thar she blows," he said, and then, "So, what brings you to town? I assume that's your buggy down the street with Illinois plates."

"That's my car. I'm going to the Black Hills and I wanted to stop and say hello to a few folks. I hoped you'd be one of them."

"I'm hanging on."

"Your family?"

"I lost Bea in thirty-five; a son since then."

"I'm sorry. My husband passed away, too."

After a dual silence for the deceased, Augusta said, "Levon mentioned that Lyn Glover died recently."

Willis dragged over a chair for Augusta and then settled into one of those swivel chairs with a spring back. Augusta had once toppled head over heels in one, a perfect summersault, the kind she'd always wanted to perform as a child but had been as leggy and awkward as a newborn colt.

"Levon said it's a sad story but she didn't explain. I feel bad I didn't keep in touch with Lyn. But life happens. I raised two daughters. Built a career. I have three grandchildren; all girls."

"A blessing. Are you still writing?"

"Freelance. I moved to Chicago."

"I recall hearing that from John. First woman at *The Tribune.*"

"My niche became crime stories."

"Ah, Carl Jess. That's what brought you here back in the day."

"It was. But about Lyn?"

Willis combed his wavy white hair with his fingers. "No one really knows why he ended up that way."

"What way is that?"

"Excuse me." Willis pulled out a handkerchief and blew his nose.

Augusta would get this story if she had to drag it out of him. She'd already decided to stay overnight, at the Windsor if it was still operating. "So, whatever happened, was it recently?"

"Oh, no; long ago, after John died. But gradually."

Gradually seemed to be the way this would proceed.

Elbows propped on the chair arms, hands folded under his chin, Willis continued. "We had Lyn over for meals, holidays and such. Other folks did, too. He socialized, for a few years." Willis smiled. "One time he came to supper wearing John's clothes, a suit, shirt, and tie."

"That was formal for Lyn."

"That's why it amused us. It was summer, a seersucker suit. He'd been to an ice cream social at the church. He enjoyed church, but he eventually quit going. Like I said, the change was gradual. The Depression came along. Tough times for everyone. You must have seen plenty of down and out folks in Chicago."

Augusta nodded, hoping to keep Willis on track without a detour through Chicago. His story had started in the middle and had only now backtracked to the beginning, after John died.

The phone rang and Willis let it ring. "That'll be for Levon. One of her gossips; er, social correspondents. Where were we?"

"I don't know," Augusta said with a laugh.

"Okay; sometime in, maybe the late thirties, Lyn got into a bit of trouble. He was in the scrap metal business and that heap of his grew to the size of the Ocheyedan Mound and folks worried about rats. The neighbors took him to court."

"Really?"

"He was acquitted, by golly. He said he'd clean up his place but that was mostly a lick and a promise. He continued collecting salvage during the war and made a decent living. After that he sold the property to the city. That's when he moved in over there, upstairs." Willis indicated with a wave of his hand a building across the street. "He'd have been . . . close to seventy."

"I'm not clear what you mean about him. Did he have physical problems, or mental?"

"Not in the medical sense. Of course, people talked about that crazy old man."

"Lyn?"

"Years back he had a ponytail and zipped around on a motorized scooter."

"That hardly qualifies as crazy."

"It's just an expression. He was peculiar, though. My best guess is that Lyn had a struggle after John died. I knew him as a kid, a teenager, and the two were always together. But you see, and I don't mean to fault John for his parenting or his devotion, but John might have suffocated Lyn."

Augusta cringed at the image and Willis took note.

"Sorry about that. Actually, that's Lou Dwinnell's theory. You remember Lou?"

"Yes; Carl Jess's lawyer."

"Right. But there might be some truth in what Lou surmised. That John so overwhelmed Lyn from the time he was a child that he didn't know his true self. At a later point in life, Lyn needed to break away from being John Glover's son. Perhaps it became . . . almost a stigma."

"That's heavy. In my view, they had a wonderful relationship."

"So it seemed. But maybe it wasn't a healthy situation. Lou believes, from a conversation he once had with John, that when Lyn decided to skip college and make a living as a mason, John was at first disappointed. But then, over time, he seemed proud as a peacock about Lyn. And I believe it was genuine. See, here's the thing, John relished his stature in the community, and let's face it, a handyman, skilled as Lyn was, does not have the cachet of a lawyer, a judge, a minister, all the things that made up John Glover."

"Wait—are you saying that John didn't want Lyn to outshine him?"

"Possibly. Lou says it seemed to him that John never let Lyn grow up. He still treated him like a kid when he was an adult. And Lyn catered to John like a kid would. Everything was done the way John wanted it done. Lou saw them as joined at the hip, and when that connection was broken, Lyn floundered."

Augusta held up her hand for a pause. "I'm trying to think of a term I heard recently."

Willis looked out the window and waved to someone. He switched on an overhead fan and the breeze rustled newspapers on the desk.

"Identity crisis," Augusta said. "A psychologist coined the term. A failure during adolescence to achieve self-identity."

"You might have hit on it."

"When John died, and Lyn was no longer John Glover's son, he didn't know who he was supposed to be."

"The thing is, he was still referred to as John Glover's son. Long after John died. As Lyn changed, the meaning changed. It was more in the sense of comparison. How could one man have been so prominent and his son the total opposite?"

"So, this was Lyn's way of gaining attention in his own right. This is who I am. I'm not my father. I'm Lyn Glover. Rebelling; something he didn't dare do as a teenager. Or didn't do out of obedience or respect for John."

"There was one time Lyn caused gossip, as a teenager. He disappeared one summer and rumor had it he'd defied John and left home, for good. John squelched that, explaining that Lyn had a job out of town. Turned out he did, construction work. He came home brown as an Indian and with long hair. But that job led to his skills."

Willis mused over that for a beat or two. "In the early years he had a reputable business. I inherited a family cottage at Lake Okoboji. It needed work of all kinds. I took Lyn over there and left him to do what he thought it needed. He turned the proverbial sow's ear into a silk purse. I still have the place."

"John boasted about Lyn's work. I remember that."

"He was never on the county dole. He ran a business ad in the paper for . . . I'd say up until about five years ago. Even after he quit paying I ran the ad. It didn't amount to a hill of beans. Only a couple of lines. Anyone who wanted Lyn knew where to find him. He was out and about every day."

Augusta took a deep breath, still rattled. "Okay, you've been saying that Lyn changed. His personality? Appearance?"

Willis rose. "Wait a minute."

———

Willis returned with a framed photograph. "I thought this might be somewhere at home but I found it in the catchall drawer." He wiped dust from the glass with his shirt sleeve. "Someone snapped the photo and brought me a copy. I'm thinking it was the mid-forties."

Augusta studied the black and white image. Of the two men facing the camera, one was Willis so she zeroed in on the other. Beneath a cap, unkempt gray hair straggled to his shoulders. His beard stopped just below the chin, a ragged fringe. Two or three layers of soiled clothing and his shoes bore what looked like paint and spackle. A pushcart of tools stood beside the men.

Augusta glanced up and shook her head. "This can't be Lyn."

Willis placed a hand on her shoulder; he didn't need to speak to confirm her thought.

"I'm shocked, and bewildered." Augusta snagged a tissue from a box on the desk and wiped her eyes. "He always dressed casually but I never saw him dirty."

"He had bathroom facilities, but it would appear he rarely used the tub. We've had a Laundromat for a few years now. I saw him there a couple of times. A woman who worked at Penney's said he'd come in and buy new work clothes and pull them on over the old ones."

"How did people treat him?"

"Some wouldn't sit at the counter over at the café because that's where he sat when he went in. Most afforded him a wide berth, but in general, he was just one of us."

Augusta glanced at the photo again and then laid it on the desk, out of sight. "I've seen hundreds of homeless people who look like this."

"I imagine so."

"Sometimes these people don't consciously choose that life style. They kind of slide into it. Social workers call it falling through the cracks."

"Meaning?"

"Someone who has a problem, mental or physical or both, but it's not bad enough for others to notice, so he, or she, blends in. He might need welfare or medical treatment but he slips through the cracks of our social department system. Does that sound like Lyn?"

Willis nodded. "The blending in, yes. Because we see mostly the same people every day we don't really see them. They're part of the background. I'm not sure I could tell you who I saw on my way here. But then, ask what I had for breakfast and I might not be able to tell you that either."

"You seem fine to me. Did Lyn develop dementia?"

"No, his mind was sharp.

"Was alcohol a factor?"

"I never knew Lyn to imbibe. Not even as a teen when kids are feeling their oats. During these last years he sometimes hung out at Massa's, but it was more of a place to land; get out of the weather and have a cup of coffee or a bowl of soup. He didn't smoke, either, nor did John. He wasn't a recluse. He chatted with folks. People he worked for liked him."

Willis paused and tipped back his squeaky chair. "Here's a funny story. In the forties, Sheriff Nicoll was re-elected by all but one vote. That vote went to Lyn Glover. Everyone talked about it so I asked Lyn if he voted for himself. He looked me in the eye and said, 'You reporters ask a lot of questions and usually get answers, but how one votes is still a private matter.' That was the end of that."

Augusta laughed. "Do you think he did, vote for himself?"

"It wouldn't surprise me. He was interesting. I kept my eye on him, physically and mentally, chatted with him at the café or on the street. I saw no sign of mental lapses. He read avidly, kept up on politics, current events. I dubbed him The Sage of Sibley and sometimes quoted him in my column. He had a folksy, homespun humor."

Willis tapped the photo. "See that leather coat? He carried it summer or winter. He said it was well-insulated, that it kept the heat out in summer and the cold out in winter. He added, and I'm paraphrasing, 'You cannot always depend on sunshine. I remember a swarm of bees in the old creamery building. It was twenty below zero and one by one the bees flew through an opening attracted by the bright sunshine, and dropped dead.' He often pulled out a story to answer a question. John did that. Always a story."

"I remember."

"One time we needed rain badly and I asked, just making conversation, really, 'Why don't we have rain? Is it because the rainmaker's source of water was exhausted in those spring floods, or what?' He went into a story, citing the actual date, October of eighteen eighty-whatever it was, when a fella, and he gave his name, was digging a well and it began snowing and it snowed a foot and the digging machine remained in place all winter. And the farmer was feeding sixty head that winter, so things could be worse, regarding our not having rain. That was the point of the story."

Willis has quite a memory himself, Augusta thought.

"Besides me, a school classmate of Lyn's looked out for him. Ross Meader owns that building where Lyn lived, rent free for, must be ten years or more. Lyn wasn't one for charity so they struck a business deal. Lyn did maintenance on Ross's rental properties."

Augusta had a question but forgot it and Willis jumped in.

"The service was at the funeral home. Quite a few people showed up. A church group. Women from the W.R.C.; some businessmen. It's odd, regardless of Lyn's situation, people seemed to respect him."

"Because he was John Glover's son?"

"I think in his own right, too. He was a pioneer and folks respect those early settlers."

"For the funeral, was Lyn cleaned up?"

"We decided on a closed casket. John had bought a burial plot alongside himself and Lyn's mother and he'd paid for a casket, too, for Lyn, and for the usual services."

"Was he alone when he had the heart attack?"

"He was working at someone's house near the hospital."

"If he'd died in his room he could have lain there for days."

"If he wasn't around, I'd have noticed, but it could've been a day or two. Like I said, we don't always see people who are right in front of us. After the funeral, I went with Ross to the apartment. I believe Lyn never disposed of a single item of his or John's. He had an extensive library, including John's law books. All kinds of vintage wearing apparel and what have you. Photos of his father, his mother, and himself. And a lawyer's diploma in Latin awarded attorney John F. Glover. The signatures were faded, not readable. The whole place was truly a curiosity shop."

"What did you do with everything?"

"It had no value; the books were moldy. We hauled most everything to the dump. A few things went to the museum. Photos and Civil War artifacts, a couple of journals from then, a locket, a lovely satin dress. They have the gown displayed on a dressmaker's form along with the locket."

Augusta sighed; today's information would take time to sort out.

"One more thing," Willis said. "When Ross and I went through Lyn's things, and they were more John's than Lyn's, we discussed that John's life, in the end, had been as spare as Lyn's. This was it, this collection in Lyn's room. Although John had contributed greatly to the community, this was what he left of himself. He and Lyn ended up pretty much the same. As Lou put it, they were both close to being paupers, but Lyn looked the part and John didn't. John lived in a nice hotel and Lyn lived in this hovel. Neither of them had but a few bucks to his name."

Willis closed his eyes, as if to block out the image. Augusta realized that this conversation had been emotional for both of them. She needed to leave but she had one more question. "On another subject, whatever happened to Carl Jess? After I left Des Moines I didn't follow up on him. Was he ever released?"

Levon interrupted, breezing into the office, chatting for a minute, and then she went to another room and typewriter keys soon provided background music.

"Ah, yes, Carl. You asked about him earlier and we got off course. He was moved from that place for children to one for adults. Then when he was still young, early twenties, there was a fire. He'd been safely outside and went back in for a cat. He died from smoke inhalation."

"Oh, no; how tragic." Could this day be any more depressing?

"His death brought a flood of old feelings to the forefront. Letters to the Editor arrived for a couple of weeks. Both sides of the controversy."

"That being?"

"The same as when he shot his father. Was he really abused or did his father simply discipline him more than he wanted? Was he smart enough to understand what he did or a simple-minded child?"

"The experts decided that. The jury agreed."

"That doesn't mean people accept it. You usually can't change people's minds once they've formed an opinion."

"True enough."

"Besides, after the trial there was talk that the outcome had been a given. Declaring that child feeble-minded ensured that he wouldn't end up in adult prison. Even the attorneys for the State were on that side. Well, you were there. You saw it."

"Yes, but did he ever grow, intellectually?"

"Not according to those who saw him."

"Then it was the right diagnosis. The right thing to do. Odd, isn't it? That mere child made an impact in a horrible way, so long ago, and here we sit still talking about him."

"Murder stays with us. We can't comprehend it. It makes us wonder about our own state of mind."

"And we're still asking the same questions. Why? What brought this about? Is any person, any age, in his or her right mind during the commission of murder?"

"It's a puzzler. Have you served on a jury for a murder trial?"

"No; but because of my profession I'd probably be struck from consideration. Have you?"

"Nope. We've had but one murder in the county since the Jess case." Willis rapped his fist on the desk, knocking wood. "It happened I'd say nineteen-twenty-nine, maybe thirty—"

Augusta smiled. "There you go again remembering dates."

Willis laughed. "Long story short; a rodeo drifter went to a farmhouse over by Harris, apparently drunk to the gills. He claimed he went there to buy liquor, but a dispute arose over money. The rodeo man pulled a gun on the man of the house; then the farm wife pulled a shotgun on the rodeo man, but he fired first and killed the farmer."

"So the wife shot the man? Double murder?"

"No; the wife was in the house and the two men were outside arguing, so the shooter got away. His wife was in the car and they fled, ended up in Worthington where the guy turned himself in to the sheriff. He was convicted of second degree murder."

"I've been covering murder for years and it's depressing, but it's also a fascinating look at people. The kind of people most of us don't associate with in life. Thank goodness."

"I know what you mean. The newspaper business, on your end or mine, is enlightening."

"No murders here in some twenty-five years."

"A sleepy little town for the most part."

"Speaking of sleepy. I'm travel weary. Is the Windsor still open?"

"It's not the hotel you knew but it's in the same location. You remember where that is?"

"I've gotten oriented."

Augusta hugged the old man. "I'm pleased to have seen you. It made my day."

"My pleasure. God speed on your travels. Don't get a heavy foot in that Packard and get a speeding ticket. You don't have John Glover to get you out of that one."

Although Augusta knew that Willis spoke with humor, it saddened her even more than she already felt. She wished John and Lyn were here. She wished they would have dinner with her at the Windsor. Make that supper. She could ask Willis to join her, but they'd pretty much exhausted their conversation and she needed time alone to sort through all she'd heard.

She hadn't told Willis about her career highlight; the murder trial she'd covered in Chicago, but as they said in the business, that's yesterdays news. A lot of yesterdays ago.

AUGUSTA DUVALL RADFORD

The Windsor had aged, but with gentility, like those stately antebellum homes in the Deep South. Modestly redecorated, the hotel seemed at once familiar and as if Augusta had never stayed here.

The young desk clerk had channeled James Dean's *A Rebel Without A Cause* look: Blondish hair poofed into a high wave, sultry eyes, pouting lips, a red jacket over a white tee-shirt, and Levi's.

Didn't hotel employees wear uniforms anymore? Well, they hadn't here even in the old days, but the question made Augusta feel old. The idea that children should be seen but not heard had been rendered obsolete. Teenagers were rebelling with or without a cause, and James Dean and Marlon Brando led the way. Lyn Glover, with his ponytail and motorbike, had been ahead of his time.

"Third floor okay?" the clerk asked.

"Sure. The last time I stayed here the third floor was for boarders."

"Really? Um, well, we don't offer that package now. But we have a nice dining room."

Augusta choked back a smile. "One night will do it."

"The suite is open. There's room to stretch."

"Great. I'll eat something first and then go up."

"If you need help with bags, let me know."

"Thanks. I can manage. I see you have an elevator now." It was one of those open cage lifts.

"Yeah, it was taken out of an old mansion in Sioux City."

"Nifty," Augusta said, and sauntered off to the dining room.

———ᴡᴡᴏᴏᴏᴏᴏᴏᴏᴏᴡᴡ———

Although Augusta had never occupied this room in the old days, she felt as if she'd gone home to her parents' house and was in her childhood bedroom. The suite consisted of a sitting room and an alcove that held the bed and bath, everything modernized fairly recently, it appeared. The overall scheme was neither feminine nor masculine; unisex was a word bandied about these days. Above the bed hung a print, a generic pastoral that could be anywhere in the Midwest. Or anywhere at all.

Augusta recalled from earlier stays a picture of a wolf standing on a snowy hilltop looking down on a village. Or was that picture in the Gill's house? Yes; Carl Jess focused on it at dinner when he wanted to avoid meeting her eyes. For a boy who had killed a man, he seemed timid as a dove. That poor child.

Wondering if this suite might have been John's, Augusta's mind again turned to Lyn. She'd half expected to learn that he'd died, but never could have imagined the story Willis related. The photo haunted her. The whole story might have been less bothersome if Willis had simply described how Lyn looked. If she had come here even a few months earlier and seen him on the street, it would have been heartbreaking. Actually, she'd have driven past him without a thought that it might be him.

Even though Willis didn't seem to think so, Augusta wondered if Lyn had suffered a mental breakdown that went undiagnosed. She'd written about the men and women who lived on Chicago's streets during the late 1920s and through the Depression. The Loop was surrounded by slums populated by transients who were either homeless or slept in flop-houses and by day frequented seedy bars and girly-show houses. With train stations nearby, these areas were the natural stop for men and women searching for something which they couldn't define if asked. They found settlement houses, missions, soup kitchens, but no jobs. They turned to panhandling, theft, alcohol, drugs, and prostitution.

Were these people simply down on their luck or were they, at least some of them, mentally unstable? As a reporter, Augusta asked the hard questions, but so far as she knew the medical community hadn't yet answered that particular question. There were any number of studies and theories and opinions.

As for mentally ill people committing violent crimes, a current study showed little connection. That made sense because most people with diagnosed mental problems were in facilities with barred windows and locked doors and not likely to be released. Serious crimes as well as petty were more likely committed by those who were homeless, jobless, without money, or under the influence of alcohol and or other drugs.

Augusta had covered a particularly grisly killing of two street people; stabbed by another homeless person. Readers didn't seem to care much when people killed one of their own—derelicts, gang members, or gangsters killing each other. If a story involved prominent rich people, even those killing their own, that grabbed attention. One such case had been Augusta's small claim to fame.

In 1924, not quite four years into marriage, she had two baby girls she adored and to whom she was a full-time mother—because she wanted to be—not because it was what the majority of women did. Yet, when her former boss at the *Tribune* called and asked her to cover what was expected to be a lengthy trial, she told Paul she desperately wanted to do it. The editor needed an educated woman's point of view. Paul immediately hired a nanny and Augusta dusted off her notebook and brushed up on her shorthand.

Reminiscent for Augusta of the Carl Jess case, this story involved teenaged boys. But unlike Carl, who had no access to his inherited money, all three of these boys grew up privileged with wealth. They were Bobby Franks, the fourteen-year-old victim, and Richard Loeb and Nathan Leopold, eighteen and nineteen years of age, respectively. The tragedy and the lurid, bizarre details about a homosexual relationship between the two older boys shocked the entire country. If ever there was a sensational story, this was it. Following John Glover's advice, and the editor's, Augusta stayed away from that style and was rewarded.

The two students from the University of Chicago, Augusta's alma mater, considered themselves superior in intellect and believed they could plan and get away with murder. Loeb in particular was fascinated with crime and had committed petty acts but none that were harmful to people, and his family bought his way out of trouble. In this case, after months of planning, the two men by chance ran across a younger acquaintance, lured him into their car, killed him with a chisel to the head, took him to a remote area, doused his naked body with hydrochloric acid, and stuffed him into a drainage culvert.

Despite their intelligence and planning, they were sloppy. They left the boy's feet exposed at the entrance to the culvert, where he was easily discovered, and one dropped his eyeglasses with an unusual hinge that was traced to the optometrist and then to Leopold.

While everyone expected the pair to plead not guilty by reason of insanity, their lawyer talked them into pleading guilty in order to avoid a jury and probably a death sentence. Therefore, although it was called a trial, it was technically a hearing; what needed to be decided was the penalty. Each defendant pointed the finger at the other as the killer. Many believed it was Loeb, the less likeable of the two.

The case became notable for the courtroom dynamics of defense attorney Clarence Darrow as he railed against the death penalty. His eloquent oratory lasted more than twelve hours, the longest period Augusta had ever sat at one time, without benefit of the ladies' room, too. More than once during the trial, she wished that John Glover were there to hear and view the drama that included all the bells and whistles of psychiatrists, called alienists then, and the language they spoke: emotional and mental instability, glandular abnormalities, insecurity, sexual longing, lack of judgment for their age, compulsion, impulse control defects, deviance, egocentricity, and belligerence, to name a few. Sigmund Freud had been invited to come and examine the defendants, but poor health kept him from accepting.

The State argued that psychiatric opinion should not be admitted because the defendants did not claim insanity. The judge allowed the testimony.

Darrow kept the pair from hanging, but they were sentenced to life in prison, plus 99 years for kidnapping. Loeb died in prison in 1936, and Augusta heard recently that parole was being considered for Leopold, who had been a model prisoner with extreme remorse for the crime. His part had been said to be a result of his wanting to please his lover, whose friendship "was necessary to me, terribly necessary."

How about that for an excuse?

For her part, Augusta received the Reporter of the Year award from the Midwest Press Association, a fairly prestigious award in itself, but she'd been the first woman to win it. She continued writing, freelance, with murder trials her specialty.

Today, thirty years later, Leopold and Loeb had name recognition. The 1948 Alfred Hitchcock movie, *Rope*, was said to have parallels to the case, but greatly fictionalized. Another movie, *Compulsion*, starring Orson Welles as Darrow, in theaters now, was loosely based on the Leopold and Loeb trial. Reviewers claimed it was more true to the story than *Rope* had been. Augusta planned to see *Compulsion* when she had a chance, and she'd seen *Rope* years ago. She'd found Farley Granger as creepy as Loeb himself, even though she thought his role was supposed to be Leopold.

Augusta had not forgotten Darrow's rumpled, wrinkled suit and shirt, as if he'd slept in it; his tie askew, his running his fingers through his hair as he gestured and paced and wore a path on the wood floor, a fan endlessly whirring overhead. One reporter who'd seen Darrow up close said there were egg stains on his tie.

Comparing him now to the man Augusta had seen in Willis's photo, Darrow might have been only a couple of laundry loads ahead of Lyn. Well, more than that.

As time passed during her career, Augusta felt as if the number of murders increased greatly each year. Her editor claimed it seemed that way only because communication was better and we heard not only local news but stories from around the country. Augusta didn't buy that. People were killing each other in all manner of horrific and devious ways.

In one case, the lawyer for the defendant claimed the man had "snapped," and then killed his brother. He couldn't help himself; he snapped.

Augusta had snapped her finger, wondering if it actually happened that fast. She did so now.

Snap—he killed his brother.

He might have been reading the paper one moment and then, snap, he killed his brother. Fratricide.

Augusta had learned the terms for relationship murders and remembered them still, even the unfamiliar ones. She ticked them off in her mind now.

A parent killing a child under one year old, infanticide. A child older than one year, felicide. Uxoricide, killing one's wife; mariticide, killing one's husband. Siblicide was easy to connect, killing a sibling. Everyone knew suicide, and the other terms were common: fratricide, killing one's brother, sorocide, killing one's sister, matricide, killing one's mother, and patricide, the one that led Augusta to Carl Jess and which, because it was her first, most interested her—the killing of one's father.

Mythology was rife with patricide. In fiction, probably the most famous patricide occurred in Dostoevsky's *The Brothers Karamazov*. In real life, the name Lizzie Borden rose to the top. As children, Augusta and her brothers, when their parents were away, sang the ditty: *Lizzie Borden took an axe and gave her father forty whacks. When she saw what she had done, she gave her mother forty-one.*

As an adult, Augusta researched the infamous Lizzie. She was accused of killing her wealthy but frugal father after a dispute about his killing some pigeons for which she had built a roost in the barn. The stepmother might have been an afterthought, collateral damage. Lizzie was acquitted of the double murder and lived out her life in Fall River, Massachusetts, ostracized by the community. Long after her death in the nineteen-twenties her innocence was still debated, as well as her mental stability, or instability, as the case might be.

Reams had been written in recent years about the mind of the murderer. One doctor studied and focused on children who kill a parent. His conclusion was that these children have a personality disorder that manifests itself in rage over real or imagined abuse from one or both parents.

Were these cases of a person snapping? They tolerate it for only so long and then strike out? Carl Jess? Did he have a personality disorder, or was he mentally deficient, feeble-minded as they said back then? The diagnosis kept him out of prison, but fate put him in harm's way in another facility.

And that other teenaged boy; the file Augusta read in Joe Gill's office, the details strikingly similar to Carl's. Carl had thought about killing his father for a year. He'd kept his resentment and anger at bay until the provocation became too great and he acted. He shot his father. Twice, to be sure he was dead.

With the other boy, there'd been no claim of feeble-mindedness or temporary insanity. His act came from self-defense. The drunken father would likely have killed him. Felicide, killing one's child. The boy had been acquitted.

Carl had been motherless for ten years; the other boy's mother testified to her husband's continual drunkenness and abuse of her and the children. Both boys put up with it until they—snapped? Was that it?

Because her coverage of the Jess case brought a relationship with John and Lyn Glover, their lives now merged in her mind.

What about Lyn's situation? Motherless at an early age. Abandoned—or so it might seem to a child. But he had one parent who loved and nurtured him. Carl had no mother, no siblings, no one to counsel him, and an abusive father. The other boy had a mother, but a father who terrorized his family. Each of those boys came to fear and hate his father enough to commit patricide.

Willis had posed an intriguing theory about Lyn. That John had sucked the life out of him. No, that wasn't the word—suffocated him.

Augusta had winced at the image. But could that be? Had John's personality, his constant presence, his drive, smothered Lyn? Later, did Lyn reach a point where he reasoned that he no longer wanted to be John Glover's son? He simply wanted to be Lyn Glover?

Did Lyn, unconsciously, or consciously, do away with John Glover? Rid himself of his father?

At first glance, it would seem that Claus Jess and his son and John Glover and his son were polar opposites. Perhaps not.

Father and son hatred. Father and son love. They are equally strong passions, and if left unbridled, one can be harmful, the other deadly.

Augusta's mind reeled. She couldn't shut out all she'd heard today. If only she could snap her fingers and turn off her confusion.

Life is a mystery. Why did Paul die from pancreatic cancer three months after diagnosis? Why did their elderly neighbor take her daily walk around the block and get hit by a car, putting her in a wheelchair?

You're on vacation, Augusta. Relax. Life goes on.

She opened a window. An evening breeze carried muted voices: laughter, a car horn, a barking dog; crickets buzzing. Compared to Chicago, the relative silence bordered on seductive. Her daughters had been so accustomed to the clamor of Chicago that when the family had gone to the North Woods of Wisconsin, little Sarah said she couldn't sleep because it was too quiet.

Across the street, Massa's Recreation appeared busy. That didn't seem like the same name it had in the Twenties, but the façade looked about right. Next to Massa's was Tossini's Tavern. That used to be a fruit and candy store. Why did she remember that? She even remembered that the owner had brought a cart to the courthouse lawn during Carl's trial.

Above Tossini's Tavern was the Garberson Hotel. Not as upscale as the Windsor, but a town needed options. Two young girls came out of the bowling alley next door and jukebox music drifted into the night: "Standin' on the corner watchin' all the girls go by. . . ." and then the door closed. Augusta didn't know the name of the singing group, one of those male quartets called The Four something or other.

Her eyes followed the girls north toward the business district, where three or four cars flowed east and west, with seemingly no purpose other than teenagers cruising on a summer night. A pickup rolled to a stop at the intersection. The girls climbed into the bed of the truck and held onto their ponytails as the driver spun wheels and carried them away.

From Augusta's third story view, she noticed the bank corner where the photo of Lyn and Willis had been taken. She imagined Lyn, without much purpose either, ambling along in that shuffle gait he had. Stopping to chat with Willis, a long-time friend. Someone took their picture. Why? Because he was a curiosity, a peculiar old man?

Melancholy from emotion and bodily tired, Augusta prepared for bed. When a knock on the door startled her, she realized she was in her nightgown but had no robe. Oh, well, the gown wasn't scanty; it was one of those shapeless muu muus women were wearing, not unlike the Mother Hubbard style of the 1920s. She crackled the door and peered out.

"Sorry to disturb you," the desk clerk said, holding out a small unwrapped box. "Willis Overholser left this for you."

She opened the door. "Oh, thanks. You could have called me down."

"He said not to disturb you. Is the room okay?"

"Yes; yes; it's lovely."

"Sleep well, then."

"Thanks, and thanks for bringing this."

"My pleasure."

Perched on the bed, Augusta pulled the lid from the box. A note lay on top of a layer of cotton. She opened and read the note.

Dear Augusta:

On returning home I remembered that I had something you might like. When Ross and I went to Lyn's apartment after his death we each took a memento. Ross chose the walking stick and I liked this antique pocket watch, initialed WLG (John's father). Dr. Winkler, who was with John when he died, told me Lyn held it in his hand that day and announced John's time of death.

I've kept it cleaned and oiled and you will see that it keeps perfect time. I enjoyed our visit but regret that my news about Lyn distressed you.

Best regards, Willis
W. W. Overholser
June 18, 1956

Augusta put the watch to her ear. From a farm in Wisconsin to the battlefields of Virginia to a small town in Iowa, four men had carried the watch. Now it had fallen into a woman's possession, a woman who would carry it with respect for its provenance. Willis knew that.

Holding the timepiece in her hand, with the chain wrapped around her wrist, Augusta slid onto the cool sheets under the cotton coverlet. When she closed her eyes, an image appeared: Willis Overholser and Ross Meader, each the father of sons they loved, each with a paternal arm wrapped around another man's son.

The imagined scene brought to mind a quote; whose author Augusta could not name at the moment:

It is not flesh and blood, but heart, that makes us fathers and sons.

Here in this old hotel, where she had met John and Lyn Glover due to an event that shattered the town's peace, Augusta Duvall Radford felt a measure of comfort. Holding the watch to her ear, detecting its nearly silent tick, she tuned her breathing to the rhythm of the timepiece, as one might set the beat of music using a metronome.

Soon she slept.

AFTERWORD

According to the online history of the Osceola County Sheriff's Department, the 1929 murder discussed by Overholser and Augusta in the latter part of this novel was the last homicide in Osceola County.

In an eerie aside, while researching the Ernest Groen patricide for this novel, I discovered that the victim, George Groen, was the maternal grandfather of a high school friend of mine.

Nearly a century has passed since the events in this book. Now, like then, rational people are horrified when a violent act is committed, and in particular when it involves children as the victim (s). Too, when the child is the perpetrator. While this novel was in progress, two 12-year-old girls in Illinois planned to kill a friend because they hoped to meet an online faceless fictional character named Slender Man. They stabbed the girl 19 times, but she survived. The defendants are undergoing mental and psychological testing. The survivor is undergoing counseling.

In Albuquerque, three teenaged boys allegedly beat to death two homeless men, leaving them unrecognizable.

Doing a word search on child murderers, I saw hundreds of hits.

An 11-year-old girl in Illinois was stabbed 40 times by her 14-year-old half-sister because the younger girl was not grateful for all the older girl did for her.

In Chicago, in a feud between two 14-year-old girlfriends, one shot and killed the other.

In California, a 12-year-old boy stabbed his 8-year-old sister to death.

Then there are mass murderers. In 1957/58 19-year-old Charles Starkweather made history with what was called a spree killing. Accompanied by his 14-year-old girlfriend, Caril Ann Fugate, Starkweather killed 11 people at random in Nebraska and Wyoming.

In Kansas, in 1959, four members of the Clutter family were slain in their farm home. Truman Capote told the story in *In Cold Blood*.

The Sixties brought the shocking drug-crazed spree in which The Manson Family, a commune of sorts led by Guru Charles Manson, killed seven people, including actress Sharon Tate and her unborn child.

The Seventies gave us serial killers Jeffrey Dahmer and Ted Bundy. About this time we became aware that children were disappearing. In 1979, Etan Patz became the first missing child whose face appeared on milk cartons across the country.

The term "going postal" was coined in the 1980s after a postal worker shot several people in his workplace. Copycat situations have occurred over the years.

In a patricide/matricide in 1993, Lyle and Erik Menendez gained fame when their defense attorney Leslie Abramson alleged that the pair was driven to kill their wealthy parents because of a lifetime of violence and abuse from both and sexual abuse from the father. The criminal records of the brothers came to light and their trials (separate) ended with deadlocked juries. In the second trials both were convicted of two counts of first degree murder and conspiracy to commit murder.

Mass murders become known by their location: The Boston Strangler, Oklahoma City, the Gainesville Ripper, The Beltway Sniper, Columbine, the World Trade Center, the BTK Killer, Sandy Hook, to name only a few. We often know the name of the perpetrator: John Wayne Gacy, Danny Rolling, Dennis Rader, but not their victims (there are too many to remember).

Within this year, defense lawyers for a 16-year-old Texas youth charged with vehicular manslaughter claimed that Ethan Couch has a rare condition called "affluenza." According to the lawyers, because of his parent's wealth, Couch had freedoms that no young man would be able to handle: money and cars, which led to irresponsible behavior and ended in tragedy. Drunk on stolen beer, three times the legal limit, he smashed into a woman whose car had broken down, killing her and two people who had come to her aid, and a passerby. Two teens in the bed of Couch's truck were seriously injured; one cannot move or talk. The judge bought the idea and gave Couch 10 years' probation but no jail time. If he slips up, he goes to jail for 10 years.

The parents of child victims have, in the past few years, become noted activists, lending the child's name to legislation and foundations that aid victims. The names that come to mind; Adam Walsh, Polly Klaas, Megan Kanka, Amber Hagerman, Matthew Shepard, and Jessica Lunsford.

Like the characters in this novel, we are still asking questions. Is there more crime today or does it seem that way because technology keeps us informed up to the minute on everything that happens around the world? I believe there is a huge increase. Many disagree with that, but it's my opinion. Added to that is the extreme media focus on such crimes, which adds to a growing fear, which adds to more people arming themselves.

In the early 1900s, George Groen and Claus Jess were both victim and villain. Rae McRae, the actual reporter for *The Des Moines Register*, wrote: "Claus was not a man of temper. He never cursed. He did not grow angry, rage about, whip the child and then repent. His was the cold, inhuman, unfeeling brutality that smiles while it lashes, that is coldly, cruelly, deliberate, and knows no remorse. It was his nature."

His nature? Or was he deranged to have been so cruel? Carl Jess, and Ernest Groen, too, might have died by his father's hand.

What compels one to murder? Heredity and feeble-mindedness, as doctors diagnosed Carl Jess? Mental disorders? Environment, upbringing, television, video games, permissiveness, liberal access to guns? Drugs?

Are those who commit murder insane, temporarily insane? sociopaths, psychopaths? Did they ingest too much sugar (Twinkie defense), or snap, or go postal? Or are they simply mean, evil, cold-hearted, deliberate killers? Are there more patricides than matricides? Do males commit murder more often than females? What about assisted suicide; once called mercy killing? Is that murder, or does it stem from an overpowering compassion and love?

Who among us might be capable of murder? Have you ever thought: If someone killed my child/grandchild I would hunt him/her down with a gun and kill him?

I've read that we all have cancer cells in our body. In most of us the cells lie dormant and cause no problems. In others, the poison races through the system and eventually takes a life.

Similarly, perhaps we all harbor murder within us. In some circumstances the act festers and erupts.

Madonna Dries Christensen was born on an Ashton farm in 1935, one of 15 children of Frank Anton Dries and Maybelle Guertin Dries. The family moved to Sibley in 1942. Madonna graduated from Sibley High School in 1953, and remained in Sibley (minus one year) until 1959.

Madonna's paternal and maternal ancestors were early settlers in Osceola County, emigrating from Germany, Ireland, and Canada. Madonna and her husband Gary L. Christensen reside in Sarasota, Florida.

In addition to compiling several volumes of family history, Madonna's writing has appeared in more than 100 publications, with three nominations for the Pushcart Prize. She's currently a columnist for *Extra Innings* and *Today's Seniors*, and Editor/Publisher of *Doorways*, a memoir publication. Madonna is the author of: *The Quiet Warrior*; *Swinging Sisters*; *Masquerade: The Swindler Who Conned J. Edgar Hoover*; *Dolls Remembered*; *Toys Remembered*; the memoir *In Her Shoes: Step By Step*; and, *The Orator And The Sage*, a biographical sketch of Osceola County pioneers John and Lyn Glover.

With the exception of *The Orator And The Sage*, all books are available on Amazon and other book sites, with royalties going to charity. *The Orator And The Sage* is available through www.magcloud.com, and all of the author's books are on the shelves at Sibley Public Library.

CPSIA information can be obtained at www.ICGtesting.com
Printed in the USA
BVOW04s0118190115

383903BV00001B/66/P

Item Price	Total
14.29	14.29

If you are not satisfied with your order, you may return it within 14 days of the delivery date. For your convenience, items may be returned to the address on the packing slip or returned to your local Barnes & Noble store (check the local store refund policy for details).

Choose a return reason below and include this slip with the item in your package. Please cut out label on dotted line and affix to carton being returned.

[ ] Wrong Quantity

[ ] Defective or Damaged in Transit

[ ] Wrong Merchandise Received

[ ] Other (please explain)_____

Pay Method: VISA   Credit Card#: 6631

From:
Sue Leu
2602 SE Covenant Dr
Grimes, IA 50111
USA

To:
Barnes & Noble.com
B&N.COM Customer Returns
1 Barnes & Noble Way
Monroe Township, NJ 08831
USA

855449264

YOU FOR YOUR ORDER!

note sales tax for the state of
collected on this order.

99050000000949076189
01/27/2015 12:00 AM   (EAD)
01/20/2015 7:19 AM   (PRINT)

BARNES&NOBLE

www.bn.com

Sold To:
Delores Truckenmiller
903 6th St. NE
Sibley, IA 51249
USA

Ship To:
Sue Leu
2602 SE Covenant Dr
Grimes, IA 50111
USA

Custo
1-800-
service

PO Nu

Your order of Jan 18, 2015   **(Order No. 855449264)**

Loc: P
Box Si

Qty	Description	Item #
1	**Patricide**	9781491743294

THA

Plea
IA w

Page 1 of 1